A Gentleman's Mistress

BY MARY BRENDAN

D1559733

ZEBRA BOOKS
KENSINGTON PUBLISHING CORP.

ZEBRA BOOKS

are published by

Kensington Publishing Corp.
475 Park Avenue South
New York, NY 10016

Second printing: November, 1990

Printed in the United States of America

Chapter One

Sarah gazed intently at the reflection staring back at her from the small oval mirror. She raised one hand, touching her face lightly and then with a quick circular movement, trying to instill some color into her pale cheeks. The large sapphire eyes accentuated her pallid complexion to a translucent beauty. She stared detachedly at each feature, studying it at length—wide blue eyes, small nose and mouth, high cheekbones set in a perfect oval face. She had never been able to appreciate her beauty as others did, feeling that her nose was the wrong shape, her eyes too large and her mouth too small. She sighed. Besides, it seemed that a beautiful face was a luxury . . . something she could ill afford, and now, being forced to earn her living in "genteel poverty," it had proved to be a positive disadvantage. "Genteel poverty." She smiled acridly; she had yet to realize what was genteel about penury.

She tilted the mirror slightly so that the blue silk gown she wore came into view. It was the only presentable evening dress she possessed, old, but of good quality, and a style that luckily had not dated too much over the past years. She smoothed a small crease in the skirt with trembling fingers, wishing uneasily that the picture she presented looked less young and attractive and more self-assured and sophisticated.

Her hair had been dressed elaborately by her employer's maid and Sarah's subsequent attempts, when she was alone, to simplify the style had merely resulted in strands of golden hair falling in loose ringlets about her ears and the nape of her neck. She tried now to secure some tendrils back in their pins, but they resisted any such attempts, stubbornly falling down after a few minutes. She looked less like twenty and more like sixteen, she acknowledged wryly to herself, her fingers still working agitatedly at the small crease. She wondered vaguely if her youthful appearance would benefit her in any way tonight, her mind shying away from the impending meeting and the apprehension it aroused in her. She turned abruptly from the mirror and moved to the window that looked out over the front of the house. Her hands clenched and then relaxed, her palms feeling slippery, and she rubbed them absently along her bare arms, embracing herself against the cool evening air that flowed, gently billowing the curtains, into the small room.

She turned back into the room longing to sit down and yet not daring to crease her dress and caught sight of herself again in the mirror. Beauty, she thought sourly, was for the privileged classes, for girls able to use it to advantage, to secure themselves a future with a man of their choice. For an impoverished widow with a small child to support, trying to find respectable employment was almost impossible, as was finding a man who would employ her for her educational abilities alone. Most men were just as concerned that her presence in their homes benefit themselves as much as it did their offspring. Sarah was at present employed as governess at Ashdowne Manor in Kent, the home of Sir Alfred and Lady Cunningham. And her mind returned to the morning last week when Lady Anna Cunningham had entered the library where Sarah was choosing books for the day's lessons, in timely arrival to witness her husband having his face soundly slapped by the young governess. Recalling the incident now, Sarah found it hard to repress a choke of almost hysterical laughter. If it had not proved quite so tragic for herself, it would have been hilarious.

Sir Alfred Cunningham—amiable and kind-hearted—Sarah had been aware of his appreciation from the moment she had met him and taken in the small eyes and jovial face lighting with a desire for more than merely making her acquaintance. She had taken pains to avoid being alone with him at any time, counting her newfound employment and her friendship with Anna Cunningham too precious to be jeopardized. When he had entered the library that morning, closing the door softly behind him, his face had been a comic study. Disbelief at his good fortune at finding Sarah alone had swiftly been replaced by a gleam in his eye that Sarah had found extremely disturbing. She had moved quickly away from him and toward the door, but he, seeing his chance for amatory pursuit disappearing rapidly before his eyes, had made a clumsy leap toward her, almost felling the object of his desire in his haste. Sarah, clutching at him momentarily for support, had merely fueled his passion, and she next felt his lips, missing hers in his frantic haste, wetly about her neck and throat. Managing to free one hand and dropping the books as she did so, she was just in the process of slapping him soundly about the face when his wife made her untimely appearance. All three had stood as though frozen for a moment, Sir Alfred unable to decide whether to nurse his smarting cheek or his crushed toes, which had borne the brunt of the books, before Anna Cunningham, in austerely polite tones, had requested her husband's presence in her parlor. Sir Alfred, looking stricken, had followed his wife's stiff figure from the room as speedily as his sore digits would allow, without a backward glance.

That day had seemed interminable to Sarah; the two girls she taught seemed more fractious and disobedient than usual, and her fear of dismissal without a reference had grown with every silent minute ticking away on the large schoolroom clock. When the summons had come after lessons that day, she was almost relieved that the inevitable had at last arrived. She went, head high, to the parlor, not about to show guilt for something of which she had been entirely blameless. She could not have been more surprised, therefore, when Lady Cunningham had asked her pleasantly to be seated and had discussed with Sarah her plans to send her two daughters, Anna and Maria, to stay with her sister in Italy for a while. She would thus not be needing a governess for some time, and Sarah's services would of necessity have to be dispensed with. Even more astonishing than her mild manner was her promise that she would endeavor to secure alternative employment for Sarah before she left the household. Sarah, unable to believe her ears, had wondered if, in fact, the older woman had misconstrued the scene she had witnessed in the library, but found it prudent to say nothing, merely thanking Lady Cunningham before escaping to her small room.

Sarah was not a fool, and she had realized at once the futility of this promise. No one in her right mind would employ a governess with her looks and youth, and one also encumbered with a young child. Sarah knew that she owed her acceptance into the Cunningham household to the longstanding friendship between her mother and Lady Cunningham and to nothing else. Anna Cunningham had been either unwilling to see, or uncaring of, the likely effect a young and beautiful woman in the house would have on her sadly neglected husband. It was highly unlikely that any other woman would risk the consequences that she had appeared so readily to accept.

Sarah's thoughts returned to the present, her fingers still working at the crease in her skirt. She looked down at the blue silk in dismay, realizing that instead of smoothing the tiny imperfection in the material, she had been pleating more creases into the gown.

Lord Mark Tarrington—she tried not to think of the name or the man who owned it.

If only there had been some mistake and she had misunderstood Anna Cunningham's fleeting message in passing that morning. She had informed Sarah that Lord Tarrington would be calling to interview her later that day regarding employment, and the news had left Sarah dumbfounded. Not so Anna Cunningham. She had seemed positively radiant, as apparently securing Lord Tarrington as a dinner guest was no mean feat.

She had hurried off, however, in pursuit of some errant servant before witnessing the distraught look that had flooded the young girl's face. Sarah, unable to believe that she had heard correctly, had spent every spare minute of the day loitering in corridors, desperately trying to intercept Anna Cunningham to gain further information regarding the plans for that evening. She had eventually asked Mrs. Robbins, the housekeeper, about her whereabouts, only to be told that she had gone out visiting and was not expected back for some time. Sarah knew Anna Cunningham well enough to guess that she, no doubt flushed with the success of securing her distinguished but elusive dinner guest, had gone to impart this news to some less fortunate crony, and she was also sure that this pleasurable task would probably keep her out until late. She had returned to her room with a sinking heart. Finally, late that afternoon, she had run Lady Cunningham to ground in her parlor, and the latter, garrulous after an extremely gratifying afternoon of nose disjointing, had been most forthcoming about her proposed plans for the evening.

Lord Tarrington, the older woman had informed her in the tone of voice used for conveying news of great import, would be dining with them later with a view to interviewing and employing Sarah as governess. The dismay she had then beheld on the young governess's face was not the reception she had expected to her tidings. Sarah's stammered comment that she was unaware that Lord Tarrington had any children had been waved aside by Anna Cunningham, and she had stated in the tone of voice reserved for those addled in the wits that, being unmarried, naturally he had no children of his own. Sarah, reluctantly bringing to mind their brief but memorable meeting, had difficulty controlling her urge to retort that the one did not necessarily preclude the other. She had listened in silence to Lady Cunningham's advice regarding her behavior and dress for the evening, and to the explanation that it was in fact the niece and nephew of his lordship who required tutoring. They had been living in London with their widowed mother, who apparently, judging by the disapproving sniff that accompanied her name, did not meet with Anna Cunningham's approval. The children would be moving to Lord Tarrington's estate in Surrey for a long stay.

Any further information to be gleaned from her ladyship had at that point been curtailed by the appearance of a sobbing kitchen maid requesting Lady Cunningham's immediate opinion on the state of the ruined syllabub. No further prompting had been necessary. Lady Cunningham had erupted from her chair with surprising agility considering her bulk, and had sped in the direction of the kitchens, muttering darkly about unreliable and incompetent servants.

Sarah halted her musings abruptly, moving back to the window. The room was cool, her arms shivering, and yet her panic at the coming meeting stifled her, making the room seem airless. She ridiculed herself for her vanity; it was a distinct possibility that Lord Tarrington, earl of Winslade, would not remember her or their previous meeting, although Sarah knew it was a day she would never forget.

Maria, the youngest of the Cunningham girls, tended to idleness, and that particular day had been

no exception. She was a likable girl with, unfortunately, her mother's looks and her father's predilection for doing nothing resembling work as often as
possible. Maria had found that leaving a required
schoolbook in her room in the morning often lead to
an amiable amble around the house on the pretext of
collecting it. Sarah, wise at last to the reason for her
young pupil's lengthy absences, had decided to accompany her to her room to fetch the required item.
Maria, sulky, but willing to admit defeat on this
particular avenue of time wasting, and Sarah, had
therefore been crossing the main hall to the stairs
when the front door of the house had opened, admit-
ting a jocular crowd of people who had obviously just
finished an early morning ride.

Sarah had frowned uneasily. She usually made a
point of avoiding the areas where guests were to be
found, feeling out of place. Lady Cunningham had
made a point, at the beginning of her residence in the
house, to draw Sarah into various evening activities
when guests were invited. Sarah, however, aware of
her uncomfortable status somewhere between guest
and employee, had evaded most of them as diplomati-
cally as possible, something that was easy enough for
a mother with a young child to carry off. She had
attempted to escape quickly up the winding stairs,
avoiding any contact with the guests below. Maria,
though, seeing an opportunity to spend the best part
of the morning somewhere other than the schoolroom,
had her own ideas. She had shot across the hall to
envelop her father in a hug about the waist and was
soon lost in the throng. Sarah had recognized Celia
Maynard, daughter of one of the neighboring landowners, chattering in a shrill tone to one of the men.

She had been wearing a peacock-blue riding habit of impeccable style and quality, her dark curls bouncing prettily beneath the matching feathered hat as she turned her head from one eager admirer to another. She was an attractive girl, of, Sarah had guessed, perhaps twenty-two, with dark hair and eyes, and she had been well aware of the effect she was having on the many attentive men between whom she was dividing her ample charms. Sarah had been struck by the picture she made, in her blue outfit among so many dark-clad men, thinking she looked like a bird of paradise surrounded by a throng of chattering starlings—or a parrot, she had mused ruefully minutes later—hearing the shrill giggle piercing the room again.

Sarah had seen Celia once or twice at the Cunninghams' before. There had been no friendliness or warmth in Celia, such as she displayed so abundantly now, when they had been introduced, only a hard stare accompanied by an indiscreet head-to-toe summary examination. A brittle smile and a dismissive toss of the head had left Sarah feeling that Miss Maynard obviously found her of little consequence.

Sarah had suddenly become uncomfortably aware that some of the pairs of eyes were now turning in her direction and that nods and interested smiles were coming her way. She had tried to attract Maria's attention as tactfully as possible to indicate that they should go, but that girl had no intention of allowing this opportunity of malingering escape and had stubbornly refused to be drawn away.

The prickling sensation of frank observation had intensified unbearably, and Sarah, acutely aware that she was being studied relentlessly, had turned slightly

13

and noticed a man standing somewhat apart from the others, talking to Williams, the butler. The first emotion she had experienced was amazement that she had not noticed him sooner. The most striking thing about him had been his manner; he had the arrogance of a man used to commanding attention, and for Sarah his presence had been magnetic. When her eyes had met his, despite her desperate urge to look away immediately, she had found she could not. He seemed able to control her will, keeping her transfixed as though mesmerized. She had returned his stare unwaveringly for a few moments and had become irrelevantly conscious of a small riding whip, gripped in one of his hands, tapping slowly against his highly polished boot.

He was quite tall and powerfully built, his shoulders broad beneath the perfectly cut and quite obviously expensive black riding jacket, and as she regarded him steadily she was instinctively sure that he was the wealthiest of this small gathering of rich and titled landowners gathered beneath the Cunninghams' roof that morning. Dusty sunlight streaming in through the open door at that moment had burnished the darkness of his head with auburn lights, making his hair and eyes look identical in color, the golden eyes seeming unnaturally light in the tanned face. Sarah had felt the blood starting to heat her face as she attempted to break his dominance, and yet still the amber eyes held hers, the hard mouth curving upward slightly in a mocking smile as he acknowledged her distress.

She had been so absorbed in her embarrassment and his amusement at it that she had not at first noticed that Celia had moved over to him and was

14

now clinging fast to one of his arms, laughing up into the dark face, which, apparently oblivious to this new female attention, was still turned Sarah's way.

Sarah had looked away hastily, but not before she had read the blatant enmity in the other girl's face as she turned her way also. Becoming desperate now in her search for Maria, she had not noticed the sly smile thinning Celia's mouth as, still clinging hard to the dark arm she was clutching so possessively, she had pulled the man across to where Sarah stood in almost rigid mortification. Celia's eyes had met hers in frank dislike, but she had smiled, turning toward her companion and saying, "Lord Tarrington, let me introduce you to Mrs. Sarah Thornley, governess to young Anna and Maria," and she had turned back to Sarah, her eyes alight with ill-concealed triumph at having declared the young woman's status, marital and otherwise.

Sarah, her composure returning speedily as her anger at Celia's spite grew, merely curtsied quickly, acutely conscious of Lord Tarrington's presence. She felt stifled by his nearness, and she backed away slightly, intent on finding Maria and escaping immediately.

Celia, however, had other ideas and her shrill laughter had trilled out again. "No need to blush so prettily, my dear; Lord Tarrington is quite used to young ladies who stare boldly at him. It is a hazard—or an advantage," she said coyly, gazing up at him from beneath her lashes, "that comes with having a title and a fortune."

Sarah, incensed now by the other woman's malicious jibes and by his lordship's unwavering scrutiny and apparent disregard of her humiliating situation, merely said with icy politeness, "My name is Sarah Thornton, and as for his lordship—I am sure he must be extremely grateful that his fortune at least renders him attractive."

The insult had been unmistakable, and she had watched with a kind of terrified satisfaction as the scorn in his eyes darkened to anger. His mouth had twisted briefly into a cruel smile, and he had inclined his head slightly in acknowledgment of her comment. Sarah had felt a knot slowly tighten in her stomach, and overwhelmed suddenly by her ill-mannered outburst, she had, in the ensuing silence broken only by Celia's contented laughter, tried frantically to think of some acceptable apology for her unwarranted insolence. But her mind refused to cooperate, and the words jumbled in her brain. She was aware only of his overpowering proximity and of the antagonism that seemed to electrify the space between them.

He had bowed slightly toward her, saying in an impassive tone, "Mrs. Thornton, I look forward to our next meeting."

Sarah, made audacious by her relief that the introduction was apparently over, met his gaze steadily, saying as calmly as she was able, "I very much doubt that my duties here will necessitate any further meeting, my lord."

He had smiled sardonically at the unintentionally barbed retort and his eyes had held a barely veiled threat. "Oh, we will meet again, Mrs. Thornton, you can be sure of it." His voice had been insidiously soft, and Sarah had felt the ice pervade her once more, her brief sense of relief evaporating slowly as she tore her eyes away from his.

Most of the other men, Sir Alfred included, had

removed to the drawing room, and she noticed that Celia, dragging playfully at Lord Tarrington's arm, was indicating that they should follow. He seemed impervious to her charm, however, remaining unmoving, his eyes still fixed remorselessly on Sarah's ashen face, and Celia, throwing one last triumphant glance Sarah's way, had swept off in pursuit of more attentive admirers. Maria had, thankfully, reappeared at that moment, and, excusing herself almost incoherently in her relief, Sarah had mounted the stairs, Maria chattering incessantly at her side. She had sensed the intensity of his scrutiny scorching her and had turned involuntarily at the top of the stairs. He was watching her still, the tawny eyes hard and narrowed, and Sarah, unable to meet the challenge further, had looked away swiftly, unable to shake off the feeling of some impending disaster.

The incident had been weeks ago and yet she had never been able to put it from her mind. She ridiculed herself again for her conceit. He had probably forgotten all about her minutes after it had happened, and yet even as she thought it, some inner self knew it to be untrue.

She had at first felt compelled to find out something about him, and Maria, eager to impart gossip despite her tender years, had informed her that Lord Mark Tarrington, earl of Winslade, had a fortune exactly matching his dubious reputation in size. It was obviously something that she had heard her mother say, and she had endeavored to enlighten Sarah further, with childish glee, as to his scandalous ways. Sarah, aware that discussing her employer's guests with the children was likely to lead to grave trouble, had soon gotten her curiosity under control and silenced Maria with a steely look and a pageful of French verbs to copy.

The light tap at the door brought Sarah's musings back to reality. The thin, pointed face of Milly, one of the young serving maids, appeared around the door. "The mistress bids me tell you that dinner is served in ten minutes and to come down now." She smiled, pleased that she had remembered her message so well, and then her eyes grew incredulous. "Cor, miss, you look really lovely," she exclaimed, and then colored in confusion. "I mean madam . . . you look beautiful in that dress." She continued to gape open-mouthed, and Sarah felt again vague stirrings of unease at the young girl's fullsome praise. She smiled at Milly and merely nodded, and the girl scurried back through the door, eager for praise from her mistress for her completed task.

Sarah looked toward the silent crib in the corner and moved as quietly as the whispering dress would allow to gaze at the tiny occupant. She lay with one small fist curled up under her cheek, pushing her mouth into an exaggerated pout, and as she watched her daughter, Sarah felt that rush of tenderness, frightening in its intensity, engulf her. She stretched her hand slowly toward the flushed face, longing to stroke it and yet not daring to wake her at this crucial time.

She moved quickly to the door, closing it with the silence born of long practice, and descended the stairs slowly, her hands slippery on the polished wood rail. Reaching the bottom step, took a deep, calming breath before moving toward the drawing room doors.

The door opened just as Sarah reached it, and Lady Cunningham, in a red silk dress that unfortunately exactly matched in color the webbing of tiny veins below her pale cheeks, stared in surprise for an instant. "Ah, Sarah, I was just wondering where you had got to. Come in, my dear." Sarah read the approval at her appearance in the older woman's face and she felt a modicum of confidence.

She noticed him at once as she entered the room. He was standing with Sir Alfred, who had obviously not seen her enter, as he was engaged in some whispered aside and good-natured back slapping. Seeing that his companion's attention was now elsewhere, Sir Alfred also looked up, and Sarah, noting his shamefaced look, guessed she had been the subject of some ribald remark. She had wondered uncomfortably whether Lord Tarrington knew of the nature of her rather sudden removal from the Cunningham household, and the scene she had just witnessed now left her in no doubt as to the answer. She could feel some of the panic she had been experiencing all day being replaced by a slow anger at what she was sure was some bragging account of her fall from grace into Alfred Cunningham's arms. Sir Alfred, looking ill at ease, shuffled away slightly, leaving Sarah and Lord Tarrington facing each other alone in the center of the room.

Anna Cunningham, not sure what was wrong but sensing the straining atmosphere, bustled over, corsets creaking. "Lord Tarrington, let me present Mrs. Sarah Thornton to you."

Sarah emboldened by the rising anger within, met his eyes challengingly before sinking into a low curtsey. He acknowledged her with a curt nod, the golden eyes mocking her undisguised anger, eroding her brief self-assurance.

"Come, Sarah, sit down. Unfortunately, Lord Tarrington is unable to stay to dine after all, so we will have to launch straight away into plans for your future employment, my dear."

Sarah sat in a chair near Lady Cunningham, which thankfully proved to be some distance from the dark figure of Lord Tarrington. She was aware of Lady Cunningham's directing some comments about mutual acquaintances toward Mark Tarrington and was glad to have some minutes to compose herself. She had hoped that the abrasive tension she had experienced at their last meeting had been merely a figment of her imagination, but she could feel it now, an almost tangible force between them. She studied her hands intently, twisting the gold band she wore around slowly, wondering why this man who was about to hold such sway over her future should arouse such hostility in her.

She glanced at him surreptitiously from under her lashes. He had the kind of imposing bearing that drew all eyes, and she noticed that both Alfred and Anna Cunningham were watching him with avid attention as he spoke. He was wearing black again—a superfine coat and trousers of equally impressive quality as the last time she had seen him—the stark whiteness of lawn at his throat and cuffs accentuating the tanned skin. He wore no jewelry, except for a large gold signet ring on one finger, and she realized that at a time when the majority of the men of fashion often dressed in colors brighter than those chosen by their womenfolk, his very sober choice of dress made his appearance even more noteworthy. His hair was thick and straight, curling only where it met the collar of his jacket, and it looked darker now than when last she had seen him. The color reminded her of an old mahogany table of her father's, so dark as to appear quite black, until the early sun streaming in through high windows glossed it titian.

She pulled herself up sharply, ridiculing herself for waxing lyrical over a man who obviously held her in contempt. Besides, she thought viciously, he looks like some lavishly dressed gypsy.

Lady Cunningham's laughter trilled again, and Sarah was caught unaware as his head turned in her direction and he saw her watching him for the second time. She looked away automatically, furious with herself for the cravenness that would not allow her to return his stare. She steeled herself to meet his gaze again, and said with a composure that surprised her, "What ages are your nephew and niece, my lord?"

"Luke is ten and Joanna is fifteen." His reply was terse.

"That is somewhat older than the children I normally teach," she said, still controlling her voice admirably.

His eyebrow rose sardonically. "Indeed? Are you indicating therefore that you think the task beyond your capabilities?"

"Not at all," she retorted, unable to keep the flash of anger from her eyes or her voice. "I was merely stating the fact that by preference I teach younger children."

He smiled at her, but his eyes remained hard. "And I, by choice, Mrs. Thornton, prefer a governess of somewhat more advanced years."

"It seems, then, that we would not suit at all, my

21

lord," she said with frosty politeness. Before he had a chance to reply, she had turned quickly to Anna Cunningham, ignoring the astonishment on that woman's face at this presumption, and said, "Perhaps, Lady Cunningham, you would be kind enough to furnish me with an open reference before I leave. I am sure Lord Tarrington must be as relieved as I am to cut short this interview."

She rose to go, but was halted by Lady Cunningham's issuing an almost choking sound and apparently speaking with great difficulty. "Sarah, I do think that it is Lord Tarrington's prerogative to draw such a conclusion."

Sarah, turning toward him, met his eyes challengingly, waiting for his condemnation of her behavior.

He was silent, however, and there was humor in his eyes, which only served to fuel Sarah's rising fury. Not content with her previous outburst, she added glacially, "I am sure you must agree with me, my lord, that employment seems unsuitable, in the circumstances."

"Not at all, Mrs. Thornton," he returned evenly. "For my part, I understand from reliable sources that what you lack in years you more than compensate for in other ways."

Sarah paled visibly, her eyes sparking and her anger obvious now as the equivocal comment struck home. Sir Alfred had also gone a strange color and was watching his friend with a look of imploring astonishment on his face. Sarah, however, determined not to be bested in this verbal battle, simply asked sweetly, her expression studied innocence, "And what ways might they be, my lord?"

Sir Alfred made a strange choking noise in his

throat and sat down in the nearest chair. Lady Cunningham, unsure why, but certain that some gathering storm was about to break, also sank lower in her chair.

Lord Tarrington, however, his eyes derisive, merely said with deceptive mildness, "Why, your excellent academic qualifications, Mrs. Thornton . . . what else? I hear from Lady Cunningham that your education would put many a man to shame."

"Yourself included, my lord?" she queried in as honeyed tones as she could manage through clenched teeth.

"I am sure there is a great deal you could teach me." He hesitated, before adding dulcetly, "I am equally certain that you will learn from me." His soft tone was belied by the threat she read in his eyes, and Sarah, aware that she had gone too far in this confrontation, yet unable to withdraw, said in a voice that had lost a lot of its temerity, "Really, my lord? I had no idea you were a scholar. What had you in mind?"

Sarah was vaguely aware that the Cunninghams were now watching them with unwavering attention. Now that the imminent danger of embarrassment for himself had passed, Sir Alfred allowed an astonished flicker of a smile. Never before had anyone to his knowledge spoken to Mark Tarrington with such asperity. Certainly not a slip of a girl about to be made homeless at any time and relying on his lordship for employment. He leaned forward slightly in his chair as his friend spoke again, as though desperate not to miss a thing.

"I think, Mrs. Thornton," Mark Tarrington said quietly, yet with an edge of steel, "that I should start with a few lessons in respectful behavior; after that . . ." He shrugged eloquently, leaving Sarah in

23

no doubt that should he decide to employ her now, she would pay dearly for this evening's folly.

She turned to Anna Cunningham, her eyes imploring, but that lady, still in a state of confusion over the ambiguities she had not quite grasped, merely looked to Lord Tarrington for some indication of the outcome of the altercation.

He turned from Sarah abruptly and extended a hand towards Anna Cunningham, saying, "I think that brings the matter to an end." There was a finality to his tone that brooked no opposition, and Lady Cunningham nodded, smiling, not daring to speak lest her dazed puzzlement became obvious. He was studying his watch thoughtfully, and then, pocketing it again, said, "Anna, I really have to go now." He replaced his empty glass on the mantel near the fire, and, turning to Sarah, bowed curtly, his expression set. She returned his gaze, aware that he was waiting for her curtsey. She would have liked to ignore the expected formalities, but she allowed her eyes to slide away from his in a mute gesture of defiance as she made a cursory bob. His mouth lifted slightly in acknowledgment of this effort, and then he was gone, striding into the hall with Sir Alfred, Lady Cunningham following unnoticed, close on their heels.

Sarah, feeling the tautness ebb from her body, sank into the nearest chair, her face dropping slowly into her hands. She knew now it was impossible; she would not work for him under any circumstances. She would speak to Lady Cunningham, beg, if necessary, for some sort of reference giving her at least a chance of employment elsewhere.

Anna Cunningham, returning to the room at that moment, stared intently at Sarah's bent head, unable to prevent a gleam of admiration from brightening her eyes. The girl had been hiding unknown talents; never before had she heard any female speak in such a way, and certainly not to Mark Tarrington. She looked at the golden head and quivering shoulders, her maternal instincts suddenly asserting themselves, and she indicated by an eloquent movement of the head, accompanied by a flapping of the hands, that Sir Alfred, who was hovering in the doorway, should remove himself. He, with a bewildered shrug, stalked off to find whether any dinner was to be had in his house that evening.

Lady Cunningham sat down with a voluble sigh, settling into a comfortable position with much rustling and creaking. Sarah, aware that her conduct warranted severe reprimand, raised her eyes to meet those of the older woman, surprised at the mild expression she read there. Anxious to press home her point while her employer appeared sympathetic, she began. "I apologize, Lady Cunningham, for my inexcusable behavior toward your guest." She faltered, searching for words to adequately express the antipathy she felt for Mark Tarrington.

Lady Cunningham, however, leaned forward, patting her hand solicitously. "I think we should have a little talk about Mark Tarrington, my dear. He has a habit of either making people like or loathe him. I have to admit, though," she added thoughtfully, "that with women it is usually the former." She halted, aware that this was not the news she had intended to impart. "Sarah," she began again, "Lord Tarrington is a very rich and powerful man. It does not do to make enemies of people who hold sway over your life. He has it within his power now to make your life pleasant, even enjoyable; on the other hand, if you continue with this unfortunate attitude, it could be that you will by your own doing, make your life unbearable."

Sarah, wanting to deliver her request for a reference before matters got too fraught, said quickly, "But there is no need, Lady Cunningham. I have decided that I cannot work or live under the same roof as Lord Tarrington and would be immensely grateful, therefore, if you could simply supply me with a reference before I leave." An abrupt, unanticipated anxiety occurred to her, noting the astonishment on Lady Cunningham's face, and she asked quickly, "I have been adequate in my duties, I hope?"

"Without a doubt, my dear. That is not the point. Lord Tarrington has made it quite clear that he expects you in Surrey at his estate on Friday. He is sending one of his own carriages to collect you." She held up a hand to silence Sarah as the young woman started to protest. "Listen to me, my dear. Mark Tarrington is rarely thwarted in anything. It is foolish to even attempt doing so. He has expressed a wish that you take up residence as governess to his niece and nephew, and I would advise you to apologize for your rudeness and settle down to enjoy the life available to you. He has one of the largest estates in the country, and the wealth to furnish and keep it in magnificent style. Why, it is a golden opportunity," she enthused. "Most girls in your place would give anything for such a position."

Sarah swallowed hard, starting once again to voice her request for a reference, but Lady Cunningham cut her short, exasperation honing her words. "You must understand, Sarah, that I cannot give you a reference

26

enabling you to disobey Lord Tarrington's express wishes, especially as I was the one who advised him of your need for alternative employment in the first place."

"I have no choice, then, Lady Cunningham, have I, for without a reference I stand no chance at all of other employment."

"You stand none anyway, my dear," Lady Cunningham said with a soft sigh. "Who will employ a widow with your looks to work as a governess in their household? And there is Emma to further complicate matters."

Sarah, seizing upon the idea at once, said quickly, "Of course, Emma. I am sure when Lord Tarrington discovers I have a child he will also want to reconsider his offer." She looked eagerly toward Anna Cunningham, sure that the requested reference would now be forthcoming. The other woman's words, however, erased the smile slowly from Sarah's face.

"But he knows of your child. I made it clear that you were a mother when I first mentioned the matter to him."

Sarah sat silent, staring ahead, her lip caught painfully between her teeth. Anna Cunningham urged gently, "Be sensible, Sarah. Lord Tarrington is well known for his fair treatment of staff and employees. Curb your reckless impulses and I am sure you will find life at Winslade Hall delightfully rewarding."

Sarah, sitting there listlessly, asked dully, "Will my presence in a bachelor's household not give rise to gossip?"

"Oh, no need to worry about your reputation, my dear. He has an aunt who resides there, quite a termagent if I remember correctly, so all the niceties of the situation are taken care of."

Sarah retorted, laughing bitterly, "But it was not my reputation that I referred to, Lady Cunningham. I am quite sure that any further damage would pass unnoticed."

Lady Cunningham, slightly disconcerted by this remark, nevertheless recovered quickly, remarking airily, "No need to worry regarding his lordship's reputation, either, my dear. I am sure he would be the first to admit that it was tarnished beyond redemption years ago." She looked quickly at Sarah, conscious that it might not have been prudent to impart such news, and added speedily "All exaggeration, of course."

Sarah read the confusion in the older woman's face and said tonelessly, "I was already aware of tales of his lecherous self-indulgence."

Lady Cunningham sighed, watching Sarah's averted face closely, and said quietly, "It is true that he has a name as a rake and a libertine. He also had quite a successful record of duels and hell-raising in his earlier years. I think a lot of the tales become enlarged in the telling, especially as he himself never seemed to bother much with repudiating any gossip. It has never worried him. Nor," she added drily, "has it dissuaded any of the multitude of hopeful debutantes and fond mamas who have hounded him mercilessly over the past ten years or so; all to no avail, since he has remained single. Wealth and position cover a multitude of sins, you see, my dear." She paused, watching Sarah steadily as she added slowly, "Besides which, he is, of course, quite extraordinarily handsome."

"Is he? I really had not noticed," Sarah returned

woodenly, unable to meet the other woman's eyes, and then continued contemptuously, "I think he looks like a wealthy Romany; he is really only lacking a gold earring."

Anna Cunningham nodded in agreement. "Yes, that heathenish color comes from too much traveling in foreign parts. He served with Wellington in Spain last year, you know." She settled into the chair comfortably, preparing for gossip. "Also," she added in a low tone meant to convey secrecy, "it was rumoured at the time that he acted as a British spy, breaking up a Bonapartiste spy ring that could have threatened the outcome of the British advance in the Peninsular." She leaned back contentedly, smoothing her dress. "Now, of course, he seems to dedicate the best part of his time to increasing his already sizable fortune. He rarely strays long from the estate. His appearances in town, except on business matters, are noticeable only by their absence, I hear."

It was a while before Anna Cunningham, still gratified by the quality of news she had just imparted, noted that Sarah's face still registered a sort of hopeless misery, and she said in an odd tone, "You do realize, Sarah, that I would have been placed in an impossible position if you had stayed here, don't you?"

Sarah smiled slightly at the older woman and said softly, "Yes, of course. You have been very kind, Lady Cunningham. I am very grateful for the time I have spent here. I just wish . . . circumstances had been different."

Lady Cunningham, anxious to bring the interview to a close before Sarah could retract this submissive attitude, said, "Well dinner is probably ruined beyond repair, but I am ravenous. Come, Sarah, let us eat."

Sarah shook her head, rising to her feet. "I do believe, Lady Cunningham, that I am too tired to eat, after all. My appetite has quite gone. I shall bid you goodnight, if I may." She started toward the door.

"I can have a tray sent up, if you prefer?" Anna Cunningham's voice followed her anxiously.

"No, really. I don't think I could eat a thing. Goodnight."

She entered her room as silently as she had left it, walking slowly toward the dark corner where Emma still lay sleeping. Her hand reached for the covers, pulling them up around the chubby arms, tucking in the sides neatly. The child did not stir, and she walked slowly to the window where she had stood what seemed now like an age ago, and, leaning her head against the wall, she stared into the silent, shadowy blackness, finally allowing the tears of desolation to fall.

Lady Cunningham sank back into her chair in the drawing room, her own appetite rapidly diminishing. She allowed her thoughts to dwell on Amelia Brent, her longest-standing friend, and Sarah's mother. She made a mental correction, Amelia Thorpe now, since she had been remarried shortly after the death of Sarah's father, Sir Paul Brent, whose unfortunate demise had left his wife and only daughter in financial ruin. She could see that for Amelia remarriage, even to a miserly tea importer, was the only escape from certain poverty, but she had been astonished when her friend had written informing her that Sarah was also to be married. The girl was barely eighteen and had not yet made her come out. The financial scandal surrounding her father's death could not erase the fact that she was gently born and certainly deserved better, in Anna Cunningham's estimation, than a hasty marriage at eighteen to a local country squire more than twice her age. This had been brought home to Anna even more forcefully when Amelia had then removed with her spouse to his residence in Manchester, leaving Sarah alone and friendless with a stranger who nobody appeared to know much of.

Anna Cunningham had always been fond of Sarah and she had made discreet inquiries regarding the nature of Mr. Charles Thornton, Sarah's husband and the squire of a small estate in Hertfordshire. She had been alarmed to find that the squire apparently spent the best part of his time dallying with women of dubious repute in London's seamier quarters, while his young wife was left alone in Hertfordshire attempting to manage his sadly neglected estate.

However, Sarah's bad luck had barely started, for Charles Thornton subsequently died in circumstances equaling the scandal that had surrounded her father's death. It also came to light when his affairs were settled that he had disinherited his young wife and child, and Lady Cunningham had been horrified to learn that there was some whisper that he had done so believing that the child was not his. Anna had never given this absurdity any credence, believing that a man of his vile character would be capable of such an act purely from spite.

Her stepfather's refusal to give shelter to Sarah and her daughter, then barely nine months old, had shocked Anna very deeply, and her respect and friendship for Amelia had sadly diminished when she realized that Amelia was not about to cross her husband in demanding some sort of home and security for her daughter and grandchild. William Thorpe's only aid to Sarah's future was to attempt to find her some form of "genteel" employment in order that she should be able to support herself, which, in the event, proved to be an almost impossible task. Anna, learning of the girl's predicament, had immediately stepped forward to offer her the position of governess. Her own daughters were sadly lacking in anything approaching educational achievement, and no tutoring so far had been able to rectify the matter. One of Paul Brent's few commendable acts had been to furnish his daughter with an excellent education, and Anna, realizing that she could indeed benefit from the arrangement, was glad to welcome the girl into her home.

She sighed now in exasperation. It really was extremely tiresome of Alfred to have made it necessary to remove the girl, doubly so, she thought acidly, as the children were at last beginning to show some signs of accomplishment. She also had the added irritation of going to unnecessary expense to send the girls to Italy for a while. She would rather that, though, she reminded herself hastily, than allow any breath of scandal to attach to the sudden removal of the young governess from her household.

Her husband's roving eye was not something Anna was unaware of. To some extent she actively encouraged it, as long as discretion played a major part in his affairs. She had been married at twenty to Sir Alfred, starry-eyed and full of romantic illusions. These,

32

however, had been brutally shattered on her wedding night, with the discovery that she found the physical side of marriage a nauseating indignity, something to be endured rather than enjoyed. Two difficult pregnancies and almost impossible births had turned her distaste for sex into frozen frigidity. Her husband, dismayed and bewildered by his wife's attitude, had soon resorted to finding comfort elsewhere, and any attempts on his part to breach the ever widening gap between them with unfortunately clumsy intimacy merely resulted in his wife's retreating behind a wall of female malaise that confined her to bed sometimes for weeks at a time. Anna was aware that most men of breeding or wealth kept mistresses at some time or other, and the knowledge that her husband was no exception did not disturb her unduly. As long as he was discreet and kept his mistresses a safe distance away in London, she was content, actively encouraging him to make London excursions whenever an unwelcome gleam started to appear in his eye at retiring time. In fact she thought with a frown, remembering her husband's recent unexpected nocturnal visits, prompted no doubt by remorse, it was high time another trip was suggested.

Her thoughts returned to Sarah and the scene she had witnessed between the young woman and Mark Tarrington. She had been amazed, not only by the electrical friction, but also by the change in Sarah. The girl was usually amenable to the point of complaisancy. Her manners were always impeccable. If Sarah's admission that she had seen Mark Tarrington only once before was true—and she had no reason to doubt her—then it seemed unlikely that there could be any valid reason for the antagonism. Her thoughts

33

stirred uneasily. Mark Tarrington's reputation with women was all too well known. Various opera dancers, actresses, and available widows had engaged his affections temporarily over the years, but nothing, to her knowledge, had ever resembled an alliance of any greater permanency. It was all of twelve years since his father had died in a hunting accident and he had inherited a fortune and Winslade Hall, all at the age of eighteen. Astute management and a keen business head had since increased his financial status, and he now had control of a fortune that most covetous mamas would have given their eyeteeth to ally their daughters with. He was still one of society's most eligible bachelors. It would not be long, she thought ironically, before the first bunch of hopefuls from all those long years ago were positioning their own earnest offspring in his path. Finding him would be the problem. He had, for the past couple of seasons now, shunned town entertainment in favor of rural life on his estate. No wonder Sarah thought he looked like a vagrant—galloping around in the open air all day with estate managers for company was hardly the life for a gentleman of his position. And yet he seemed to prefer that now.

If Sarah had any notion that Lord Tarrington's interest in her exceeded that of her abilities as governess, then Lady Cunningham was not so sure that the same ideas were not crossing her own mind. Ridiculous as it might seem that he would bother to go to such complicated lengths to ensure a new mistress. Anna considered Sarah, and any idea that it was beyond credibility began rapidly to diminish. The girl possessed a rare loveliness, and coupled with her superb intelligence and her obvious dislike of him, she could prove to be the kind of challenge a man like Mark Tarrington would find irresistible.

Anna sighed heavily. Her head was beginning to spin with the strain of making sense of it all. She stood up, all thought of food vanishing, deciding that an early night for her also was in order.

She reached for her reticule just as Sir Alfred entered the room.

"Fine dinner, m'dear. Syllabub tasted a bit strange, though," he added reflectively. "Shame Tarrington had to miss it." He scanned the room. "Where is Sarah?"

"Oh, she decided not to dine tonight; overcome with emotional strain, no doubt." The subtlety was lost on Sir Alfred, who, still relishing the food he had just consumed, said, "Are you going in to dinner, m'dear? I was too famished to wait any longer, I'm afraid."

"No, I think I shall have an early night; my appetite has quite disappeared also." She turned as if to go, but her husband had stepped forward, a familiar glint in his eyes.

"I think I might join you in an early night, m'dear. Quite worn out myself." He sighed indicatively, making a maladroit attempt at catching one of her hands in his.

"Good idea, Alfred," said Anna noncomittally, disengaging herself at the same time. "On your way, would you ask Maggie to prepare me one of her potions? My head is about to split, and I do so need an uninterrupted night's sleep." She smiled sweetly, ignoring her husband's dejected look, and made a hasty withdrawal. Stopping at the door, she turned back to Sir Alfred still standing glum-faced in the middle of the room, saying, "I hope it will not inconvenience you, Alfred. . . ." She hesitated, hoping for some reaction.

"What's that m'dear?" he said, with an ill-concealed display of the sulks.

"I did so hope you might find time to pop to London—on an errand—I thought if business were to take you there soon . . . ?" She let the question hang in the air. He looked thoughtfully interested suddenly, so she continued, pressing home her advantage. "I need some fripperies collected—something I ordered a while ago from Madame Claudine—only if it is no trouble, of course."

"No trouble, my love," he said, with what he hoped was repressed vigor.

"Thank you Alfred. Goodnight." She turned before the relief became too betraying, closing the door quietly behind her.

Sir Alfred sank into one of the armchairs, resting into it with much squeaking and wheezing, smiling with pure satisfaction. He reached for the decanter at his side, and examining a glass, poured a measure into it. He settled back, congratulating himself on his impeccable diplomacy, which had kept his wife in ignorance over the years of the amorous peccadillos that so enhanced the carrying out of her little errands. He raised the glass to his lips, savoring the burning liquid, and with smug anticipation made plans for his excursion.

Chapter Two

Sarah folded the last of the print baby dresses into a neat pile. The room was littered with small stacks of clothing all awaiting packing into her battered trunk. She looked at the open trunk and at the stacked clothes, not wanting to finalize this act of departure just yet.

Turning away from the depressing sight she looked out of the window. She let the gentle breeze disturb her hair, lifting the weight of it away from her face. She pushed a hand across her eyes, feeling the weariness of lack of sleep overtaking her slowly. She had not slept properly for several nights now, not since the visit of Lord Mark Tarrington had robbed her of her peace of mind. She tried to erase the thought of him from her mind, but it was something that she was finding increasingly hard to do. Dark features, cruel and gloating, seemed to haunt her waking and sleeping moments alike. She shook herself mentally. This was ridiculous—she was becoming obsessed with the odious man.

The fatigue was beginning to show in her face, the sapphire of her eyes emphasized by the shadowing of similar color beneath them. She pushed the heavy cloak of her hair back from her shoulders, luxuriating in the soft air cooling her skin, letting it fall back caressingly against her neck. Her hair was undoubtedly her best feature, something she had always been unconceitedly proud of. It was thick and straight, yet felt as fine as wet silk and shone with the rich gold color of precious metal. Any attempts made to style or curl it had always been a disastrous failure, and Sarah therefore wore it loose, or, for a more formal appearance, twisted at the nape of her neck into a simple knot. For the future, she thought bitterly, she would be wearing it almost unfailingly in the less attractive manner.

A slight noise made her turn, and she sighed in exasperation at the sight of Emma, chubby hands clinging to the bed for support, slowly knocking pile after pile of neatly arranged clothes to the floor. Aware that she was being watched, the child laughed with impish glee, equally aware of her bad behavior.

"That will not benefit us at all, I am afraid to say," Sarah chided her with mock severity, swinging the child high in the air before placing her firmly in front of her wooden toys. "Now these are yours—do not touch the clothes." She wagged an admonishing finger in front of the child's face, but Emma merely giggled, trying to grab the waving finger.

Sarah sighed, starting to collect the strewn clothing, straightening as she heard Lady Cunningham say in astonishment from the doorway, "Good grief, what are you doing with your clothes, my dear?"

Sarah laughed, "Emma wanted to help pack—or unpack, perhaps I should say. I think the child has more sense than I credit her with," she added wistfully.

Anna Cunningham looked despairingly at the girl. "Now, come along, Sarah, I thought we had agreed that this opportunity is definitely worth some enthusiasm." Her sharp tone was belied by the concern in her eyes. "Besides, I have a suggestion I think you may like." She resumed quickly before the gleam of anticipation in Sarah's eyes became too pronounced. "Anna and Maria will be leaving for Italy next week with my sister Lucy and her husband, the count. They have been staying in London with some friends for a while, and when they return they will take the girls with them. It is all very convenient, as it means that I shall not be required to travel with them—thank God," she added, her pale cheeks tinged with grey at the thought of sea travel. "They have no children of their own, and they are quite keen for the girls to stay for at least six months, probably longer. It is an ideal opportunity for them, really. Anyway, I shall not now, of course, be requiring the services of Maggie, their maid. I thought, my dear, that perhaps you would like her to accompany you on your journey to Surrey? She is so good with Emma, and who knows, perhaps if you handle the situation correctly," she glanced sideways at Sarah as she spoke, her meaning crystal, "you may be able to keep her on with you, for a while, at least. I am sure Mark Tarrington would not object to a short stay until you have settled, especially as I have no desperate need for the girl here now. He would probably not even notice another member of the staff in that colossal place of his." She stopped, noticing with relief the look of delight on the girl's face. Realizing that this would be as a good a time as any to restate her advice, she added firmly, "Remember, my dear, the more cooperative you are in your dealings with Mark Tarrington, the better life will treat you."

Sarah grimaced wryly, but she was not about to let any thoughts of the arrogant Mark Tarrington dampen this heartening news. Sarah liked Maggie.

She had always been amazed at the difference in attitude of the servants in this house to those she had known as a child. Here they seemed happy, pleasant, and eager to help. In her father's house they had been sullen, bad-tempered, and more often than not quite blatantly insolent. With hindsight, she realized that their attitude had probably been governed by the erratic nature of their wages. Money, or the lack of it as a result of her father's gambling problems, had always been at the bottom of their troubles, she remembered.

Maggie was a cheerful, attractive girl who she guessed to be about the same age as herself. She was taller than Sarah, dark-haired and plumply curvaceous, with a ready smile and a quick wit. Emma had taken to the girl straightaway, and she had been a great help to Sarah when the child, fretful with teething pain, had needed attention during lesson time.

Sarah finished packing quickly, some of her lethargy vanished now. Anna Cunningham, aware that this simple kindness had rendered the girl almost speechless with gratitude, bustled out suddenly, muttering that she had to check on the girls' packing, clutching a scrap of lace to her suspiciously and suddenly mote-ridden eyes.

The coach lurched suddenly and the three occupants were thrown together in an undignified heap. Maggie, clutching Emma concernedly, muttered, "These roads will kill us all; that is the third time she has knocked her head."

Emma was apparently oblivious of this solicitude and continued with her attempt to remove the limbs from her wooden doll. Sarah stirred on the seat. The coach was comfortable, luxurious even, but the journey was beginning to tell on them all now. Traveling with a young child was certainly trying, she mused, remembering Emma's tantrums when her attempts to clamber through the window had been thwarted. She closed her eyes, letting her head fall back against the cushioned squabs of the coach, allowing weariness to possess her momentarily.

Parting with the Cunninghams had been quite traumatic. Anna and Maria had clung to her tearfully, their small faces a mixture of sadness at her departure and thrilled anticipation at their own imminent journey. Lady Cunningham and Sarah had embraced each other emotionally, their eyes overbright as they made the usual vows of promising to write, and to visit when possible. Sir Alfred had shuffled about uneasily, looking quite relieved when the party finally boarded the coach.

Sarah wondered now whether Lady Cunningham would, in fact, write to her. Her mother had made the same promise over two long years ago when she had left her daughter in the care of a lecherous old man. Sarah could not recall the number of times her mother had written in those years—she only knew that months of waiting fruitlessly for the post each day had taken their toll on her. In the nine months she had been employed at the Cunninghams', she had received only four brief notes, usually filled with uninteresting news of the state of the tea-importing business and her husband's meanness with money. There were only rarely queries about her own or Emma's health or happiness, and the pathos of the letters left Sarah in no doubt as to the success of her mother's second marriage.

Sarah was brought back from her reverie sharply with the sound of John, the driver, booming out, "Just entering Lord Tarrington's estate now, madam."

41

She shot forward in her seat, peering out at the rolling countryside, unable to reason why the sight of his land should fascinate her so. She peered into the distance, scanning the horizon for some sight of Winslade Hall. Lady Cunningham had been full of praises for the house, and yet Sarah hoped now, illogically, that she would be unimpressed by it.

She was not. It came into view suddenly as they rounded a screen of tall poplars. It was more magnificent than she could ever have imagined. It was built in late gothic style, and although it had obviously been improved on and maintained extensively since its original construction, it was without any of the over-elaborate and fancy additional architecture that often marred so many houses of that period. Not only was the structural appearance immaculate, but everywhere there was evidence of meticulous and constant care. As they drew closer she could see that everywhere were clipped, smooth lawns and weed-free beds of roses, shrubs, and late summer flowers. A large part of the stonework was covered in a well-pruned mass of golden honeysuckle, intertwined here and there with splashes of dark red and pink, which she guessed to be climbing roses. Several areas of the garden were being tended as they arrived, and she could see curious workmen watching the progress of their coach as they rolled steadily nearer.

Sarah sank back into the cushions, strangely disappointed by the splendor, aware that Maggie was still gazing at the scene, mouth agape.

"Do you think this is it?" she asked in an awed whisper.

Sarah laughed shortly. "Unless the master of Winslade Hall has two such residences, I should say, yes, it is." She could feel some of the panic starting to stir again, and she breathed deeply, attempting to calm herself.

Before leaving the Cunninghams' she had settled on a course of action for her new life at Winslade Hall. She was determined not to give Lord Tarrington any further cause for complaint, either with her duties as governess or with her attitude toward him. She was a good tutor, and she was well aware of the fact, and she had decided that cold efficiency at all times, even under provocation, would soon show him that she was not prepared to be drawn into any further verbal wrangles. She would be cool and polite when in his company, but she knew with unwavering certainty that she would be scrupulous in avoiding him as often as possible; something that, thankfully, should prove to be quite simple in a house of that size. She hugged her strategies close about her, bolstering her courage as the coach drew to a halt outside the massively impressive great door.

A man in an immaculate black butler's uniform, and a woman, her round face and friendly smile contrasting sharply with her severely dressed black figure, stepped forward to meet them as they alighted.

"Mrs. Thornton? I am Matthew Davis, the butler at Winslade Hall. I hope your journey was not too uncomfortable?" His expression was one of polite inquiry, and Sarah realized that he was, in fact, quite genuinely interested in her reply.

"The journey was quite surprisingly quick, thank you."

Sarah turned to the woman standing smiling still at his side, and he said, "This is my wife, Matilda. She is housekeeper here."

The woman's smile deepened, and Sarah could feel some of the nervous apprehension within her easing; they, at least, seemed amiable and pleasant enough. Matilda Davis looked at the child still sleeping in

Maggie's capable clasp, her expression softening visibly, and Sarah warmed to the woman at once as she indicated silently that they should follow her into the house.

If Sarah had been overawed by the magnificence of the building itself, she was doubly awed by the interior. She could not help but stand entranced for a few moments looking around the vast hall in all its splendor and she knew that in no way had Lady Cunningham exaggerated the impressive opulence of Lord Mark Tarrington's stately home.

Mrs. Davis was used to seeing new guests and employees alike being rendered speechless by their first sight of Winslade Hall, and she allowed the two young women to stand in silent appraisal for a few minutes before saying pleasantly to Sarah, "I shall show you to your room, Mrs. Thornton; I expect you will want to freshen yourself before dinner. The little mite looks completely worn out." She indicated Emma with an inclination of her head and then started across the great hall to the widely sweeping curve of stairs. Sarah followed her starch-murmuring figure, her eyes darting from side to side as she examined minutely the luxury that was to be her new home.

The room allocated to Sarah was unexpectedly beautiful, and she turned at once to Matilda Davis in embarrassed confusion and queried quickly, "But surely there is some mistake?" The other woman frowned uncertainly and said, "Lord Tarrington was very specific that you should have this one." She looked concerned suddenly and said, "It is satisfactory, I hope?"

Sarah laughed, ill at ease. "Yes, of course, it is very beautiful. I had not expected any such room—that is all."

Mrs. Davis bustled forward, pleased that her welcoming touches were obviously appreciated. "There is a cot in this corner for the baby. If you like I could have it moved into the dressing room?" She indicated a door off the main room.

"No, I would really prefer her to stay in here with me." Sarah smiled her thanks at the woman.

"Now, let me find your traveling companion somewhere to sleep for the night. I expect you will be needing to refresh yourself before the return journey." She indicated that Maggie should follow her, unaware of the consternation that suddenly flashed across that young woman's countenance at her words. Maggie looked toward Sarah questioningly, hoping that the housekeeper was to be informed that she was to stay on with her new mistress, but Sarah merely indicated with a slight movement of the head that she should say nothing yet.

Matilda Davis stopped at the door, saying, "I almost forgot. His lordship is out dealing with estate matters at the present. He said he would be back to welcome you at dinner tonight."

She sailed out then with a parting beam, her starched uniform rustling busily, and Maggie, placing the still sleeping Emma in the crib, followed, with one last forlorn look at Sarah.

Sarah sank onto the massive, soft bed and looked around with slow incredulity at her room. The walls were covered in a pale gold watered silk, and the curtains and bed draperies were of an exactly matching shade. The floor was almost entirely covered, except for a small border of polished wood around the perimeter of the room, in a luxurious deep blue carpeting. She sank the points of her shoes into the rich pile, watching as the fiber reshaped slowly. There was a small, light mahogany escritoire in one corner with paper neatly arranged on top, and highly polished light mahogany chests of drawers and wardrobes. She let her gaze come to rest on a mahogany chair, marveling at the wonderfully intricate brass inlay design worked into the back. A tiny, exquisitely crafted table and chair in another corner was obviously intended for Emma's use, and it seemed that every available surface was filled with vases of freshly cut late summer flowers.

As Sarah sat surveying the unaccustomed splendor, she felt suddenly ashamed of her uncharitable feelings toward Mark Tarrington. She was well aware that she had already been treated far better than a governess had reason to expect. A plush traveling coach, and now a room of this beauty. But as she allowed her gaze to roam the room once more, she was not sure whether this unexpected consideration rendered her grateful or troubled.

She moved from the bed and to the open window. Her room looked out over the back of the house. More immaculately tended gardens were spread out below. A small fountain spat a jet of crystal water gently into the air, and the last of the day's sunshine fell in a myriad of rainbow-sparkling droplets. Further in the distance she could see what looked like a small lake, with a tiny island near the center abundant with trees and shrubs, the surface of the smooth water dotted here and there with white and colored shapes that she guessed to be ducks and swans.

Turning back into the room and walking to the large bed, Sarah started unpacking her meager possessions, wondering what to wear that evening at dinner. She had only the blue silk dress she had worn that fateful evening at the Cunninghams'. Her other clothes were simple everyday styles in dull, practical colors, ideal for her role as governess but not suitable for wearing to dinner.

She shook out the blue dress and hung it up, hoping that some of the creases would shed before the evening, making an unconscious choice as she did so. She smoothed the skirt with slightly trembling fingers, wondering whether she had the courage to ask for a tray in her room that evening, pleading travel fatigue. She dismissed the abject notion instantly and let her mind escape along the avenue of her future pupils. She wondered if they would take to her or if they would be resentful of her youth; she was, after all, only just five years older than the girl she was to teach.

Mrs. Davis, reappearing with a tray of tea and small cakes, cut into her musings, saying, "I expect you are famished." She lowered her tone, espying the still sleeping child, and continued, "I have brought the baby some milk."

Sarah smiled her thanks and watched Matilda Davis retreat softly from the room. Then she relaxed back onto the bed, removing her shoes. She reveled in the luxurious softness for a few minutes before starting on the tea and cakes, but the nervous exhaustion of the past few days had taken its toll, and after a mere sip of tea and a few mouthfuls of delicious honey cake, her weariness overcame her appetite and she slept.

Chapter Three

Sarah woke, stretching lazily. Her eyes roved slowly around the unfamiliar, lavish surroundings, and she sat up with a startled exclamation. She sat staring ahead, allowing her memory to catch up with her racing thoughts, and then she relaxed back onto the pillows.

A lamp was burning softly by the bed, casting a golden glow over the room. Turning toward the window, she saw that a russet dusk was deepening to ochre. She must have been sleeping for hours. She threw back the covering blanket and paced softly toward the cot. Emma was gone. Sarah panicked slightly before realizing that whoever had covered her on the bed and lit the lamp must also have taken Emma; Maggie had obviously taken the child to her room. She sat down in front of the gilt-framed mirror, her memory clear and troubled now by the imminent dinner summons. She wondered hopefully whether she had perhaps missed the meal, but she drew little comfort from the idea, and as though in answer to her unspoken query, there was a soft tap at the door and Mrs. Davis entered.

"Ah, I see you are up, my dear. I did not like to

wake you earlier, you looked completely exhausted. Your companion has taken the baby to her room for a while—such a dear little thing," she enthused. She moved quickly about the room lighting lamps and closing the heavy window drapes. "Dinner is almost ready; I can help you dress and freshen yourself, as your maid is busy with the child."

Sarah, biting off unuttered an excuse about exhaustion having completely removed her appetite, smiled thanks at the woman, allowing her to comb her disarranged hair into some sort of order.

Mrs. Davis sighed enviously. "What hair!" She ran her hand down the satin smoothness of it. "You are quite the prettiest girl I have seen in a long while."

She broke off suddenly as a loud gong sounded downstairs. "Come along now. I shall show you the way to the dining room."

Sarah followed in apprehensive silence, conscious of an unwelcome sensation writhing in the pit of her stomach. Mrs. Davis stopped in front of a large door, and seeing the young girl's frightened look, said gently, "Go on in dear. I expect Miss Joanna and Master Luke will be in there first. His lordship is usually late for meals." She raised her dark brows heavenward, as though his tardiness was of some exasperation to her, and hurried off muttering darkly about ruined dinners.

The brightly lit dining room was just as impressive as the rest of the house that she had seen so far. A huge, highly polished walnut table, set with gleaming china and light-reflecting silver, dominated the room. She thought, with immeasurable relief, that she was alone as she entered. The room seemed deserted, and she moved slowly toward the magnificent table, the tips of her fingers brushing lightly along the satiny wood. A slight sound behind made her turn with such haste that her straying fingers caught against the coldness of the cutlery and a fork knocked noisily to the floor. She spun round feeling foolish at her clumsiness.

Mark Tarrington was watching her, smiling slightly, and as her discomfort at her ungainliness grew, so it seemed, did his amusement. She realized he had been in the room all the time, and swallowing a retort about people who crept up on others unobserved, she quickly bent to retrieve the utensil, at the same time attempting to recompose her fraying nerves. She rearranged the fork with elaborate attention, more to occupy her shaking fingers than from any care for the table setting. Aware of his intense scrutiny and unable to bear it longer, she turned towards him, her eyes meeting the amber depths of his, and said, "I apologize for my clumsiness; I had thought I was alone—you startled me." Her tone was studied politeness; Lady Cunningham would have been proud of her, she thought acidly.

He bit his lip for a moment, as though to quell a smile, before saying solemnly, "It seems to be a habit I have, Mrs. Thornton."

She could feel the color starting to creep up under her skin and turned with relief as she heard the door open and saw two young people enter.

She was immediately aware of the similarity between the two. They both had dark, glossy hair in abundance, and eyes of a deep brown color and clear, pale complexions, accentuated by the darkness of their hair. The girl was fairly tall and walked with a graceful ease. She was quite obviously beautiful, and yet there was a sullen twist to her mouth that detracted from the otherwise lovely features. She studied Sarah intently for a moment, but there was no friendliness or welcome in her eyes, and Sarah's hopes for a good relationship with her new pupils started to sink. The boy, she could tell, did not have his sister's calm self-assurance, and he hovered near the door, obviously unsure of himself.

Lord Tarrington, moving forward at that moment, beckoned the apprehensive boy forward, and turning to Sarah, said, "Mrs. Thornton, this is Joanna and Luke, my sister's children. They will be staying at Winslade Hall for some time. . . ." He ignored the flash of unmistakable annoyance on Joanna's face at these words, staring hard at her until she flushed and looked away. "While their mother is in London," he finished. He paused and then added, "After dinner, Joanna, perhaps you would show Mrs. Thornton the schoolroom and any other parts of the house she may like to see."

The girl looked positively unenthusiastic, but nodded with bad grace and sat down at the table, obviously dismissing Sarah's presence.

Sarah's blue eyes met Lord Tarrington's over the top of the boy's dark head, and he smiled at her for the first time with warmth and a certain amount of sympathy, as though apologizing silently for his niece's atrocious manners. Sarah, confused by this display of friendliness, turned quickly to the silent boy, smiling kindly at him, and the boy flushed with pleasure and sat down next to Joanna, a pink glow staining his cheeks.

The meal looked delicious, and yet Sarah found she could barely eat. She was aware of Joanna's coolly appraising gaze throughout, and several times, meeting her watching eyes, she smiled, but gained little response from the sulky girl. She was also conscious that Mark Tarrington's eyes rarely left her face, and the combined scrutiny of the two diminished her appetite completely.

51

Lord Tarrington, however, managed to keep the conversation flowing reasonably, asking her about the journey, the Cunninghams, and various other topics of general interest, and Sarah realized that it was the first time they had managed to converse freely, without the dialogue's being strewn with barbed remarks or veiled insults.

The meal ended at last, and Joanna, obviously eager to escape, excused herself saying that she had a letter to write, but would meet Sarah later in the sitting room if she wished to see the rest of the house. Sarah realized from the tone of the invitation that it had only been issued under duress, and she refused the offer, saying that she would rather leave it until tomorrow. Luke also showed signs of disappearing, and Sarah, with no wish to test this newfound amity with her employer further, also rose with the mumbled excuse that she had unpacking to see to.

His next words however stopped her short. "I have a few things I wish to discuss with you, Mrs. Thornton, if you would care to come to the study for a few minutes." He had moved to the door without waiting for or expecting a reply, and Sarah, slightly nettled by his high-handed manner, preceded him reluctantly through the door.

The house and its splendor still fascinated her, and she walked leisurely, her eyes darting from side to side as she examined different aspects of the architecture and the various paintings decorating the walls.

He noticed her perusal and said, "The house interests you?"

"Very much so; it is beautiful."

"Good."

Sarah looked at him quickly, but he was opening the door of a room slightly down the corridor from the dining room and on the opposite side, and as she walked hesitantly into the room he indicated that she should be seated in a wing chair and sat down himself in a leather swivel chair behind a large mahogany desk, scattered with papers and open ledgers.

The room was almost a personification of himself, she realized idly: dark, totally masculine, and with none of the softening touches that could be glimpsed in the other rooms she had seen. She guessed the servants were probably rarely allowed in to clean. It smelled of leather furniture and had the scholastic scent of the schoolroom—ink and old bookbinding. There was a small leather sofa along one wall, and she thought at first that the room seemed badly lit, but realized that it was the darkness of the wood paneling covering each wall that made it seem so.

There was a large decanter half full of brandy in the middle of the desk, and he sat now pouring himself a measure. When he spoke it was without looking at her, as though her presence was of little interest, something belied by the expression in his eyes when they eventually met hers.

"I hope your room is satisfactory?"

"Of course. It is lovely."

He smiled and nodded slightly. "I thought it would suit you." He swirled the golden liquid around in the crystal goblet, watching the amber swell, before raising the glass to his lips, his eyes meeting hers over the rim. The silence was lengthening uncomfortably, and Sarah found herself examining her nails with nervous attention.

"I expect you will have plenty to do tomorrow settling yourself and your daughter." Sarah noted the reference to Emma. It was the first time he had acknowledged her existence. "I think, therefore, you can commence your duties here the following day. It will give you a chance to get to know Luke and Joanna

53

slightly better, also. She is quite a pleasant girl really." he paused, adding drily, "Beneath the veneer of spoiled brat."

The silence recommenced, and Sarah wondered whether he was expecting some comment from her regarding her future pupils.

"I shall expect you to dine with the family in the evening."

Sarah, not sure that she could face that ordeal, replied quickly, "It is very kind of you to offer, but I really would prefer to eat with my daughter in my room, if that is convenient."

"It is not, Mrs. Thornton. I expect you to eat with the family. Sometimes it is the only opportunity I have of seeing Luke and Joanna during the day, and it enables me to catch up on family matters and their progress . . . or the lack of it," he remarked with a wry smile, "in the schoolroom."

Sarah, resenting his manner, merely replied stiffly, "Very well, my lord, if you wish."

"I do, Mrs. Thornton, and just to relieve you somewhat I should add that my presence at dinner rarely occasions more than three or four times a week. Estate matters keep me out quite late sometimes." He was watching her with sardonic amusement, having judged correctly by the slight flush enhancing her complexion that it was his presence rather than any sense of maternal duty that would keep her in her room at mealtimes.

"You have not yet met my aunt, the Dowager Alice Milbrook. She is indisposed, I hear, at the moment, so you have been spared the ordeal for a while at least." He spoke ironically, and yet his face had softened when speaking of her, and Sarah felt mildly surprised that he could display fondness for anyone.

Sarah saw his hand go to a silver knife lying on the

54

desk in front of him, and he ran his thumb caressingly along the edge, saying evenly, his eyes fixed relentlessly on her face, "I have no idea what governesses expect in the way of remuneration for services rendered. You shall have to advise me."

She stared at him for a few moments in blank surprise, and then as it dawned on her slowly that he was, in fact, giving her the opportunity to name her own price, a writhing uneasiness stirred in her stomach. Noting the derisive inquiry in his eyes, she knew instinctively that his generosity had nothing to do with any appreciation for her educational ability.

She glared at him, not wanting to examine too closely the reason for this unexpected offer, and retorted swiftly, her tone stinging, "I would not, of course, expect any more than I was paid at the Cunninghams'."

He was silent for some time, as though giving her the chance to change her mind, and she was aware of the veiled amusement in his eyes as he sat watching her unwaveringly, his fingers running the length of the silver dagger. Unable to look at him further, she studied her hands abruptly, trying to swallow her rising fury at what she was sure was some subtle and insulting proposition.

He spoke at last, asking easily, "And how much were you paid at the Cunninghams'?"

Sarah swallowed, feeling ridiculously embarrassed at uttering the figure. She knew that she had been badly underpaid for her services at Ashdowne Manor, but had been so desperately grateful for any employment and shelter at all that she had never felt able to broach the matter and try to negotiate more. The fact that Anna Cunningham was a family friend and treated her in every other respect with every possible consideration, had added to the reluctance Sarah had felt to upset her benefactress in any way. She murmured in a rush, "Forty pounds."

He appeared to consider this for a moment and then asked evenly, "Forty pounds half-yearly?"

"Per annum," she managed stiffly.

She watched his eyes widen with exaggerated surprise and humor and his bottom lip thrust slightly in amused thoughtfulness, and then he said with slow emphasis, "You sell yourself too cheaply, Mrs. Thornton. I would have rated your qualities as worthy of far more."

"I was quite satisfied with the arrangement," she lied quickly in clipped tones.

"Perhaps, but I have no intention of being accused of exploiting slave labor. I think forty pounds half-yearly would be a fairer sum." He halted, watching her, but she remained silent, her eyes lowered, and he added quietly, "For which you will tutor Luke and Joanna for an unspecified period of time."

She still did not reply, but sat there, her mind in turmoil. She wanted to throw the offer back, still uncertain what was really prompting the generosity, but the extra, unexpected money was tempting and needed desperately. She had nothing in reserve at all, and as she sat, her emotions warring silently, he said mildly, "Do you want a written contract?"

She shook her had once and then, looking up at him steadily, said firmly, "Thank you."

Their eyes held for a few moments, and then he looked at the silver knife beneath his fingers and his mouth distorted in a half-smile, his head inclining in acknowledgment of her gratitude as he murmured, "Not at all."

He made to rise abruptly, saying, "I hear from Mrs. Davis that you traveled here with a female companion. I have made arrangements that she shall

56

return to the Cunninghams' tomorrow afternoon. That should give her ample time to rest between journeys. Perhaps you would inform her of this."

He had turned, the matter obviously dismissed, and Sarah, seeing her chance to speak for Maggie's retention in the household, said hastily, "I had hoped, my lord, that Maggie might be allowed to stay on here. She is a very experienced nursemaid and is a great deal of help to me, especially during lesson time when my daughter needs attention."

His expression was impassive as he turned to her now. "That is no problem, Mrs. Thornton. There is an old retainer here by the name of Mary; you will no doubt meet her soon. She was nurse to both my sister and myself and also to Joanna and Luke. She has stayed on here, I think, in the unlikely hope that her services will be required again. I am more than pleased to provide her with the means of earning her keep once more."

He had turned away from her again as though indicating that there was nothing further to say on the matter, and Sarah, not sure why Maggie's presence in this house was of such vital importance to her, but knowing only that she desperately wanted her to stay, added swiftly, "But my lord, Maggie really is quite indispensable. She not only helps with the child but . . . but she reads tolerably well also, and can assist with lessons if I should be indisposed. . . ." Her words faded as she saw the frank disbelief in his eyes and she at once wished the lie unuttered as she noticed the dark brows lift in mock amazement.

"Really Mrs. Thornton? That is indeed unusual; quite an achievement, I should say, for a maid to be capable of reading lessons. I must meet this intellectual paragon."

He moved leisurely to the bell pull, and almost

immediately a liveried servant appeared. "Be good enough to ask Mrs. Thornton's companion to join me."

Sarah felt her tension release slightly, sure that when he met Maggie the girl's amiable personality and friendly disposition would win him over and he would allow her to stay. It could matter little to him, after all, that there was one more mouth to feed in a house of this size. She found she could not meet his gaze, though, and the silence between them seemed to stretch interminably. Sarah began dearly to wish that she had not mentioned the matter at all.

The door opened and Maggie, looking nervous and overawed but with a ready smile and deferential bob, entered the room.

Sarah, feeling slightly more confident with her arrival, smiled reassuringly, and Mark Tarrington turned to the girl, his smile friendly and his voice smooth.

"You must be Maggie. Mrs. Thornton has just been enlightening me as to your many worthy capabilities."

Maggie smiled contentedly, sure she was about to hear that her future was settled favorably. "I always try to please my employers, my lord," she said shyly.

"I am sure you do, Maggie." He looked at the book he had been turning over slowly on his desk, and picking it up, walked round to stand just behind Maggie. Opening the book, he held it slightly in front of her. "Your mistress tells me that you read exceptionally well; I would like you to read to me." He flicked the page in front of her. "Just a paragraph so that I can judge this extraordinary talent for myself."

Sarah stood numb. Maggie could not read a word, and she knew now that he was just as certain of it. His eyes met hers over the top of Maggie's bowed head, and Sarah looked away hastily, ashamed of being caught out with so obvious a lie.

Maggie, looking uneasy and smiling nervously, watched Sarah, waiting for some sign that this was merely an unappreciated jest, but seeing the forlorn dismay and a slight, hopeless shake of the head, she realized, horrified, that it was not so. Lord Tarrington's silken voice close behind her made her start in fright. "Come now, Maggie. There is no need to be shy; just a few lines."

The young woman's head bent lower, and Sarah, unable to bear Maggie's obvious humiliation at this ordeal, stepped forward, ready to admit her deceit. She began to speak, and at the same time the book lying open on the palm of Lord Tarrington's hand was snapped shut abruptly, cutting off her words. Maggie, her nerves at full stretch, uttered a small, suppressed scream at the unexpected noise, and he walked back to the desk, dropping the book onto it, saying scathingly, "No doubt overcome by modesty; well, another time, then. You can go Maggie."

Maggie, with one last bewildered look at Sarah, almost ran from the room, and he turned to Sarah, standing white-faced, the sapphire eyes bright with mortification. But she raised her chin, defiant even in defeat. Their eyes met and held, and he smiled slightly at the intensity of her aggression before saying, "If you are determined to continue with these willful battles, my dear, I suggest you improve your ammunition somewhat." His voice was smoothly sarcastic, and she flinched despite herself at his scorn.

He picked up the book and tossed it across the desk to where Sarah stood, biting her lip to control her temper.

"Teach her something from that by this time next week if you want her to stay." He sat down in the leather swivel chair, turning it so that he was facing the window with his back to her, and Sarah, almost faint with relief that she was obviously dismissed, picked up the book and said, "Yes, my lord," unable to keep the note of insolence from her voice, and then retreated to her room with all due haste.

Chapter Four

Sarah gazed through the windows, watching in drowsy fascination as the wind whipped a whirling mass of russet leaves high into the air and then abated, allowing them to spiral back to earth. It was only mid-September and the leaves were falling already, their colors gaudy against the emerald grass. She sighed, turning away from the colorful scene and back to the two bent heads, apparently absorbed with their work.

She had been at Winslade Hall nearly a week now.

Her gaze encompassed the large, bright schoolroom. It was set on the ground floor at the back of the house, with views of panoramic beauty across rolling Winslade land. How anyone was expected to do schoolwork when there was such diversion, Sarah could not imagine. She had several times looked up from marking books whilst the children had set work to do and found Joanna gazing sightlessly through the windows and across the countryside. She seemed to live in a world of her own for the best part of the day. Her apparent diligence with her work in the morning wavered as the day passed, and her attention wandered once again through the large windows, a secretive curve to her mouth.

Sarah was beginning to like the girl. She was hardly a girl, either, Sarah acknowledged; she was a young woman, and as such resented the fact that she was still in the schoolroom, tutored by someone barely older than herself. But their relationship had improved tremendously, and Sarah felt that Joanna was even beginning to warm to her.

Not that it was possible to instill much of educational worth in that pretty head, Sarah thought. The girl seemed to have an inbuilt resistance to learning or understanding anything. However her sketching had shown promise, and Sarah had asked them both if they would like to sketch out of doors one day if the weather proved clement. She had thought the idea a reasonable one, and was surprised at the enthusiasm the children expressed at this idea of escaping from the schoolroom for a few hours.

Luke, however, seemed to have a natural aptitude for schoolwork. He was quick and bright, with a keen memory and a natural desire to learn.

Their widowed mother apparently spent the entirety of the social season in London amidst the fashionable whirl offered to the favored few. The season was now at an end, and Joanna had intimated, without much enthusiasm, that her mother would probably be coming to stay at Winslade Hall soon for the winter months. It appeared that Lady Susan Morton was quite prepared to allow the upbringing and responsibility of her two children to rest on the broad and capable shoulders of her younger brother.

Sarah's musings at this point were brought sharply back to reality, as they inevitably were when her mind dwelt on Mark Tarrington. Fortunately, after the episode with Maggie in the study, she had seen little of him. His insistence that she dine with the family had not, in fact, been such an ordeal, for he had been quite truthful about his late absences from the house several times a week. Sarah found herself wondering acidly whether he had been just as honest in explaining the reasons for the absences, and she decided that, judging by his reputation, he was probably not just attending to estate matters. She refused to think further about it however, convincing herself that she was merely grateful for his absence, whatever the reason. When he had been present at mealtimes she had been studiously polite and coldly withdrawn, something that had seemed to amuse him to some extent, and she often found it extremely difficult not to rise to the very obvious and tantalizing bait he threw her way.

Sarah's thoughts turned to Emma, and, as always, her expression softened. Her daughter had settled down remarkably well in her new surroundings. Spoiled and petted by the servants, she was becoming more independent and willful all the time. Mary, the old nanny, had turned out to be an Irishwoman of extremely ample proportions, with maternal instincts of equally generous size, and she had clucked and fussed so over Emma when they met that Maggie had laughingly declared that she would find herself redundant and her services dispensed with, if she was not careful. This thought had moved the girl to inquire tentatively whether Sarah had heard anything of Lord Tarrington's decision regarding her future. Luckily Sarah could answer quite honestly that she had not, although the memory of that evening's humiliation still lingered painfully in her mind.

Sarah's attempts to teach Maggie to read had drawn a total blank. She seemed unable to recognize even basic words, no matter how painstakingly often they sat poring over the books in the evening. She had, paradoxically, managed to write her name tolerably well after only a few short lessons. Sarah dreaded the time when Lord Tarrington would remember his ultimatum, and she hoped desperately that he might forget the incident completely.

She had yet to meet the indomitable old lady of the house. Joanna and Luke referred to her as Great-Aunt Alice, and she could tell by their expressions that they were both extremely fond of her. She had apparently taken to her bed with a chill just before Sarah's arrival at Winslade Hall, but Joanna had informed her that morning that the old lady was eager to meet the young governess and would be dining downstairs with them that evening. She had her own suite of rooms in the east wing of the house and apparently stayed there for a good deal of the time, even entertaining her own friends and acquaintances there and holding much-vaunted card parties.

Sarah was brought back to the present sharply by the sound of Joanna's voice. "Mrs. Thornton?"

"I am sorry, Joanna, my mind was far away."

"I know, Mrs. Thornton. I feel the same way most of the time." She sighed deeply. "I was just saying that there is a village fête at the end of the week. The servants are usually allowed to go, in a rota, some in the morning and some in the afternoon; I wish Luke and I might be allowed to go." She looked wistfully at Sarah.

Luke snorted suddenly in disgust, saying, "You know very well Uncle Mark would never allow it. It is not even worth thinking about." He sounded suddenly angry, as though it mattered to him.

Sarah cut in quickly before the atmosphere became too frigid. "Why will your uncle not let you go, Joanna?"

"He never needs a reason," Joanna returned petulantly. "Just the fact that we would like to go is reason enough. Perhaps if you were to ask him . . ."

Sarah interrupted quickly, ignoring the last remark. "That is not fair, Joanna. Your uncle may be a lot of things," she continued hastily, before Joanna asked for any further explanation, "but petty, I do not think is one of them."

"I am flattered by your championship, Mrs. Thornton, and intrigued also to know what the other things you refer to are. We shall have to discuss them at further length another time." Mark Tarrington walked further into the room, stopping by Sarah's desk and picked up a book of Shakespearian prose, apparently studying it. He looked up slowly, well aware of the scarlet-faced dismay he had caused by his untimely entrance, and Sarah swallowed her compulsion to make some disparaging remark about his amazing aptitude for creeping about silently. His dark gaze held hers for a few moments before he walked leisurely into the schoolroom, stopping behind the two bent heads displaying a sudden conscientious diligence. He bent over Joanna, watching her write, her hands shaking visibly with the effort.

Sarah had never before been quite as aware as she was then of the awesome respect the two children felt for their uncle, inspired merely by his presence. He walked past Luke, and she saw the boy's pallor increase, and then back to where Sarah sat, her composure regained slightly.

"What was it you wanted to ask me, Mrs. Thornton?" His voice was expressionless, and looking past him, she could see that Joanna's and Luke's eyes were now fixed on her face. She knew that attempting this small kindness for them could mean a lot to their relationship, and she let her eyes slide back to his and said in a rush, "We were wondering whether we might visit the fair in the village at the end of the week. Educationally it would provide good essay material for the children." She faltered, aware of Luke and Joanna watching her with awed admiration. Their trust added to her determination, and she continued quickly, "We would only require half a day. Perhaps the morning, and they could write about the experience in the afternoon."

His face was unreadable, although she thought he smiled slightly before saying solemnly, "Well, Mrs. Thornton, as you seem to think the trip of benefit—educationally speaking, of course—I cannot think of any reason to deny you. I might accompany you, I think. It is a long time since I visited the village fête." He turned as though to go, and then stopped, asking evenly, "And how is Maggie progressing with her reading?"

Sarah could not prevent a slight nervous laugh. "Not at all, I am afraid, my lord. She writes very well, though. I could get her to copy the required passage from the book, if you wish." She met his gaze challengingly, aware suddenly of a new intensity in the golden eyes, which made her turn away sharply. He did not answer, but walked from the room, leaving the three occupants gazing at each other in unabated relief.

Dinner that evening was an animated affair. The Dowager Lady Alice Milbrook graced them with her presence, and Sarah, at first startled by the old lady's appearance, nevertheless warmed to her quickly as the evening progressed. She was a complete enigma. Petite and small-boned, she nevertheless had a voice that could, Sarah guessed, shatter glass at fifty paces. Although she must easily have been seventy years old, her hair was still predominantly black, streaked here and there with large bands of silver; her face quite smooth in places and yet deeply etched with lines in others. Her dress was of fine crimson satin, bedecked with various feathers and sequins. The whole should have looked ridiculous but in fact looked quite effective, in a rather outlandish fashion. Her mind was sharp and her wit athletic, and she kept Sarah enthralled throughout the meal with anecdotes of life when she was a girl. Judging by the expressions on the faces of Luke, Joanna, and his lordship, they had heard the stories many times before, and yet they humored her fondly.

She turned to Mark Tarrington suddenly in the middle of some tale saying, "Gel's got sense; not many youngsters know what I am talking about when I speak of life fifty years ago."

She was watching him shrewdly, black eyes narrowed into slits. "Picked for her educational abilities, you say? Well, I have to admit that unlikely as it may seem, it could be true. She certainly is a cut above the average simpering female." She turned to Sarah abruptly. "You are very pretty." It was an accusation rather than a compliment, and Sarah flushed beneath the old woman's piercing scrutiny, merely managing to murmur, "Thank you," and not noticing the astute gaze and ghost of a smile that twisted the thoughtfully puckering mouth as she looked again at her nephew.

He appeared unmoved by the old lady's suggestive remarks, merely returning her stare with equal intensity. She laughed suddenly, and turning back to Sarah, said, "I hear you have a daughter, my dear. Unusual for a governess to be encumbered with her own offspring as well as someone else's. Like to meet her sometime. Must visit me in my rooms; got lots to show you."

She rose then, irritably waving away a servant who had sprung forward to assist her. "Had a tiring day. Have to rest if I am to entertain my cronies tomorrow. Don't forget, my dear, visit me soon. I shall expect you."

She turned to Mark Tarrington, saying enigmatically as she left, "Treat her well, Tarrington." He merely smiled blandly as the old lady disappeared, but Sarah, for some reason she could not understand, avoided his eye with increased zeal for the remainder of the meal, and, excusing herself as soon as possible, returned to her room and Maggie's and Emma's calming influence.

Chapter Five

The day of the fête dawned bright and clear.

Joanna, in high spirits, was knocking at Sarah's room before she was even dressed. The young girl was becoming more amiable all the time, and the relationship between them had become more one of friend and companion rather than governess and pupil, even to the extent that Joanna had fallen into the habit of calling her Sarah instead of Mrs. Thornton.

She was dressed in a pretty lemon-colored muslin dress, which accentuated her dark good looks to perfection. She bounced onto the large bed, saying eagerly, "What are you going to wear today, Sarah?"

Sarah, mentally discarding all her well-worn dresses as unsuitable, sighed. "Well, I have not much choice, really." She opened the wardrobe door and looked at her small collection of clothes. She pulled out a pale blue walking dress, old, but still reasonably presentable, one eyebrow raised at Joanna in query.

The girl looked positively unenthusiastic. "Are they all the clothes you have?" She sounded incredulous.

"I am afraid so. Governesses do not need much in the way of elaborate gowns, mind you," Sarah said with a wry smile.

"Why do you not ask Uncle Mark for an advance on your salary? I am quite sure he would not mind, and then you could have some clothes made at the dressmaker's in the town. She is quite good, really; I had a lovely pink gown made once. . . ." She had begun to sound quite excited about her proposal, and Sarah cut in more sharply than she had intended.

"No. I mean, I really do not need any other clothes, and besides, Emma needs dresses before I do. She is outgrowing her clothes almost before she has worn them." She laughed, shaking out the blue cotton dress and laying it on the bed.

"I could lend you something. I have plenty of dresses that I never wear." Joanna spoke doubtfully, not sure whether her offer might offend.

"No, thank you all the same Joanna," Sarah continued quietly, "It is very kind of you, but I would rather have my own things; perhaps next month I might have something."

Maggie entered at that moment with the chattering Emma, precluding any further comment on the subject, and she dressed quickly, brushing vigorously at her hair and leaving it loose for a change. She saw Joanna watching her in the mirror and smiled at the girl.

"You have got such lovely hair, Sarah. Why do you scrape it into that knot all the time? If I had hair like that," she said dreamily, "I would wear it loose all the time."

"Well, I have always wanted dark hair, especially with a curl in," Sarah said, pulling gently at a dark ringlet as she passed Joanna. The girl flushed, pleased with the compliment.

Sarah, lifting Emma into a tight embrace, said, "And you, young lady, will have to do without Maggie for the morning. She is coming with us."

Maggie laughed. "She will not even notice that I have gone. Mary is absolutely delighted; she cannot believe that she has got her all to herself for the morning. I saw her just now carrying two platefuls of honey cakes into the nursery. She will be uncontrollable by this afternoon," she remarked with mock severity.

"I have a few things to get from the schoolroom before we go, Joanna. I am not hungry, so I shall do it now. You have breakfast and I will see you after."

Sarah made for the schoolroom, Emma in her arms. "You, I think, can spend some time with your mama before she goes to the fête. I don't see very much of you, do I?" She kissed the pink cheek gently, sighing as she acknowledged the fact that her daughter was learning to need her less and less.

Note pads and pencils were stacked into a pile on her desk, and Sarah turned, calling to Emma. She picked up the items, looking around the room. She had left Emma with a pencil and scrap of paper, sitting on the floor. The paper and pencil were discarded and there was no sign of Emma. She called louder, her voice slightly harsh with panic, just as Maggie appeared at the door.

"Have you seen Emma? She was here a minute ago, she cannot be far." She hurried out of the door, not waiting for a reply, unable to shake off an unreasonable fear. The child was probably just along the corridor, but she felt suddenly chilled at her disappearance, nevertheless. She hurried toward the front of the house, Maggie taking the opposite direction.

Mark Tarrington, carrying a riding whip and dressed in dusty riding clothes, and another equally grimy man whom she had never seen before, were walking toward her, engrossed in conversation and, she slowed her pace as they looked up.

She saw Emma at the same time as he did. She was sitting in a small alcove, barely a yard from where he was standing, examining her toes with great interest. Sarah darted forward suddenly, catching the child up in her arms as though removing her from some menace.

"I am sorry," she said breathlessly. "It will not happen again. I had not noticed that she was missing until just now."

The golden-brown eyes were studying the child intently, and Sarah unwittingly clutched the baby protectively closer.

"She is your image," he said slowly, his eyes still on the oblivious child.

"Yes, she is very like me." Her voice sounded strained.

"How very fortunate." His voice was softly insinuating, and she could feel the color staining her cheeks and her temper rising.

"In what way, my lord?" she returned coolly, meeting his gaze challengingly.

He was looking at her now, and his eyes were dark with amusement. "You are very beautiful Mrs. Thornton, as I am sure you are well aware. Your daughter has obviously inherited your good looks." He turned abruptly to the man standing silently at his side, indicating that the incident was closed. "Let me introduce you to Stewart Palmer. He is estate manager at Winslade Hall."

Sarah smiled quickly at the fair-haired man. He

looked to be in his late twenties and was slightly taller than Mark Tarrington, yet slimmer, with the wiry strength of a laborer. He smiled easily, and Sarah noted that he did not seem affected by the strained atmosphere. The introduction was brought to an abrupt halt with the appearance of the disheveled and breathless Maggie, rounding the corner at great speed.

"Have you found . . ." She froze into silence, seeing the two men standing with her young mistress.

Sarah saw a sudden spark of interest light in the blue eyes of Stewart Palmer as he took in Maggie's disarranged curls and heaving bosom, and she felt a vague stirring of alarm at the fair man's speculative gaze. Looking at Maggie, she knew the girl was also aware of the nature of his scrutiny, but judging by the shy smile and pink glow staining the girl's cheeks, she was not particularly displeased by his attention.

Mark Tarrington had also noticed the reason for the young girl's self-conscious shuffling. Turning to Stewart Palmer, he said, with the suggestion of a smile, "This is Maggie. She came with Mrs. Thornton from the Cunninghams'. Maggie acts as nursemaid to the child while Mrs. Thornton is otherwise occupied." He halted, staring hard at Sarah before continuing with exaggerated irony, "Apparently her true vocation lies in teaching in the schoolroom . . . something Mrs. Thornton is actively encouraging, I believe." He turned, his eyes taunting as they met hers fleetingly, and then he had entered the study before she could think of some equally caustic remark. Stewart Palmer followed close at his heels, and then, just as he was about to close the door, he grinned at them, his eyes lingering on Maggie, much to her red-cheeked confusion.

The coach arrived promptly at the front of the house at ten o'clock, and Sarah, Luke, Joanna, and Maggie set off for the fête in a jocular mood. Mark Tarrington had made it clear previously that he would make his own way to the village later in the morning, and Sarah knew that each of the coach's occupants in his/her own way, was silently hoping that he would either forget about his promise or find something more important to do. Sarah smiled wryly to herself, realizing the prospect of a morning spent in idle pleasure.

They passed many other vehicles on the road, mainly farmers and laborers' carts, and she noticed that their crested coach attracted quite a few inquisitive glances. Village fêtes, she knew, quite often drew a certain amount of curious gentry, but she was surprised, nevertheless, to see several other coaches of quality making their way in the same direction at this early hour.

The stalls and sideshows were already set up around the village square, and upon alighting she gathered Luke and Joanna to her side, amazed at the thronging mass of people already assembled.

"Keep close to me. We do not want to be separated in this crowd." Joanna appeared to be otherwise occupied, her dark eyes scanning the faces around closely, as though expecting to see someone she knew.

"Joanna." Sarah shook the girl's arm slightly to draw her attention. "You must stay close or you will get lost in the crowd, and that would certainly preclude any further outings, as far as your uncle is concerned."

Joanna nodded, but seemed distant still as they started off on a circular tour of the entertainment.

Sarah was entranced. There were stalls selling every

conceivable kind of ware, from pots and pans and ribbons and laces to hot pies and pasties, fruit preserves and cakes.

Maggie and Luke had walked ahead slightly, while Sarah waited for Joanna to select ribbon from one of the stalls. The sun was rising, the day becoming quite hot now, and Sarah was glad she had chosen the cool cotton dress as she lifted the heavy mass of hair away from her shoulders for a minute. She was just about to move to Joanna's side to examine what she had purchased when she noticed the girl was no longer alone. She was gazing into the face of a young man who looked to be about Sarah's age. He was quite tall, with light brown hair and a distinguished face, which, together with the cut and quality of his clothes, marked him as a member of the nobility.

Joanna, becoming aware that they were being watched, said something to him quickly, and with a light, almost imperceptible touch on the arm, moved back to where Sarah stood, smiling overbrightly, as though nothing was amiss. She proferred the pink ribbon she had chosen in a distracting manner, chatteringly requesting Sarah's opinion, but Sarah stared past the girl still, noting the young man still watching Joanna's retreating figure, his face tense and anxious.

Preoccupied with the incident, Sarah did not at first notice the slight change in the heavy atmosphere. The noisy hum of activity was receding in slow waves as all eyes turned in the direction of two men dismounting at the far end of the square.

Mark Tarrington and Stewart Palmer were laughing at something another man had shouted, apparently oblivious of the awed quiet accompanying their arrival. They had started to move slowly around the square, Mark Tarrington stopping to greet various

75

acquaintances, peasant and gentleman alike, as he strolled.

The buzz of activity had resumed slightly but the atmosphere was subdued, the populace respectful of the distinguished visitor in their midst. As he approached the spot where Joanna and Sarah stood, a crowd of well-dressed young people approached noisily, and Sarah heard a female voice she recognized trill, "Why, Lord Tarrington."

He turned, frowning, and Sarah saw Celia Maynard, immaculately dressed in lilac muslin. She and a group of friends milled about him.

Joanna, for some reason eager to escape, was about to disappear in the opposite direction when she saw her uncle looking directly at her. He beckoned silently and she went forward reluctantly, pulling Sarah with her.

Sarah noticed the young man she had seen with Joanna earlier and understood the girl's reluctance. He was staring unflinchingly at her, and she, in return, was doing her best to ignore him. Celia's voice carried on the hot air. "Yes, Mama and I are staying for a few days at the Ashtons', so for a while, at least, we shall be neighbors." She glanced up coquettishly at Mark Tarrington from beneath dark lashes, but he did not respond to this information, and she turned to Joanna, her face dimpling in welcome. Her expression changed drastically, however, when she espied the young girl's companion, and she was not quick enough to prevent the flash of astonished dislike in her eyes.

"Why, Mrs. Thornley, the governess, is it not? What are you doing here? I had no idea the Cunninghams were visiting you, Mark." She turned, tapping his arm gently with a small parasol, looking at him coyly and gazing around in exaggerated fashion. "Where are the Cunningham girls? I do not see them."

"Mrs. Thornton is in my employ now. She is governess to Luke and Joanna." He spoke quietly, his eyes on Sarah's face.

Celia's face registered stupefaction, quickly followed by malicious fury, and she turned to Sarah with a taut smile. "Well, Mrs. Thornton, how very enterprising of you. I noticed last time we met that you seemed particularly interested in his lordship." She had spoken with pure venom, aware that others in her party had heard her words and were tittering.

Sarah, humiliated beyond bearing, merely said in an unsteady voice, "It was not a move I would have made by choice Miss Maynard, I can assure you." She turned away quickly, saying, "Excuse me, there were some other stalls I wished to see."

She walked blindly past the various displays, stopping at last near the far edge of the square. She looked at the nearest stall, touching the lace and ribbons tentatively. It was then she noticed the doll. It was propped at the back of the stall, its delicate china features curved into a painted smile. It was wearing a white satin gown, trimmed with pink ribbon and lace, and she felt a stirring of memory, vaguely remembering a similar one she had owned as a child. The face had smashed, if she remembered correctly, falling downstairs in some game, and Sarah had been desolate for months afterwards. She stretched out a finger, touching the smooth china face lightly, letting her hand drop to the frothy dress. She suddenly felt an aching need to have something that reminded her of her youth and the security she had taken for granted, and as an uncontrollable surge of nostalgic tears stung her eyes, she inquired softly of the hovering stallholder "How much?"

"Well, let me see now." He stroked his chin thoughtfully. "It's worth a great deal, as you can see; it's quality, as a lady like yourself would know." He continued hastily, seeing Sarah's hand withdrawing from the doll, "A sovereign—it's worth more, you know, but I will let it go for . . ."

She shook her head slightly, smiling ruefully, unaware at first that Mark Tarrington was staring over her shoulder. She backed away from the stall quickly, recognizing the deferential silence of the stallholder too well. She had not expected him to be standing so close, and she felt his hands on her shoulders, steadying her as she knocked into him. His touch seared through the thin material of her dress, and for a moment she was aware of nothing except his closeness and her inability to move away from him. He released her at last, at the same time flicking a gold coin into the air and into the deft clasp of the gaping stallholder. He reached across her, brushing her lightly with his arm and picked up the doll from the stall.

She turned quickly, staring at him as he held it out to her, unable to take it and desperate for some reasonable excuse for refusing. "You should not have . . . I cannot . . ." She stammered into silence, aware that the stallholder was watching them with fascinated curiosity.

"Come now, a sovereign will not render you under any obligation, you know." He spoke softly, his eyes mocking her distress "Besides, I have no intention of spending the remainder of the morning with a china doll under my arm." He pressed the doll into her arms saying, "Here, a gift for your daughter," before walk-

78

ing away slowly, smiling exaggeratedly at the gaping merchant, who managed to stutter, "Your lordship," and make a form of jerking bow before turning around in self-important satisfaction to see who else had noticed the monumental event that had taken place at his stall.

Sarah, aware that they had probably given the man enough material to keep him in free drinks and gossip for the rest of the day, followed slowly, the doll clutched tightly between her hands. He stopped suddenly, allowing her to catch up, saying, "I do believe my presence here is dampening the festivities somewhat. I cannot remember a fête as subdued as this one."

She laughed, glad of the release of tension between them. "I have to admit it was livelier before your arrival."

They walked in silence for a while. She had not seen Celia or any of her friends again, and he had not mentioned the incident further. Sarah became suddenly conscious of a girl walking slowly toward them, carrying a tray of some pastries or pies, her large, startlingly green eyes fixed intently on the man walking at her side. She was quite stunning, and for a moment Sarah stared at her mesmerized as she moved leisurely closer. She was dressed in a vivid emerald gown, the bodice so tightly laced that her breasts were pushed high and almost naked, and she was swaying her hips provocatively, her skirts swinging and curving against the brown legs. Her mouth was parted slightly in a flirtatiously vague smile, and as Sarah watched her unfalteringly the girl shook her glossy russet hair back from her face and large gold earrings bounced brightly against her burnished skin. Sarah was certain from her dark good looks and her striking

79

dress that she was Romany, and she was uneasily aware of the girl's eyes sliding to meet her own in frank challenge before returning to the man at her side.

Sure that the situation was about to become unbearably embarrassing as she realized that the girl was walking directly in their path, Sarah made to move quickly to one side, in apparent fascinated examination of the nearest stall. As she started to move, she felt his hand grip her wrist firmly, and he murmured, his eyes fixed expressionlessly on the girl, "We do not want you getting lost in the crowd, do we?" Sarah could sense the humor in his tone and knew instinctively that he was well aware of her reason for trying to disappear so hastily.

The Gypsy's eyes moved back to her face and Sarah cringed slightly at the expression there, and then she felt him move closer to her as the girl brushed hard against him in passing. He said nothing, his composure unaffected, and Sarah, acutely conscious of his fingers burning her wrist, attempted to slip her hand hastily from his grasp, but he retained his grip and started to move away from the main area of the square to where there was a small boxing ring set up and two men, surrounded by a throng of shouting and cajoling spectators, were engaged in bare-knuckle fighting. As they moved closer, the raucous advice ebbed slightly, and the crowd parted, allowing him passage to the front. But he remained near the back, watching the two assailants still. Realizing from the intentness of his gaze that he was quite genuinely interested in the outcome of the spectacle, Sarah said coldly, "I have no desire to watch this barbaric display," and endeavored once more to remove her hand from his hold. She saw his mouth curve in acknowledgment of her comment, but he remained silent, his eyes still on the grunting and sweating men.

An abrupt loud cheer went up, and Sarah saw one of the men, his face bloodied badly, reel to the dusty ground. Feeling nauseous at the unnecessary cruelty, she made an exasperated sound and turned away. As she moved she noticed the girl again, standing now just to one side of them, the feline eyes narrowed and concentrated on the earl still, and then she stared at Sarah, the hostility unchecked. Sarah winced again as the blatant hatred stung her and turned back hastily toward the fight. As she did so she heard him say, without looking away from the contest, "A friend of yours?" His tone was vaguely amused, and Sarah realized at once that he was well aware of the girl's presence and of her interest in him. For some inexplicable reason it infuriated her to impulsive rashness and she retorted with vicious sweetness, "No. I thought perhaps a relative of yours." Almost before the words were uttered she regretted her stupidity. She bowed her head slightly, hoping desperately that he might somehow have misunderstood the obscurely personal insult, but as she felt his fingers cut lightly into her wrist she knew he was well aware of her meaning. She examined the doll clutched in her free arm, wondering, horrified, how she could have insulted him so when he had just bought it for her, too conscious that he was staring hard at her averted face. She raised her eyes to meet his against her will, and as she did so he laughed softly and then looked back at the boxing ring, and the mirthless sound made her freeze.

He released her then and his hand went to his pocket. She saw him throw some coins toward the victor, who was strutting proudly, before he turned

81

and merely said, "Come," as he passed her.

The girl, as though sensing the friction between them, moved forward again also, smiling suggestively, and Sarah hesitated, about to make some detour back to the village square, but he turned slightly, catching her wrist again and pulling her forward. The girl, obviously furious now at his lack of interest, snorted loudly in disgust as she passed him, and picking up one of the pastries from the tray she held, slapped it into his free hand before she flounced off, muttering in an unintelligible tongue. Sarah saw him look at the cake frowningly for a moment and thought he was about to throw it away. Then, releasing her again, he broke it in half and held out a piece to her and started to eat the other, totally unperturbed.

About to knock his hand away contemptuously, Sarah became abruptly aware at that point that practically everyone within reasonable visibility was watching them with ill-disguised gawping astonishment, and not yet feeling courageous enough to insult him further, she took the food with bad grace and stony silence.

He smiled, saying in a laughing tone, "It's really not bad."

She looked at the pastry and then started to eat it, and realizing as she did so that not only was it quite delicious but that she was ravenous.

They moved back slowly around the square, and she saw Maggie and Stewart Palmer standing just ahead, with Luke and Joanna close by attempting to eat their way through enormous hot pies. Maggie was laughing shyly at some remark the fair man had made, and Mark Tarrington murmured, "It looks as though your scholastic friend has made quite an impression there."

"Yes." Sarah could not keep the troubled note from her voice.

"You do not approve." It was a statement rather than a question.

"It is not for me to choose her friends, I fear," she returned tartly. "I would not like to see Maggie hurt, that is all."

"What makes you think she will be?" His voice was mildly inquiring, and she looked up to find the golden eyes regarding her steadily.

She took a deep breath, but was unable to prevent herself saying slowly, "Perhaps because he spends so much of his time in your company." She turned away quickly, not giving him a chance to reply, saying brightly to the children, "Well, if you are to write essays this afternoon, we should be going now," and ignored the glum looks that were the result of this suggestion.

Chapter Six

It was early November and the mildness of autumn was turning slightly to a chill but bright early winter. The days were getting shorter, and the time Sarah spent less and less time out of doors.

The children both enjoyed their sketching sessions on the grounds, and Joanna was showing a definite talent that Sarah knew equaled, if not exceeded, her own. The girl seemed to live for the trips out to the woods and rolling countryside, sometimes so eager to discover new species or items to sketch that she would disappear suddenly on her own, much to Sarah's fretting dismay, returning late, breathless but bright-eyed, clutching some twig or leaf. Sarah was suspicious that the girl's excitement was not wholly due to her nature studies, but she said nothing, merely trying to keep the girl at her side for as long as possible.

Luke was becoming more withdrawn and pale as the days passed, and Sarah, at a loss to know what ailed the boy and getting no response from him when she asked him, said to Joanna one day, "Do you know why Luke is so fretful?"

"Oh, that," said Joanna airily. "He is worried about school."

"What school Joanna?" Sarah asked in surprise.

"Uncle Mark arranged ages ago that Luke would go to Eton after Christmas. He is terrified of going, of course, but it will make no difference. He will still have to go." She sounded quite unconcerned about the whole incident.

"But that is absurd. He cannot know the boy is making himself ill. If he does not want to go so desperately, surely it would be easier to have him tutored at home."

"Of course," returned Joanna, "but if Uncle Mark wants him to go to school, then that, of course, is that. He gets his own way in all things," she added bitterly.

Luke entered the classroom at that moment. Seeing the two occupants staring at him, he knew at once that he was the subject of discussion. Sarah, approaching him quickly, said, "Joanna tells me you are to go to Eton after the Christmas holidays, Luke." The boy's bottom lip had begun to tremble, and he sat down at his desk and said with childish bravado, "I won't go. No one can make me."

Joanna snorted her disgust at this remark and busied herself with her own books, dismissing the topic contemptuously.

"Surely, if you really do not want to go Luke, your mother would speak for you about this. She must have some say in your education, surely?"

Luke turned his overbright gaze on Sarah. "She is not bothered what happens to me—us—she is only concerned with herself and her life in London. She leaves everything up to Uncle Mark. Why," he continued heatedly, "she has not even visited us now that the season is finished—she has gone to stay with some 'admirer' "—the emphasis he put on the word made Sarah flush—"at his country home. We shall be lucky

85

to see her before Christmas—or unlucky, perhaps I should say." He finished on a note that sounded suspiciously like a sob, and Sarah felt her heart go out to the young boy.

She had purposely seen little of Mark Tarrington over the past month, managing to work out the days he was most likely to be seen in the house and studiously avoiding places they were likely to meet. He, for his part, had not seemed to seek her out, either, and she was glad, finding the continual skirmishing between them distressing and exhausting. She knew now, though, watching Luke's all too obvious misery, that she ought, at least, to try to speak for the boy on this matter and resolved to do so later that day, before her courage failed.

She knocked lightly at the study door, loathing herself for the rising panic that made her wish desperately for no reply. The impatience with which she was commanded to enter made her swallow hard before doing so.

He looked up scowling, surprise and some other emotion showing on his face as he saw her before his eyes shuttered. He leaned back leisurely in the swivel chair, saying coolly "Well, well. I am deeply honored, Mrs. Thornton, that you should seek me out. Some catastrophe has occurred, no doubt, that you should take this unprecedented step."

His sarcasm was biting, and she could sense her temper rising in retaliation. "I do wish to speak with you on a matter . . . if you have the time." Her tone was glacially polite.

He indicated with a brief movement of his hand that she should sit down and picked up the half-empty glass on the littered desk.

She launched straight into an attack, saying, "Luke tells me he is expected to go to school after Christmas, much against his wishes." She hesitated, aware that his eyes and mouth had hardened at her words.

"I do not think you can realize how it is affecting him," she resumed quickly. "He looks pale and is withdrawn and his schoolwork has been suffering. . . ."

He cut in harshly. "If you are concerned about your own prospective employment, Mrs. Thornton, I can assure you that Joanna will still, of course, require your services, for the time being at least, and I therefore suggest that you leave the planning of Luke's future to me."

Sarah felt her hands clench in impotent rage, and she said with barely repressed insolence, "I thought you were well aware, my lord, that termination of my employment here would suit me admirably, much as I like the children. I am concerned merely with Luke's happiness and well-being, something which you, quite obviously, are not." Her anger had made her reckless, and she continued heatedly, "You, of course, are only interested in your self, imposing your will on others and getting your own way in all things, insensitive to the hurt you cause." She was so incensed by her feelings that she did not at first notice that he had risen and moved around the desk. He pulled her sharply to her feet, one hand gripping her wrist viciously, while the other slid into the silken mass of her hair, preventing her from turning away. She had never seen him look so furious and realized with dawning horror that she had so far barely skimmed the surface of the dark side of his character. He smiled slightly at her fear and said with menacing softness, "If that were true, Mrs. Thornton, believe me, you would by now have had firsthand knowledge of it."

She stared at him, mesmerized, as the hand in her hair drew her inexorably closer, the sapphire and amber eyes meeting in silent contest for a few moments, and then, as she became aware of his gaze moving across her face, lingering on her mouth, she instinctively attempted to draw back and turn her head away. But he held her unmoving for a few pulsating seconds more, and then pushed her back into the chair abruptly and slammed out of the room, leaving her shaking with some suppressed emotion that she refused to analyze.

Chapter Seven

The mildly chilly weather continued into mid-November, and Sarah sat gazing through her bedroom window, watching the bobbing white blobs moving slowly on the distant lake. It was Saturday afternoon, and she and the children had free time. Luke and Joanna were probably out riding. They had asked her several times if she would like to ride with them, but as yet she had not found enough courage to do so.

Her riding experience was almost nonexistent. As a child of about eight or nine she had had her own pony, but she had soon outgrown it, and with her father's predilection for gambling and losing, the stables were the first area to be deprived of anything of value. She would have dearly loved to ride again, but had avoided doing so, feeling embarrassed at her inadequacy. She pushed to the back of her mind any other reasons revolving around the fact that Mark Tarrington spent the majority of his day around the stable area. After the episode in his study when she had dared to question him about Luke's education, her avoidance of him had been meticulous.

Dinner that same evening had been a nightmare. It was usually a night he was late home, and she had thought herself safe in eating with the children. The dowager had also been present at the meal, and his entry into the dining room just after her own left her with a sinking heart and a complete loss of appetite. She knew there was no way she could retreat to her room without making the reason obvious, and had therefore sat through the meal, eating little, aware of his murderous gaze directed her way for the duration. The atmosphere was strained overtight this time, Luke and Joanna even becoming aware of the throbbing silence. Only the dowager, conscious of the electrical friction between her nephew and the young governess and apparently amused to some degree by it, ate heartily, attempting to maintain a semblance of normality despite the monosyllabic conversational replies from the other two adults present.

Sarah sighed and turned to Emma playing noisily on the floor with her wooden top. The child was becoming bored, and she lifted her onto her lap, saying, "Shall we go and find Mrs. Davis?" Emma's face lit with excitement; any trip to see Mrs. Davis was likely to result in her being given tasty tidbits from the kitchen.

Sarah's contact with a lot of the servants had been limited, and she was quite eager to meet some of the others who worked in the kitchen area all the time. She had not even met the cook yet. She stood up, Emma in her arms clutching a favorite rag doll, ready to explore the kitchens via the back stairs, the thought making her realize that she was quite hungry herself. Besides, it seemed a shame to waste time in her room, when she had seen the reason for her self-imposed imprisonment riding out with Stewart Palmer some time earlier.

They reached the stairs just as Mrs. Davis appeared at the top.

"Hallo, Mrs. Davis. We were just coming to visit you. Emma is quite keen to sample some of your kitchen delights again."

The older woman laughed, holding her arms out for Emma as she did so. "Come on then, my love, let us see what Cook has got today."

The kitchens were light and spacious and gleamingly clean, copper pots and pans shining brightly the entire length of one wall. The door leading out to the kitchen garden was open, and yet it still felt quite oppressively hot.

Sarah noticed curious glances directed her way as she entered, and she smiled at the new faces. Mrs. Davis bustled over to the enormous scrubbed wooden table in the center of the room, placed Emma on it, and turned to an extremely plump woman with a huge bosom and quivering arms.

"Martha, this is Mrs. Sarah Thornton, the new governess, and her little girl, Emma. They have come to meet you and sample some of your wares."

Martha laughed, shaking her massive bulk and chucking Emma beneath the chin. Smiling in friendly fashion at Sarah, she said, "You will be in luck in a few minutes, for there are some batches of scones and currant buns in the oven ready for tasting."

Some of the other female servants had come forward now, their smiles amiable, and were fussing around Emma, touching her golden curls. Martha, wagging an admonishing finger in mock annoyance at the baby, said suddenly, "You won't have to come too often, my girl. You have brought activity in my kitchen to a complete standstill, I'll have you know. His lordship will have my hide."

Sarah noticed that the mention of his name brought quite a few pairs of eyes swiveling her way, and she wondered what gossip regarding their fiery relationship had reached their ears.

A young boy of perhaps ten was standing by a huge bowl peeling potatoes, and Sarah smiled at him, saying, "What is your name?"

"Tom, ma'am," he said shyly.

"That is Kathy Clark's boy," said Martha indicating with a nod of her head a dark-haired woman in the process of pouring milk into a small mug for the spoiled Emma. "He helps his ma in the kitchen. They have a cottage on the estate. Lost his pa last winter, so he is the man in the house now, aren't you Tom?"

He was washing his hands, indicating that his task was finished, and Sarah saw his face flush red with pleasure at Martha's comment. He walked toward the table looking at the chubby little girl and Emma, obviously delighted with the sudden male interest, held her plump arms out to him to be picked up.

"Cor, Tom, you have made a conquest," bellowed Martha, her ample frame shaking with the intensity of her mirth.

Tom, reddening but not unpleased, turned to Sarah, saying, "May I take her for a walk in the garden? I will look after her well," he added importantly.

Sarah hesitated for a moment, but seeing the look of hurt mortification starting to steal across the boy's face, said quickly, "All right, but not far. She can be quite a handful sometimes."

The boy, taking the chubby fingers in his, lead the willing Emma, still clutching her ragdoll, out through the kitchen door and into the garden.

Sarah settled into a hard kitchen chair, and Martha pushed a mug of steaming black coffee in front of her. The atmosphere was relaxed; the kitchen staff resumed some semblance of activity.

Sarah looked around at the friendly faces. The

majority of those who were not engaged in kitchen duties were gossiping quietly, and the door was constantly opening and closing, with new arrivals just finishing tasks and others just commencing theirs. She noticed that the majority of the girls were young and that some were quite pretty, and she found herself wondering whether any of them had been singled out for particular attention by the master of the house, not knowing why the thought should disturb her newfound contentment. She chided herself; it was no concern or interest of hers what he did with his staff, but looking again at the girls she realized suddenly that it was unlikely. None of them had the look of smug self-importance that usually accompanied the position of favorite.

She thought of the man she had married and the young kitchen maid who had become his mistress shortly after he had brought his bride home. The girl had never made any secret of her relationship with Squire Thornton. She had been brazen in her attentions to him even in Sarah's presence, and sullen and insolent when asked to do anything resembling work. Sarah smiled at herself at the recollection, wondering whether the girl would have been quite as pleased with herself had she realized that her lover's wife was more than pleased with her husband's extramarital activities.

Her musings were cut short abruptly by the appearance of a panting and distraught Joanna in the kitchen doorway.

Sarah stood up, ice surrounding her heart, knocking the wooden chair over in her haste. "Emma," she breathed and knew from Joanna's frantic nod that some disaster had occurred.

"Sarah, I think Emma is going to fall into the lake." Joanna's voice had risen almost to screaming

93

pitch in her hysteria, and Sarah, not waiting to hear more, pushed past her in the doorway, running as fast as her hampering skirts would allow in the direction of the lake.

She saw them at once. A small boat, which Tom apparently had been rowing was now about forty yards from the shore and yet still a good distance from the small island rising out of the middle of the lake.

Tom was wailing in fear and panic, holding on to Emma who was also sobbing hysterically, dangling over the edge of the boat, her body trailing in the water.

Sarah's eyes closed momentarily with the sheer weight of her terror. She could feel her heart beating a slow, thudding rhythm in her throat, and she felt as though she were slowly choking. "Tom!" she called out, trying to keep the hysteria from her voice. "Tom, try to pull Emma back into the boat if you can. Quickly, before she wriggles free." She steadied her rising tone, not wanting to frighten Tom further with her panic. She could see the boy's hands gripping and regripping at Emma, but the baby's struggles were defeating him, and as the boat gave a sudden lurch he sank back into it, his wails increasing. "I can't. She is slipping, she is slipping."

Sarah, aware now that the majority of the servants had joined her and were gazing in horrified disbelief at the scene, said wildly, "Can anyone swim? I cannot swim," and then repeated through chattering teeth, "Can anyone swim; someone must be able to!" She stared at the silent, grim-faced men, watching them shake their heads in hopeless negation. She swung round, tears of helpless frustration sliding down her cheeks, and then, prompted by a fresh bout of hysterical screaming from Tom, ran to the water's edge and started to wade out toward the boat.

Although the day was quite mild the water was icy, and she felt the chill of it spreading slowly through her legs and thighs. She clenched her teeth to stop their chattering, as much from the freezing water now as from the rising panic. She had always had an unreasonable fear of water, hating the feel of it in her eyes and ears even when bathing. She closed her eyes, swallowing her rising nausea as her feet slid and slithered over the slippery surface. She could feel the mud sucking and tugging at her shoes, and as she moved slowly forward could feel the hampering drag of her many petticoats and heavy skirt, which was now completely water-logged. She could see Tom watching avidly as she moved closer and realized that her attempts to reach them had, at least, calmed him slightly. She called out to him through frozen lips. "Hold on Tom, I will soon reach you," but even as she uttered the words she knew the futility of the promise. The water was already past her waist, and the boat still bobbed twenty yards away, at least.

So obsessed was she with keeping her balance and watching the peril ahead that she had not noticed the black horse thundering toward the lake's edge, sending a spray of greyish water high into the air. Looking up suddenly, she saw the figure swimming toward the boat from the opposite direction and stood petrified, willing him to reach the terrified children before it was too late. She saw him surface by the boat, shaking water from his head as he did so. He was attempting to put Emma back into the boat, but she, clutching at him with a tenacity born of sheer terror, refused to let him go. He said something to Tom, the boy almost fainting with shock now that the realization of inevitable retribution for his folly had penetrated his immediate fear, and he nodded and started to row the boat back slowly to shore, still sobbing raucously. She watched Mark Tarrington push away from the boat, Emma still clinging to him desperately.

Sarah stood motionless for a moment, shaking from head to foot with reaction and cold. Her thoughts turned to her own predicament and she closed her eyes, attempting to turn slowly to face the way she had come. She shuffled around slowly, her head bent, endeavoring to watch the movement of her feet hidden in the murky depths. The attention she afforded this futile effort made her oblivious of his presence until he was only a few yards away, and she raised her head suddenly at his approach, her face pallid with exhaustion and shock. They stared at each other in taut silence for a moment, she with increasing terror as she noted the unchecked fury blazing from the tawny depths of his eyes. She wanted to thank him for what he had done, but the look of intense, almost tangible rage on his face left the words unuttered. He had moved closer now, and she quickly looked down at her hidden feet again, apparently absorbed in their progress. He caught her arm, jerking her closer, and gritted out with cutting sarcasm, "I have no doubt you have a perfectly reasonable explanation for this afternoon's lunacy." She looked at him, trying to think of words to explain the situation, and finding none looked away again, feeling the tears of humiliation and frustration start into her eyes. She blinked them away quickly, not wanting to let him see her distress.

"Take off your petticoats." His voice was abrasively autocratic. She stared at him as though unable to believe that she had heard correctly and saw his mouth curl into a cruel sneer. "It is quite all right, my dear, I do not have any designs on your virtue; leastways not in the middle of a lake with the best part of the servants in attendance. I do not intend carrying you and a goodly part of this lake back to shore." His calculated scorn incensed her, and she felt her own fury rising. Her teeth were chattering so much now that she could barely speak, yet she attempted to push past him disdainfully, saying, "That is quite unnecessary, my lord, I made it this far on my own, I am sure I can make it back the same way." She moved forward abruptly, sensing her footing slipping away from under her as she did so and the icy water closing about her head.

He let her submerge almost completely before hauling her up unceremoniously, and she clung to him despite herself, trying to wipe the water from her smarting eyes.

"Well?" His voice close to her ear was scathingly mocking. "Are you going to do it, or shall I?" She glared at him through a blur of angry tears, thankfully hidden by the water dripping from her hair, and she knew he would be quite capable of it. She fumbled at her waist, watching as the white mass of material floated slowly out of sight, and she stepped out of the garments, grabbing hard at him as she moved. He swung her up suddenly and with such ease that she realized the increased weight would have mattered little, and they started back to shore.

The servants, now that the imminent danger was well past, were watching the scene with the fascinated relish of those afforded some unexpected but nevertheless extremely welcome diversion. Not since Becky Smith's father had chased his daughter and the head groom from the stables, that man not having found it prudent to allow the unlucky pair to dress themselves first, had there been such gratuitous entertainment. They watched entranced as the earl of Winslade, dripping wet and with murder in his eyes, deposited the equally wet and furious Sarah on the shore next to the still wailing Emma.

Sarah, kneeling next to the child, clasped her tightly to her, rocking her back and forth in her arms. The child, however, was attempting to break free, gesticulating wildly at some point in the lake. Sarah, attempting to quiet Emma before his lordship's sorely tried humor was finally exhausted, tried to lift her, but she refused any such attempts, wailing quite clearly now, "Dolly! Me want it."

Mark Tarrington, attempting to dry his soaking hair by rubbing it vigorously with his fingers, muttered with unconcealed impatience, "What ails the child now?" And Sarah, unable to reply for fear of provoking unthinkable consequences, merely tried to soothe the baby with whispered endearments.

But Maggie, as she tried vainly to wrap the wriggling Emma in a large towel, answered in a trembling voice, "Her doll, my lord. It is floating in the lake."

He turned back, scanning the water with narrowed eyes, espying a small red object floating near the island. Sarah, looking up at that instant, met his eyes with an unconscious plea, and he stared at her for a long moment and then turned his head away savagely, standing unmoving for a few seconds before striding, cursing, back to the water's edge.

The servants, unable to believe their eyes, gaped in open-mouthed astonishment at the sight, and Sarah became suddenly aware that there were two other riders approaching on horseback. They had moved around from the far side of the lake, leading the black stallion. One was Stewart Palmer; the other man she did not recognize at all. He was quite short and plump, elaborately dressed in riding clothes, and at the moment was almost in an agony of mirth. His eyes were streaming, and he held a scrap of lace to them, dabbing ineffectually as guffaw after guffaw brought forth further moisture. He was bent almost double in his uncontrollable laughter, and she noticed that his hands were holding his quivering sides as though he was in physical pain. Stewart Palmer was almost smiling with unconcealed amusement at the spectacle.

Mark Tarringon, reappearing at that moment, dropped the sodden doll at Sarah's feet, and turning to his florid-faced friend, made some vicious remark, rendering him illegitimate and his mother of dubious virtue.

Sarah, colored hotly and held her breath, expecting some retaliation, but this insult served only to fuel his friend's amusement further and his hilarity erupted again in a loud snort. She became uncomfortably aware suddenly, as did Mark Tarrington, that most of the men present, his laughter-ridden friend included, were now studying her with avid attention. Her wet skirt, without the added bulk of her petticoats, was clinging to her slim form like a second skin. She attempted to peel the material away from her legs, shaking it out, her face crimson.

Mark Tarringon, looking around at the assembled servants, said with treacherous softness, "Well, I had never realized before just how acutely overstaffed I appear to be." His wrath was uncontrollable suddenly, and he added with menacing quiet, "All of you with apparently nothing to do are dismissed." He ignored the looks of amazed horror that flashed from face to face and turned to Kathy Clark, who was alternately hugging and cuffing her still sobbing son around the ear, saying with icy calm, "I will see you in my study in half an hour." The distraught woman opened her mouth to say something, but he strode away, saying over his shoulder to Sarah as he passed, "You also, Mrs. Thornton."

Sarah stood ashen-faced, watching the servants

springing belatedly into a veritable hive of activity. She saw Mrs. Clark look her way, her face grey with fear, and then turn away, leading Tom back to the house.

She had brought about disaster for all the servants, and the knowledge made the nausea rise into her throat again. She returned to her room filled with a dull misery. An attentive Mrs. Davis and Maggie were soothing and fussing over Emma who, blissfully oblivious of the mayhem she had caused, had discarded the ragdoll in the corner.

Maggie looked at Sarah as she entered, her face anxious, and whispered, "What is going to happen?"

Sarah, unable to speak, merely shook her head and started to strip off the wet clothes with unsteady hands.

Matilda Davis, attempting to smile, said, "He has these fits of temper; he will soon forget about his threats . . ." But her voice trailed off into strained silence, and Sarah buried her head beneath a towel and rubbed vigorously at her hair.

She dressed slowly, not wanting to rush the dreaded confrontation, and then when her hair had dried slightly, forming a fluffy golden halo about her face, she made her way downstairs, trying to force her brain to formulate some acceptable and suitably humble apology.

She tapped lightly at the door and it was opened almost immediately by the man she had seen earlier, his mirth seemingly under control now. He smiled at her good-naturedly and bowed slightly, indicating that she should enter. His eyes, skimming her now drily clad form, were appreciative, and he said laughingly, "I am Sir Joseph Ashton, a neighbor of Lord Tarrington. You must be Mrs. Sarah Thornton."

Sarah smiled nervously and moved tentatively further into the room, her eyes drawn at once to the figure standing with his back to her by the window, his dark hair curling wetly onto his collar. He turned abruptly, and with an almost imperceptible movement of his head toward the door indicated to Sir Joseph that he should go. That man, with one last rueful smile at Sarah, closed the door quietly behind him.

Sarah, feeling light-headed and sick, clutched at the chair in front of her and stood gripping it, studying the whiteness of her knuckles intently as she started haltingly. "I am sorry . . . I apologize for my . . . for the . . ." She stammered uncontrollably to a halt, aware that he had moved away from the desk and was now standing silently somewhere behind her.

"You are not really going to dismiss all those servants, are you?" Her voice was barely a whisper, and she swung round, staring at him white-faced, her bottom lip caught between her teeth in her distress. But he returned her gaze impassively, his expression unreadable.

"It was not their fault. It was especially not Mrs. Clark's fault or Tom's." She rushed on hastily, afraid he might silence her. "Tom asked me if he could take Emma out in the garden. I just did not realize what he intended. It was probably Emma's doing; she can be very tiresome and difficult to handle if she cannot get her own way."

His mouth twisted in sardonic humor. "Some trick she has no doubt learned from her mother," he returned scathingly.

Sarah, wincing at the sarcasm but unable in her anguish to do justice to the taunt, merely repeated imploringly, "But it is really not the servants' fault; you should not blame them. If anyone is to be dismissed, it should be me."

He laughed then and with a trace of real amusement. "If you are the one to be punished, Mrs. Thornton, perhaps we should think of something a little less to your liking."

He was standing only inches away now, and as she saw his hands reach for her and his head nearing hers, she realized his intention and averted her face quickly so that his mouth merely brushed the softness of her hair. His hand moved to her face, spanning it and turning it back with slow deliberation, and his eyes locked with hers for a few seconds before she felt his mouth bruise her own.

The sensation was so new that for a moment she remained unresisting. Sarah's only experience of being kissed was limited to the foul-breathed, slobbering wetness of her late husband, and Alfred Cunningham's equally salivary but less successfully placed attempts some months ago. This time there was nothing nauseating about it at all. His mouth felt warm and dry, and there was no intrusive tongue battering at her, just a barely perceptible touch as it moved lingeringly along her bottom lip. She realized detachedly that he had somehow managed to part her mouth by moving her face with his hand, and had done so with such skill that she had not even been aware of it. As though sensing her entrancement, his mouth softened, became caressing, but the knowledge that he was aware of her weakness made her push hard against him suddenly and try to twist her face free again.

He released her then, turning away from her, and moved back to the window.

"We shall call that a first installment, until such time as I decide to collect in full." His voice was gratingly harsh with some emotion, and she made immediately and hurriedly for the door, the back of one hand pressed hard to her throbbing mouth, unable, in her mortification, to retaliate in any way.

Mark Tarrington sat down in the swivel chair, his booted feet coming up onto the desk in front of him, and he leaned his head back against the cushioned leather. He hooked the decanter with one foot, drawing it close, and poured himself a measure into the crystal glass.

His thoughts turned to Sarah, something they were doing with alarming regularity, he reflected acidly. He was becoming obsessed with her, and the knowledge irritated him. He was used to women a lot more responsive to and grateful for his attention. He realized the antagonistic barrier she had thrown up between them was a shield with which she could keep him at arm's length. The puzzling thing was why. If it was some lengthy and involved game she was playing to increase his desire . . . he scowled; it was working admirably. He could not remember ever wanting a woman as much as he wanted this one. She was not even the type that would normally have interested him: too young, small and slight to the point of thinness. Her face, though . . . he smiled wryly to himself. She was beautiful, there was no doubt of that.

He tipped the decanter again, aware once more of the dull ache that consumed him whenever he thought of her. He pushed the chair away from the desk abruptly in irritated frustration and stood looking over the garden.

She was a penniless widow with a small child, something which usually would have precluded him getting involved at all, with a reputation that did not stand too much close inspection. He had made inquiries about her background before the opportunity to employ her had even arisen. Rumor had it that her husband had disinherited her and the child because of his belief that the child was not his but a lover's, a fact that was given credence by her refusal to contest the will. A muscle in his jaw hardened at the thought of her with anyone, and he could feel the unreasonable fury pervading him, not wanting to examine why it should disturb him so.

He dwelt on the circumstances that had made her removal from the Cunninghams' necessary, and his grip on the glass tightened. Not that he was unaware of the sorry state of the intimate side of Alfred's marriage. His friend's roving eye and exaggerated accounts of his various amorous accomplishments were a standing joke amongst most of his peers. He was sure that Alfred's version of the incident probably bore little resemblance to the truth, and yet it still rankled bitterly that his friend could possibly have gained more response from her than he had so far managed to do. Nor had it prevented his being sorely tempted to stop Alfred's bragging with more effective means than a politely worded rebuff. If anything, he realized he should be grateful Alfred had made unnecessary any more devious means of having Sarah removed into his care.

Any other woman in her position would by now have made some conciliatory move, indicating in some way that she was not completely adverse to his attentions. He was not particularly vain, but he knew well enough that his wealth and title and his preference for mistresses rather than a wife made him a prime target for women who were forced to support themselves . . . and for quite a few who were not, he reflected drily. His generosity was well known; indeed, his sister had once remarked that most of his discarded mistresses were financially better off after his protection had ceased than during it.

His intentions in bringing Sarah to live beneath his roof had never stemmed from any obligations duty he might have felt toward Luke and Joanna, and he knew she was quite aware of the fact. Her reluctance to come to Winslade Hall had seemed genuine enough, but his experience with women had left him cynical; he had known mistresses who could protest innocence and virtue while removing their clothes with indecent haste. Yet he was uneasily aware that she still seemed to be avoiding him at every possible opportunity with almost fanatical zeal.

He tossed back the remainder of the amber liquid, resolving to find Joseph Ashton. He needed a night out on the town; some diversion to put her from his mind. Perhaps he would find that this obsessive need was merely something of his own making and another woman would serve him equally well. It had proved that way in the past. He had felt a few times that there was someone special, but his affections had always strayed eventually, and he had found that a tearful and sordid severing of the relationship could usually be avoided if the payoff was generous enough.

He turned at a slight tap at the door as Joseph's head appeared around it. "Your young governess gone, then?" He winked salaciously. "What is a girl like that doing teaching in the schoolroom? I could think of a much better way to keep her employed." His voice was sly. "Or perhaps you have already done so, Mark, eh?" He laughed, slapping the other man hard on the back. "Wondered why you have not been seen in town for so long."

Mark Tarrington, ignoring his friend's suggestive remarks, said, "I was just thinking, Joe, it is about time we had a night out. Make it tonight?"

Joseph nodded. "Good idea. But look Mark," he

hesitated, his expression serious now, "if you are not interested in Sarah Thornton," he looked hopefully at the dark face, "I would like to approach her, take her off your hands, you know. After all, the children are practically past needing a governess. Be glad to . . ." He halted abruptly, aware of the dangerous darkening of his friend's eyes. "Well, just a thought. I shall meet you in town later."

He sauntered to the door, humming some tuneless melody, Mark Tarrington watching his departure with scowling intensity.

Chapter Eight

"Joanna." Sarah's voice cut, mildly exasperated, into the silence of the room.

The girl looked around sharply. "Joanna, you have been gaping through that window for the past ten minutes. You will never finish that exercise at this rate." She walked slowly toward the vacant-faced girl, saying, "Luke finished twenty minutes ago. Is there something wrong?" She looked searchingly at Joanna's face, seeing a wary light appear in the girl's dark eyes.

"No. Why should there be? I am bored, that is all. It is Christmas next week. I think lessons should be finished with now until after the holidays." Joanna looked sullen and uncooperative, and Sarah was sure there was some other reason behind the girl's recent change in attitude.

"That is for your uncle to decide, I am afraid."

"I do not see why Mama cannot have a say now that she is here," Joanna cut in. Sarah, knowing well enough that Lady Susan Morton was more than willing to leave all decisions requiring even a minimum of thought to her brother, merely sighed and

107

said to Joanna, "Off you go, then. We shall leave the rest of that page until tomorrow."

The girl disappeared with a smile, her face brightening slightly, and Sarah collected the books together and stacked them on her desk.

Lady Susan Morton had arrived at Winslade Hall a few days ago to spend Christmas with her family. She was a dark-haired woman of perhaps thirty-four, who looked, by quite strenuous design, quite a lot younger. She had a vivacious beauty and the same lustrous dark eyes and abundance of glossy curls as her children. She was friendly and charming, and Sarah liked her instantly, despite the knowledge that she neglected her children quite appallingly in favor of pleasure-seeking, for a good part of the year. The children had, before Sarah arrived, been tutored for the best part of three years in London by various governesses. Their mother, conscious that her life was not ideally suited to the raising of children, had approached her brother to take the children to his country house, where he now seemed to spend the majority of his time, to finish their studies. She had made her request pessimistically, and had been amazed at the readiness with which he appeared willing to take them, and had not dared to jeopardize her luck by questioning him about it further.

She was quite open with Sarah about the life she lead and the gentleman protectors she had encouraged since the death of her husband some three years previous. Sir Alexander Morton had been considerably older than his young wife and had loved her dearly, he had died of a heart attack in his fifty-eighth year. Although Susan spoke quite fondly of him, she did not seem in any way put out by his demise. He had left her quite a sizable fortune to use as she would, and she had systematically frittered the majority of it away on clothes and luxurious excesses, so that she was now almost entirely dependent on the generosity of her wealthy brother, when unsupported by other male generosity.

She had certainly livened the place up, Sarah thought, smiling, although she had noticed in Susan, even in the few days that she had been resident there, a tendency to restlessness, as though she longed for a far more active existence.

Susan had eventually persuaded Sarah to ride with herself and the children, and had selected a small grey mare for Sarah to use that was fairly docile and easy to handle. She had insisted that Sarah use one of her discarded riding habits, which she had admitted, with a grimace, was too tight anyway. Sarah had soon relearned the basics of keeping a seat, but she realized, ruefully, that she would never, by any means, make a good rider. She merely enjoyed the outings and the nonstop chatter of the woman beside her as she described London life. Joanna usually rode ahead, apparently bored by these anecdotes, and soon disappeared from sight, something which did not seem to bother her mother at all. Luke, still fretting about his imminent departure for school, had withdrawn into a kind of silent misery, which his mother had either not noticed or was ignoring.

Sarah closed the schoolroom door and made her way to her room. The house was alive with the sights and smells of Christmas preparation. Holly and ivy were being collected to decorate the rooms, and the servants seemed even more animated and cheerful than usual. The aromatic scent of baking invaded every room, sharpening the senses and appetites, and Sarah felt herself being drawn into the joyfully expectant atmosphere. Her abandoned good humor, she knew, was not wholly unrelated to the fact that Mark Tarrington had left for London on business shortly after Susan's arrival. He would, apparently, according to Maggie who was kept informed by Stewart, not be back before Christmas day, if then.

Christmas morning dawned crisp with frost, but palely sunny.

Joanna bounced into Sarah's room early, with gifts for herself, Maggie, and an excited Emma, and they went downstairs to wish Christmas cheer to the others. Emma, inundated with gifts, did not know which to open first, or where to turn; her small pink face was alight with agitated excitement. The dowager, Susan, Luke, Joanna, Maggie, Mrs. Davis — all had in turn given her some gaily colored item to unwrap. Even Martha, the cook, had brought her a beribboned box of small iced cakes.

Susan arrived at that moment, her arms full of gaily coloured parcels.

"Look, Stewart gave me these. They must be from Mark." She dropped them on to the cushions of the settee, spreading them out.

Joanna pounced on one with her name and then picked up another, smaller parcel, studying it. "This one is for you, Sarah." She turned to the young governess, holding out the package.

Sarah stared at it for a long moment and then took it tentatively, not wanting to open it, for some reason. Susan, leaning over her shoulder with avid curiosity, said, "Let us see, Sarah." Her excitement was infectious, and Joanna, also with wide-eyed eagerness, prompted Sarah to open it. She did so slowly, carefully unwrapping it and lifting the lid of the small box.

110

A gold filigree necklace lay on black velvet. It was quite obviously expensive, yet simple enough in style, and without any ostentation that would have rendered it too unacceptable. Sarah heard Susan's breath catch in her throat as she murmured, "It's lovely," and noticed that the older woman was looking at her now with speculative interest.

Joanna touched the gold circlet lightly and said, "It is beautiful, Sarah. Put it on."

Sarah, feeling an odd constriction in her throat, said, "Later," and snapped the box shut with trembling fingers.

She had prepared small presents herself for the other members of the family, but had got him nothing, feeling incapable of the hypocrisy. In any case, she thought now uncomfortably, there was nothing of worth that she could have afforded to buy him.

Emma was unwrapping a large doll, almost identical to the one Mark had bought for Sarah at the fête, and she realized that he had known all along that her interest in the doll had been purely personal rather than maternal. She had kept the doll herself, knowing that Emma, with her sudden tantrums, could break it quite easily.

Collecting together the strewn gifts she and Emma had been given, Sarah excused herself, saying she would take them to her room. She left Emma amusing herself with shredding the colored paper into tattered strips, the majority of the toys she had been given forgotten. In her room she placed the box on the dressing table, opening the lid again carefully. The gold gleamed dully against the black velvet, and she lifted it out, feeling the weight of it resting on her fingers. She wanted to put it back, leave it unworn, but she could not. It was the most beautiful thing she had ever owned, and she undid the clasp involuntarily and fastened the necklace about her throat. She caught sight of her reflection in the mirror and her fingers went up to touch the delicate design. She unfastened the bodice of her gown, slipping the necklace inside, feeling the coldness of it settle against her skin, and then rebuttoning her dress and pushing the empty box into a drawer, went back downstairs.

He arrived back early that evening.

Sarah had been sitting with Susan, Joanna, and the dowager in the drawing room, the old woman attempting to teach her and Joanna the basics of playing loo and whist. They had been enjoying themselves immensely when Sarah, not wanting any meeting with his lordship that night, had risen suddenly as she realized the day was lengthening, excusing herself with an exaggerated yawn.

She had gained the middle of the hall when the door opened, and she knew he had seen her. Aware that there was no way she could disappear without being unforgivably rude, she stopped, cursing silently that she had not retired just five minutes earlier.

He walked toward her slowly, tossing his coat to the waiting Davis as he did so.

Since the fateful day when Emma had nearly drowned, there had been no physical contact between them at all, although she was well aware of the expectancy that strained the atmosphere whenever they met by chance.

He was standing quite close now, and she said, slightly unsteadily, "Good evening, my lord." She continued in a rush, eager to get away, "Thank you for the gifts; it was very kind of you." She had half-turned, wanting to escape now the necessary formalities were over, but he caught her arm, turning her back toward him. The golden eyes searched her face, and he touched her throat lightly with one finger. "You are not wearing it." His tone was impassive, and she could not tell if he was annoyed or merely stating a fact.

"No," she lied quickly, looking away, and then as the ensuing silence lengthened uncomfortably, added simply for something to say, "I did not get you anything . . . I'm afraid there was nothing I could think of that you would need."

She wished the words at once unsaid as hard mockery colored his eyes and words.

"Indeed?" He paused, his mouth twisting sardonically. "You should have asked. I might have been able to suggest something." The vehemence in his tone made the color start stingingly to her face and she tried to move quickly away from the restricting hand on her arm, but his grip tightened and he leaned closer, brushing her mouth lightly with his.

"Merry Christmas, Sarah." He released her abruptly, and she turned hastily, making for the stairs, acutely aware, by the absence of any noise from the hall, that he was watching her.

January was passing slowly.

Luke had gone to school at the beginning of the month. They had watched him being driven away in the crested carriage, his small face white and pinched with trepidation. Stewart Palmer had accompanied him on the journey, but even that did not seem to afford the boy any comfort. Sarah felt her heart go out to him as the coach rolled out of sight and he could wave to them no more. Mark Tarrington had not been present; only Joanna, Susan, and herself, and she knew that of the three of them, she was the most

113

distressed by his departure.

Joanna still seemed preoccupied with some inner anxiety she was unwilling to share. Susan had left for a rout at a friend's manor in Kent a few days after Luke's departure, and Sarah could see the relief this afforded the woman. She had been becoming more restless as the days passed, and Sarah knew she longed to mix socially again. The schoolroom seemed depressingly empty to Sarah now, and with the emptiness came the knowledge that her thoughts would soon have to turn to her own future again. Joanna would be sixteen soon, and well past the need for a governess. She had pestered her mother mercilessly while she had been at Winslade Hall to let her make her come out soon, but Susan merely prevaricated, saying she would speak to her brother about it.

She and Joanna still rode together in the mornings before lessons, and Joanna seemed to disappear with an alarming frequency on some errand of her own. Sarah had tried to question her about this, but she became sullen, unwilling to comment further than saying she needed time on her own. Joanna was an experienced horsewoman and there was no way that Sarah could keep up with her if she wished otherwise.

Sarah realized that once Joanna's schooling was finished her need to find other employment would be an acute problem. She tried to push the fear to the back of her mind, hoping that a recommendation from Mark Tarrington would provide her with some other employer, yet knowing also the futility of that hope.

Sarah started from her reverie, suddenly aware of the scorching sensation which usually heralded Mark's arrival. She was still amazed at the way he could approach so noiselessly. He rarely visited the schoolroom now, and she did not turn but looked ahead at Joanna, still oblivious of his arrival but, thankfully, apparently engrossed in study. Her dark head was bent over a book and she was reading diligently. Mark walked past Sarah, and although his footsteps could be heard quite clearly now, Joanna seemed deaf to, or uncaring of his approach.

She looked up suddenly as he stood by her desk and made a quick, desperate movement, trying to cover what she had been reading. He was too fast, though, and Sarah saw the girl's face take on a look of almost incredulous dismay as he turned over the closed book. He examined it with minute interest for a few seconds, saying, "Jane Austen—I had no idea this was in the school curriculum."

Joanna made a clumsy snatch for the book, but he held it out of her reach, saying over his shoulder as he walked away, "I shall keep it for a while and read it myself, as it appears to be so engrossing." He changed the subject abruptly, saying, "I hear from your mother that you wish to make your come out soon."

Joanna merely stared at him, her face ashen.

"Well?" the steely impatience in his voice at her silence was evident.

She merely nodded, her eyes still intent on the book, which he clasped in one hand and tapped slowly against the other.

"Your mother seemed to think that you would welcome the suggestion with slightly more enthusiasm. Obviously, she was wrong. We shall leave it for a while, then," he said, and with barely a glance at Sarah, strode from the room.

Sarah moved concernedly to Joanna, her face anxious. "What is the matter? You look positively ill."

The girl shook her head as though unable to speak,

115

and jumping up suddenly, rushed from the room.

It was quite late in the afternoon now, and Sarah tidied away the books, deciding any further study that day would be impossible.

She guessed Joanna would have gone to her room and followed her there slowly, trying to make some sense of the girl's distress. It obviously had to be more than just losing a copy of a book.

Joanna was lying across her bed sobbing noisily, and Sarah went to her hurriedly, trying to make her sit up so she could question her. The girl let her face fall into her hands and shook her head slowly from side to side, saying, "He will kill him—I know he will."

Sarah, completely at a loss to understand what this meant, said impatiently, "Come, Joanna, you will have to explain better than that."

Joanna sat up suddenly, her tear-streaked face gazing beseechingly at Sarah.

"That book . . ." She hesitated as though uncertain whether to continue. "There was a letter in it. That is what I was reading."

Sarah looked puzzled. "Well that is all right, surely. Your uncle will return it soon. He will probably not even read the book. You will get it back tomorrow."

Joanna's sobs increased. "You do not understand; the letter was from . . . Paul Ashton." She looked away, her face registering shame. "He is Joseph Ashton's younger brother," she explained. "We have been meeting for some time now in secret. When we go riding I meet him sometimes near the boundary of the two estates." She looked up, defiance flaring in her eyes. "He loves me. He said so. And I love him. We want to be married soon." The defiant flicker died suddenly, and she repeated with a whimper, "He will kill him."

Sarah felt all at once unaccountably cold as she remembered the young man at the fête and the look on his face. She said calmly, "What was in the letter, Joanna?"

The girl's averted face and scarlet cheeks made Sarah's heart sink. "You have not done anything . . ." she stopped, searching for words, "anything too indiscreet."

"No, not that—well, not quite, I don't think," Joanna said in confusion. "He loves me; he said so," she repeated stubbornly. "When Uncle Mark finds out what has been going on he will call him out—I know he will. There will be a scandal and he will kill him . . ." She broke off, throwing herself back onto the bed and weeping into the covers.

"Perhaps he will agree to your being married." Sarah said, trying to instill some optimism in her voice. "After all, you have only been meeting him out riding. There is not a lot that can happen in broad daylight, is there?"

"There is a small summerhouse we go to," Joanna said, unable to meet Sarah's eyes. "He has only kissed me, and . . ." she stopped, unable to go on. "I have not even made my come out yet. He will be really furious, I know he will."

Sarah, not knowing what to say to comfort the girl, said with little hope, "Perhaps he might not see the letter; he might not even open the book." But even as the words were uttered she knew the futility of any such expectation. "You will have to try and get the letter back, Joanna. The book is more than likely in his study. He will probably leave it there, and you can take it out when he goes out."

The girl shook her head miserably. "He has taken it to his room. I saw him go in there with it a while ago."

Sarah bit her lip, trying to think clearly. "Well, he will not be in there forever. You could get it later this evening."

"I cannot. Mary always visits my room after bedtime, and his valet is nearly always there until well after nine o'clock." Her face became animated suddenly, and she looked at Sarah, her eyes glowing. "You could get it," she breathed. "He always goes out with Stewart Palmer and Joseph Ashton on Thursdays without fail. They go to town whoring or gambling."

Sarah was stunned, as much by the girl's choice of words as by what she was suggesting.

But Joanna hurried on, unheeding. "His valet will be in his room all day until he goes out, at about nine-thirty, I think. Then he goes to the kitchens. For diversion of his own," she added with a watery smile. "That is the best thing. You could go to his room—it is always unlocked. Get the letter and destroy it."

Sarah's face registered sheer disbelief at what the girl was saying and then shock as she realized she was quite serious. "I cannot, Joanna. I am sorry, but I cannot do it."

Joanna looked bewildered and then her face crumpled. "You will not, you mean. You do not care about what happens to me any more than mama does, or he does," she added vehemently and threw herself back onto the bed with a theatrical show of weeping.

"Joanna, can you not go yourself after he goes out?" Sarah's tone was desperate.

"No. Mary's room is just down the corridor. She will be in fussing and getting me ready for bed at nine, and she always pops in several times during the evening and I never know when she is coming. She will raise the roof if she cannot find me." She looked at Sarah beseechingly. "You could do it, Sarah. His room is just below yours. It would only take you a few minutes to get there down the back stairs. No one would see you."

Her voice was pleading, and Sarah nodded, white-faced. "You are sure he goes out?" she asked Joanna, unnecessarily, as she knew already herself that it was his habit to do so.

Joanna sat up, her face regaining some color, and her gratitude, pathetic in its intensity, made Sarah swallow unuttered her misgivings about the whole thing.

Chapter Nine

It was ten o'clock.

Sarah was sitting by the window in her room. She had seen Stewart Palmer and Mark Tarrington leave some time earlier, but nevertheless she waited, her heart in her mouth, just in case they should return for some reason.

She stood up as Maggie entered, glancing toward the cot. "I see Emma is asleep. I will help you with your dress."

She started to unfasten the back of Sarah's dress and Sarah moved away quickly. "No, it is all right. I can do it. You go to bed now."

The maid was not about to be put off, her fingers still busy, and Sarah snapped, "Leave me alone, Maggie."

The young girl looked up, startled.

"I am sorry, Maggie." Sarah smiled at the girl as apologetically as her fragmented nerves would allow. "I am on edge tonight, that's all."

Maggie smiled sympathetically and continued unfastening the dress. She was aware of the fraught situation between Sarah and Lord Tarrington. According to Stewart, his lordship was also displaying signs of severe emotional stress.

Sarah allowed the girl to help her slip into her nightgown and she belted her robe over the top and went back to sit by the window. "You go to bed Maggie," she said quietly. "I am not tired. I shall stay up for a while, I think, and read."

Maggie retreated softly to her own room, her thoughts troubled, leaving Sarah white-faced and shaking slightly with cold and reaction.

She shook herself mentally. It was ridiculous; she had seen him go out quite clearly earlier. It should be childishly simply to retrieve one small piece of paper.

She thought of Stewart Palmer and wondered what Maggie felt about his trips to town. She knew the girl was falling in love with him. She put the thought from her mind; there were more pressing things to think of now. She got up and left her room, then made her way silently along the corridor and down the back stairs. There was no one to be seen anywhere.

She tapped lightly at the door, her mind working feverishly for some excuse should the valet prove to be there still. There was no answer. The silence was oppressive, and she opened the door holding her breath, but it swung inward silently.

There was a fire burning in the large hearth and a muted glow from some lamps. She walked forward quickly into the room, avoiding looking at the massive bed that dominated the room. Her eyes scanned quickly along the most likely surfaces and she saw a pile of books lying on a desk in the corner. She moved swiftly, picking them up one at a time. None were right. She moved toward the bed, noticing more books on a reading table, her shaking diminishing slightly as the time passed.

She picked up the books, studying them, sitting down on the bed as she did so. She looked around the room objectively, trying to estimate where else the book might be, and then looked back at the titles in her hand.

She was unaware the door had opened until a slight flickering of one of the lamps made her look up. Mark Tarrington, with a decanter and glass in one hand and his coat in the other, was entering the room, the valet following.

The valet suddenly stood still, his face a study of incredulous astonishment, quickly masked by a look of bland indifference. Mark, noting the change in the man's attitude, turned into the room, and for a few moments he and Sarah stared at each other in pulsating silence. Then, with a few low words to the valet, he kicked the door shut after the man's hurriedly departing figure.

He turned back toward her, and although the room was too shadowy for her to clearly see his expression, she knew instinctively that he was smiling.

It seemed that for a few moments she did not breathe or function at all, merely sat rigid with shock, acknowledging objectively that despite all her frantic endeavors to prevent this moment's ever occurring, she had been caught out after all by her own foolish recklessness.

He started to walk slowly into the room, and still Sarah sat, numb, too stunned to feel anything. She attempted to bring her frozen mind into some semblance of action, with the dawning and horrified realization that he had not seemed that surprised to see her there. She jumped off the bed quickly and stood facing him, the tip of her tongue running nervously along her parched lips.

"I can explain . . ." She halted, unable to think of anything else to say, and moved away from the bed as she did so, making a detour of the furniture toward the door. She could still not see his face clearly but she thought he smiled slightly as he said, "There is no need."

Her mind ferreted deliriously for some words to account for her presence on his bed at this time of night but they jumbled and spun in disorder and she merely watched in mesmerized terror as he walked closer.

He placed the decanter and glass on a table and threw his jacket toward a chair, and as he did so she made a sudden, furious dash for the door, trying to evade him.

He caught her easily, dragging her close, and said with frightening quiet, "It has taken you long enough to get here—I think you should stay for a while."

"You do not understand . . . Joanna's book . . ." She struggled wildly, but his mouth stifled hers into silence and she was futilely aware of his hands loosening the robe she wore. She felt it slide slowly and inexorably to the floor. She tore her mouth away from his, attempting to push herself back from him, throwing her head back with the effort. She was almost sobbing with desperation now, and she started to utter some incoherent explanation, but he silenced her again, lifting her, his mouth hard, and, following every fierce evasion with relentless accuracy, he carried her to the bed. He allowed her to fall with such force that she sensed the wind knocked out of her, and she lay there gasping for a few moments, trying to regain control of her breathing. She felt the downy covers beneath and all around her and pushed herself up quickly, acutely conscious now that he had removed his shirt and was sitting on the bed and was in the process of removing his boots.

She made a lunge for the opposite side of the bed, but he caught her with one hand, pushing her back down into the smothering softness with insulting ease. She was shaking violently now, and steadying her voice with supreme effort, she managed, "Please, I can explain . . ." before she felt him pull her roughly toward him, one hand holding her face still while the other checked the renewed thrashing of her limbs. He pulled her under him slightly, curbing her struggles with the partial weight of his body, and kissed her with a kind of brutal sensuality. Her mouth bruised beneath his, and she fought with hopeless desperation, one hand coming up to claw at his face. She heard him swear beneath his breath as her nails caught his cheek, and then she felt the thin shift she wore rip beneath his fingers. His hands felt cool against her feverish skin, and she twisted and writhed beneath him in an effort to break free. One hand trailed to her throat, his fingers tracing the line of the gold necklace she still wore, before moving lower. She caught at his hand, moving it away, and he allowed her to hold it, moving the other down instead, and, realizing his motive, she flung it away from her in savage disgust.

She stilled at last from sheer physical exhaustion, her breath rasping painfully in her throat. She lay quiet, aware of nothing now but the movement of his hands and mouth against her skin, and in her lassitude she felt an insidious warmth stirring, spreading through her, bringing new and unwanted sensations. She wanted to struggle free, to repress these frightening feelings, but her limbs felt leaden, intoxicated with the skill of his stroking fingers. Somewhere on the edge of her consciousness she was aware that she should make some last effort at resistance, but she felt drugged with fatigue, and as her clenched hands against his chest started to relax, clutching at him rather than pushing him away, she felt his body slide to cover her completely, forcing her further into the yielding softness of the bed.

She cried out suddenly in pain and panic, her befuddled senses straining for control, her hands pushing ineffectually at his arms as she tried to twist herself free. For a moment she thought he was in fact going to release her; he lay unmoving, his head falling forward slightly, almost touching her shoulder, as though in indecision and disbelief. Then his hands caught in the tangled mass of her hair, stilling her wildly turning head, and his mouth covered hers again, the ruthless plunder still present but tempered now with a kind of seductive persuasion. His hands and mouth moved coaxingly, slowly and with practiced art, clinging and caressing, erasing some of the pain, until she sensed the tension within beginning to ease and a familiar fiery pleasure heating her blood.

His hands slid beneath her, lifting her against him and pressing her close. She felt herself being molded to the hardness of his body, and as he moved her slowly with him she felt as though she were being completely absorbed. She held her breath with the intensity of her arousal, afraid that he might move away before the throbbing pressure building within her was released. She clung to him tenaciously, her hands sliding from his chest, moving up around his neck and into his hair, and she pulled him closer, arching into him as she did so.

But the violence of the pleasure became too intense and she attempted to break free again, unable to bear the contact longer, and he stilled slowly until he was lying unmoving on top of her.

Her breathing quietened, and with her self-control came the realization of what had happened. She opened her eyes, seeing the dark head close to her face, and noticed her hands, half lost in the glossy

125

mass of his hair. She pulled them away quickly, as though they were scalding, and the abrupt movement seemed to rouse him, for she felt his head starting to move back. She shut her eyes and turned her head away quickly, unable to meet his gaze. She knew he was watching her, and after a few seconds she felt the weight lift from her and the bed ease as he got up.

She lay motionless, her eyes and mind tightly shut, not wanting to acknowledge what had passed between them. She listened, straining for some sound to indicate that he had gone, but there was none. It was silent, and she lay with the blood heavy in her ears, waiting for him to leave so she could get up. The soundless minutes passed, and she opened her eyes at last, scanning the shadowy room.

She was surprised that her shame and humiliation had not left her feeling feverishly hysterical; instead she felt icily cold suddenly and detached, as though remote from the incident. With her new clarity of thought came the realization that he was probably waiting for her to leave; it was his room, after all.

She sat up, pressing the back of one hand to her mouth as the agony between her thighs raged, and as she did so she noticed the blood streaking her legs and the sheets. She wondered with frozen calm how he would explain that away to the servants, and she slid her legs over the edge of the bed tentatively.

Her robe was thankfully lying quite close by, and she belted it tightly with shaking fingers. One slipper was by the bed, and she picked it up, scouring the floor quickly for the others. There was no sign of it, so she left the one she had found and started toward the door silently.

She noticed him as she approached it, and her steps faltered slightly. He was fully dressed now and standing by the dark window watching her. She looked away, aware suddenly that he was walking toward her, and she quickened her pace, reaching the door and managing to open it slightly before his hand, going over the top of her head, pushed it shut again.

She moved away from him back into the room slightly, unable to bear his closeness, and said with iced calm, "Was there something else?"

He ignored the comment, saying quietly, "Why did you not tell me that it was your first time?"

She looked at him, unable to keep the loathing from her eyes, and asked acridly, "Why, would it have made any difference?"

"Of course."

His tone was impassive, but she knew he meant it, and the knowledge made her retort harshly, "I am so sorry, I hope I was not too much of a disappointment to you." She had spoken with bitter sarcasm, intentionally misunderstanding him, but it sounded like a whining plea for reassurance, and she wished at once that she had remained silent.

He said nothing, his expression unreadable in the shadowy room, and she looked away unable to meet his eyes as her humiliation started to burn remorselessly, threatening her shaky composure. She made for the door again, murmuring, "Emma. I have to go."

His arm barred the way as she moved, and she recoiled from the threatened contact.

"You keep quite exalted company, my dear. A virgin birth—I have only heard of the one before. I am skeptical of that, too."

She stared at him, stunned as much by the blasphemy as by the sudden realization of what he knew. She tried desperately to think of something to say that would satisfy him and let her escape to her room, but she was silent, and his voice cut in softly, "Well, whose child is she?" She rounded on him suddenly, and said with quiet vehemence, "She is mine."

"Physically impossible, I should say." His voice was soothing, and it only served to fuel her agitation further.

"It is none of your business," she flared at him and saw through the gloom the dangerous spark that illuminated his eyes at her words.

He said with a hard edge to his voice, "You are wrong. Everything and everyone in this house is my concern. I make it so."

She glared at him, biting her lip in frustration, knowing that there was no way she could get past him, and knowing also that he would not let her go until she had told him what he wanted to know.

"It is a long story and very boring," she said, trying to dismiss it flippantly.

"I shall let you know if I am in danger of falling asleep," he returned drily.

She could think of nothing else to say, and with one beseeching look that afforded her nothing, she began the story that she had never before told anyone.

She picked up one of the books lying on a nearby table, unable to meet his eyes as she spoke, and began turning it over and over.

"My father was Sir Paul Brent. He died when I was just eighteen, leaving my mother and me penniless. He had always gambled and there were always unpaid debts. It was something my mother accepted because she adored him so. After his death, when we were settling his affairs, it came to light that a lot of the outstanding accounts were in fact dressmaker's bills, but for clothes which my mother had never had. The realization that he was not only a gambler but a whoremonger completely shattered her. She had trusted him implicitly, and the knowledge broke her.

"Our relationship had never been very good; she

resented the time he spent with me and the money he put by for my education. She thought it should have been spent on other things. Shortly after the funeral she met an acquaintance of his who had visited to express sympathy at our loss. William Thorpe was a tea importer from Manchester, and he was apparently attracted to my mother at once, although he took pains to let her know that she was lucky he had rescued her from imminent poverty. They were married quite shortly after, and although he was prepared to offer a home to my mother, he made it apparent from the start that his generosity did not extend to an eighteen-year-old daughter.

"I had received several offers from a neighboring landowner, Squire Thornton. When my father was alive he had merely laughed at what he called the man's presumption, but my stepfather made it clear that I should accept this offer or find myself alternative means of support. The fact that Squire Thornton was forty-two and a renowned lecher made no difference, and so I, not knowing how I could begin to earn my own living, agreed to marry him."

She stopped there, aware that he had made no comment, but, unable to look at him, she resumed quickly, "We were married shortly after, and I went to live at Thornton Manor. It was a very small estate, run down with neglect. He drank excessively, which proved to be quite fortunate for me. On our wedding night I retired early and locked the door. He came up some while later almost senseless with drink, and he soon gave up any attempts to get into the room. The second night was the same, and after that, when he had realized that retiring at the same time as I did might afford him entry, I pleaded illness. I managed to draw that excuse out for a week, by which time I was aware, from the gossiping of the servants, who took no pains to hide the fact, that he was finding comfort with one of the young kitchen girls. At first I could not believe my good fortune, but I knew that sooner or later he would demand his rights—as his main reason for remarrying was his obsessive need for an heir.

"I had managed to build quite an effective barrier between us, and I knew that his interest in me was beginning to wane. I think he quite regretted marrying me at all. He returned to London when I next pleaded illness and was gone for two months, leaving myself and a foreman in charge of the estate. When he returned he informed me that his mistress was pregnant. He was pleased and excited about it, and I thought he was probably in love with her. He wanted the child desperately as his heir, and suggested that if I would soon agree to announce a pregnancy, toward the later stages his mistress and I would be packed off to some remote spot, supposedly for my health, and she would apparently nurse me. The child would be mine, and he would have his legal heir. I agreed, because I knew that any interest he had in me was likely to vanish completely, and also because I thought I owed him that, at least.

"The woman and I and an old and trusted servant of his went to a small coastal village when she was six months pregnant. Fashion being what it is, it was easy enough to hide her increase in weight and add to mine. Her name was Caroline Brown; she was about twenty-five, I think, and a widow. That is all I know about her, although we became quite close. I was aware from the way she spoke that my husband was not her only lover and she did not feel any particular fondness for him. She was merely grateful that this inconvenience in her life was being disposed of.

"The child was born two weeks early. My husband

was visiting the cottage at the time. When he learned the news that it was a girl he was beside himself with rage. He looked at her once and left for London the same day.

"Caroline and he were both dark-haired, with brown eyes, and Emma is fair and blue-eyed. It seemed an incredible twist of fate that the child I was supposed to claim as mine resembled me minutely. My husband was obviously aware as soon as he saw the child that it was not his.

"Caroline left for London as soon as she was able to travel, and I returned home with Emma a few weeks later. Scandalous gossip was rife, of course; everyone was eager to view my supposed daughter. After they saw her no one questioned her legitimacy again, and I noticed quite a few shamefaced looks.

"When Emma was six months old my husband wrote to me from London informing me that his finances were exhausted and that he was coming home and expected my cooperation in producing an heir. A week or so later I learned that he had fallen downstairs at some bawdy house and broken his neck."

She stopped abruptly, acutely aware of his silence, and said with a bitter laugh, "I told you it was tedious."

His voice sounded distant. "On the contrary, my dear, I cannot remember hearing anything so fantastic in a long while."

She stared at him, the sapphire eyes huge in her white face. "You do not believe me." It was an unemotional statement.

"Not at all; no one would attempt to create anything so ridiculous. Where is this Caroline Brown now?"

"I do not know. I heard nothing more from her; she was simply glad to be rid of the encumbrance of a

131

child. I do not know who the father is. After taking so many elaborate pains to have the child accepted as mine, I think my husband was too embarrassed or humiliated to admit that he had been duped himself. There was nothing he could do. I dreaded his coming home, in case he should harm Emma in some way. When Emma was baptized the birth was registered with myself as mother and Charles Thornton as father; neither was correct. I found out after his death that he had disinherited us both in favor of some male relative and that he had instigated a rumor that Emma was mine but not his. There was very little left of worth to wrangle about, and besides, I did not think that either of us was entitled to anything."

There was silence for a few moments, and Sarah, realizing now that she was light-headed with exhaustion and pain and shivering with cold, asked tonelessly, "Am I free to go now?" She had moved forward slightly, but still kept out of his reach.

He picked up the book she had been turning over while speaking and held it out to her. "Do you not want this?"

She looked at it with numb stupefaction. It was Joanna's book. She reached for it automatically, wanting to hurl it as far as she could, but she merely took it from him, saying nothing.

"I have removed the rather interesting note inside. As you seem privy to this deceit, perhaps you would tell Joanna to see me first thing tomorrow morning in my study. She has brought this matter to a head somewhat before I anticipated."

She stared at him stupidly, and he laughed softly, saying gently, with a vague note of real surprise, "Come, Sarah . . . you did not really think I was unaware of what was going on?"

She felt tears of desolate misery behind her eyes at

the realization that everything that had occurred that evening had been for nothing.

He was watching her closely and said quietly, "Are you crying for her or for yourself?"

She sensed her throat closing, and, uncaring now, pushed past him and ran blindly out into the corridor.

She heard him call her name with such imperious command that she would usually have stopped dead, but she continued to run, her face wet and cold, until she gained her room. She slammed the door, locking it with shaking fingers, and leaned against it for a few minutes. Then, with a wretched sob, she sank onto the bed and buried her face in the covers, weeping until at last exhaustion afforded her the comfort of sleep.

Chapter Ten

Sarah stirred, not wanting to move, vaguely aware of a noise that had been gnawing at the edge of her consciousness for a while. The sound came again. A soft insistent tapping at the door.

She sat up, gasping as an aching agony consumed her body and her head swam

"Who is it?" Her voice was a cracked whisper.

"Joanna. Let me in." The girl sounded breathlessly anxious, and Sarah pushed herself away from the bed slowly.

She had been sleeping without covers, and she felt chilled and her body was raw.

She looked toward the crib. Emma was sleeping still, a thread of saliva spreading onto the sheet from her tiny mouth.

Sarah opened the door quietly and Joanna hurried past her.

"I am sorry if I have woken you, Sarah. Have you

got it?" She could not keep the note of excited impatience from her voice. She pounced on the book lying on the bed where Sarah had dropped it the night before, not waiting for a reply.

She lifted it by one cover, shaking it vigorously.

"It is not there, Joanna." Sarah's voice was colorless.

Joanna looked at her blankly. "What do you mean?"

"He knows. He already knew about your meetings with Paul Ashton. He has taken the note." Sarah sat down heavily on the side of the bed, crossing her arms and rubbing them absently to warm herself.

"He was there?" Joanna looked incredulous and then frightened. "Are you sure he knows about us?" she whispered.

Sarah nodded, feeling unable to comfort the girl in her distress.

Joanna started to sob quietly, rocking herself back and forth, her arms clasped about her.

Sarah moved around the bed to her, her arms going around the shaking form.

"He wants to see you in his study this morning."

"I cannot go. I shall have to run away." She said it with dramatic hysteria. "Paul and I could run away." A hopeful glimmer was beginning to spark life into her eyes, some of the tears drying.

"You are being ridiculous, Joanna. Where would you go? You need money and a place to live. Look," Sarah tried to continue hearteningly, "he must have known for a while, and he has done nothing so far. Perhaps it might not be so bad." She hesitated as her own memories surfaced, conscious suddenly of Joanna staring at her.

135

"You . . . you do not look well this morning, Sarah." Joanna was gazing at a mark, livid against the whiteness of Sarah's shoulder, revealed by the gaping robe. "What did he say when he found you there? He did not hurt you, did he?" Her voice rose slightly in disbelief.

Sarah pulled the robe quickly about her, rebelting it. "No. No, of course not. You had better go and see him. The sooner it is over with the easier your mind will be." She smiled encouragingly at the girl, who was still looking at her uncertainly.

"What time is it, Joanna, do you know?"

"About seven-thirty, I think. I could not sleep. I have been awake all night," Joanna added slowly.

Sarah, noticing the dark circles beneath the young girl's eyes, could believe it.

"Go on," she murmured again, pulling Joanna gently off the bed. She wanted her gone for reasons of her own, too. She needed time to try to compose herself for the day ahead.

Joanna, with one last anguished glance Sarah's way, shut the door softly behind her.

Emma was beginning to stir now, and Sarah knew Maggie would soon arrive to help them both dress.

She let her robe slip to the floor and stripped off the torn shift, throwing it violently into a corner without looking at it. She washed and dressed as quickly as she could and sat in front of the dressing table studying her face in the mirror. She looked awful. Her eyes were dull from lack of sleep and weeping and her swollen mouth looked vivid in the pallor of her face. There were bruiselike marks at the sides of her neck, and she shook her hair forward abruptly, not wanting to look at them, and picked up her brush, starting to drag it quickly through her tangled hair.

Maggie came in just then, and Sarah kept her hair covering her face and neck, not wanting to expose herself to Maggie's sharp scrutiny.

Maggie, chattering incessantly about plans for the day, picked up the gurgling and fully awake Emma, oblivious of any change in Sarah.

"Would you take Emma to breakfast, Maggie? I have a few letters to write this morning and I am not very hungry."

Maggie went readily enough, still murmuring in babyish tones to Emma.

The door opened minutes after Maggie had left, and Sarah turned to see Joanna reentering. The young girl looked dazed, and Sarah felt lead settle in her stomach. "That was quick; have you seen him?"

Joanna nodded, still looking stunned. "Everything is all right. He is going to speak to Paul—I think he meant lecture," she said with a grimace, "about a betrothal, and see if Mama is agreeable to a betrothal and come-out party on my sixteenth birthday in June." She laughed then, her face registering stupendous relief, and Sarah laughed with her, her joy infectious.

"That is marvelous, Joanna. I am very happy for you."

"Oh, he was angry," the girl continued airily, "but he could tell that I was adamant about marrying Paul; so, there is an end to it . . . thank heavens," she added forcefully, sinking casually onto the bed. "Oh, I nearly forgot. He wants to see you now."

Sarah stared at the girl for a long moment before turning away. "Tell him I cannot come Joanna, will you. You were right, I am not feeling very well this

137

morning." She ran a slightly trembling hand through her hair, despising her cravenness in avoiding the meeting.

Joanna looked doubtful, but nodded, too absorbed with her own happiness to perceive Sarah's misery.

She was back within a few minutes, saying with an uncertain frown, "He said you have ten minutes to come down, or he will come up."

Sarah closed her eyes and nodded, knowing that he would do just that. "Thank you, Joanna. You go and get your breakfast. I shall see you later."

She sat down at the dressing table, trying to marshal some courage. She started to brush her hair absently. What did it matter? He was probably going to dismiss her. She would not be needed now Joanna's future was all but settled. The opportunity was too good for him to miss. She threw the brush despairingly onto the dressing table and made her way downstairs.

He was standing by the door of the study with Stewart Palmer, and she saw him look up still talking to Stewart. Her steps slowed, and she felt her body starting to throb with an emotion that was not wholly fear.

Stewart passed her, his smile sympathetic, and she wondered with frozen detachment if he knew. Of course, the valet. Her face started to burn with uncontrollable humiliation. No doubt the story of how the earl had found the young governess waiting on his bed for him was the talk of the kitchens by now, and she was sure with some elaborate embellishments.

She was aware that he was waiting for her, and swallowing hard, loathing herself for her cowardice, she made to turn.

"Sarah." Just her name, quietly spoken, but the warning was implicit, and after hesitating momentarily she moved forward again slowly, through the door he opened for her, unable to meet his eyes.

"Sit down." She obeyed automatically, keeping her face turned away in studied contemplation of her hands. She had expected the interview to be concise and brief, sure he would want to finalize things as quickly as possible, but he was silent, and she was acutely conscious of his gaze.

He moved to the desk and leaned against it, his hand going to her face, turning it up to his.

She kept her lids lowered, her lashes shielding her eyes, and she heard him say softly, "Can you not look at me, Sarah?"

She met his eyes fleetingly, looking away again hastily, alarmed at what she read there. She felt his fingers extend, brushing softly against the side of her neck, and she winced from the light touch, realizing that he had noticed the bruise.

He released her, moving away slightly, and said, "Are you all right?"

She remained silent, concentrating on the gold ring spinning feverishly beneath her fingers.

"Are you bleeding still?"

She sensed her cheeks stinging furiously and shook her head quickly, averting her face further.

"Do you want me to apologize, Sarah?" He sounded vaguely exasperated, as though her silence irritated him, and she flared impulsively, "I doubt you would know how." She halted abruptly, aware that he was smiling, and he said softly, "Better."

His ability to manipulate her was infuriating, and she vowed she would not give him the satisfaction of

139

dismissing her and said in an unsteady voice, "I want . . . I would like a reference. Now that Joanna's future is settled, I should like to attend to mine."

He said nothing, and she looked up quickly, wondering if he had misunderstood.

"I will decide when your stay in my household is to be terminated." There was slow resolution in his voice, and he continued evenly, "I shall be going to London on business for a week or two. . . ." His mouth twisted immediately and sardonically at her undisguised relief at this information. "We shall discuss your future when I return."

She stood up, making for the door, her thoughts racing. She knew with sudden, simply clarity that she would be far away by the time he returned.

"Sarah." His tone was a gentle threat. "Do not be foolish enough to try to leave before I return." She saw one side of his mouth lift almost imperceptibly. He was well aware he had read her thoughts, and she left quickly, unable to prevent herself banging the door shut as she did so.

He was away for three weeks, during which time Sarah passed some of the happiest days she had known since childhood.

The weather was still clement for February and early snowdrops and daffodils were dotting color into the verdant landscape. She and Joanna still rode in the mornings, and now that the young girl's need for secret excursions had passed, they settled into a comfortable amity, enjoying each other's company immensely. Joanna chattered endlessly about the proposed plans for her betrothal and even the wedding.

140

Her gown for her betrothal ball, her wedding gown, all were described in minute detail, and she and Sarah rode slowly, discussing all conceivable aspects of the dressmaker's skills. Sarah's uneasiness about Joanna's enthusiasm over all these plans was soon put to rest by the appearance of the young man. Paul Ashton visited several times with his elder brother Sir Joseph, and the ardent adoration he had for Joanna was plain for all to see. Sir Joseph's obvious cynicism about all this slavish devotion manifested itself in the expressive raising of his eyebrows in Sarah's direction, after which he commenced to indulge in a discreet flirtation of his own. His personal interest in Sarah was growing steadily, and he knew she was aware of it. It irked him that he felt incapable of taking this passionate impulse further because of his absent friend's disapproval. From the flashes of apprehensive concern that showed in the girl's eyes at any mention of the earl, he was quite sure that she was not romantically entangled with him. She seemed quite disconcerted just by his name, usually changing the subject speedily whenever it arose, and Sir Joseph determined to broach the point again with his friend when he returned.

Sarah, for her part, would have been more than happy to have allowed Joanna to meet with the Ashtons alone when they called, but she knew that propriety called for the young girl's being chaperoned. Joseph Aston's attentions, although always charmingly proper, were beginning to grate on her already sorely tried nerves, and she always felt a distinct sinking of the heart when she knew that they were visiting. She had been, at first, reluctant to see them at all, sure that her presence would evoke barely concealed leering smirks. But she had been wrong.

141

They both seemed to treat her with every respectful consideration.

The same had been true of the servants. After the episode with Emma at the lake, the majority of the servants had started to treat her with a kind of awed deference. Many of them had believed their employment in certain jeopardy, and they knew that it was she who had seemingly brought about the earl's change of heart. None was sure how this apparent miracle had been achieved, but they were content enough that the outcome of the incident had not proved to be the disaster they had feared. Kathy Clark's gratitude had reduced her to tearful incoherency when she had realized that she and her son were not about to be turned out of their cottage following his reckless and stupid behavior.

Sarah, sure that her disgrace would have by now become common knowledge, had avoided all the servants with meticulous care for some days after, not wanting to read the contempt in their eyes. But she had been mistaken. Their attitude toward her was unchanged. She had watched Matilda Davis closely, searching for some hidden spark of contempt in her eyes, but there was nothing. The woman treated her with the same casual friendliness as before. Even the valet, bringing Sarah to scarlet-cheeked confusion the next time they had met in the corridor, had merely greeted her with bland courtesy. The realization dawned on her slowly that the man had obviously been threatened with dismissal if he mentioned the incident, and this she was sure with vehement malice, was to protect the earl's credibility rather than her reputation.

The days since he had left passed enjoyably, but

slowly. She had passed a lot of the time catching up with her letter writing. She had written to her mother shortly after taking up residence at Winslade Hall, informing her of her changed circumstances, and had received a brief note in reply, filled with bitter complaints about the cold, damp climate in Manchester and various other items of contention, William Thorpe being the chief protagonist. Sarah wrote to her again now, feeling obliged by some filial duty rather than by any real sense of interest or concern, keeping the content brief and general. She also replied to Anna Cunningham's last letter, informing her quite truthfully that she was still enjoying life in Surrey, but avoiding replying once again to the many queries from the older woman as to the state of her relationship with the earl. She was unwilling to examine it too closely herself, and was certainly unable to describe it at all to someone else.

She and Luke had exchanged letters since his departure for school. In his first two weeks of school life he had sent four lengthy missives, and on reading them Sarah's heart had sunk. They had been full of his misery, barely concealed beneath a veneer of forced gaiety. But as the weeks passed, the tone of his writing had changed slightly. There was a boy in his dormitory with whom he was becoming particularly friendly, and also an older boy in the school who had apparently taken him under his wing and prevented his being subjected to the worst of the usual humiliating bullying meted out to those just embarking on new school life. He had mentioned once briefly that the prefect was, in fact, the son of one of his uncle's close friends, and Sarah realized, slightly shamefacedly, that Luke was being protected from the cruel initiation into boarding school life not so by any true camaraderie, but probably at Mark Tarrington's instigation. His newfound friendship had now blossomed to the extent that he informed her he would be spending the Easter holidays with the other boy and his parents, as long as his mother and uncle had no objections to the plan. This last news finally convinced Sarah, much to her chagrin, that his arrogant uncle had, in fact, been correct in his estimation that he knew best as far as Luke's education and future were concerned. The knowledge that she had spoken out of turn should have made her feel irritable mortification, but she felt too much relief at Luke's newfound peace of mind to allow herself to dwell on it further.

Sarah found that when she was in the schoolroom with Joanna her eyes would turn incessantly to the large windows, watching for some sign of his return, unwilling to acknowledge that his could be for any reason other than her mounting apprehension regarding her future security and employment. The relief she had felt at first at his departure had slowly eroded, leaving her with an inexplicable sense of emptiness, as though part of her was absent also.

Sarah, Maggie, and Emma often visited the dowager in her rooms, and Sarah had been amazed at the treasure trove she had collected there. Furniture, jewelry, and ornaments of every description, from every conceivable corner of the world. Things she and her late husband had accumulated during their travels. They had never had any children of their own, and Sarah guessed that they traveled extensively to fill this void in their lives, although the dowager never made any remarks about her childless state. Her

144

husband, the late Lord Ralph Milbrook, had died of a consumptive illness some six years ago, leaving his wife without any close relatives, and her nephew had immediately asked if she would prefer to move to Winslade Hall than live alone. Sarah became aware, as the dowager spoke of him, of the close bond that existed between her and the earl. She guessed this to be a result in no small part of the fact that after Mark and Susan's mother's death, when Mark was very young, the dowager and old Mary had between them taken over the role of surrogate mother to the two small children.

Alice Milbrook had been sister to their mother, Elizabeth Tarrington. She had been frail for some years after the birth of her only son and had died when he was three, leaving her husband distraught. Sarah found herself wondering idly whether this lack of proper maternal influence was responsible for Mark's quite obvious cynicism where the majority of the female sex was concerned. His father had never remarried and had died fifteen years after his wife in a tragic hunting accident. Apparently a new and inexperienced horse he had bought only weeks before had shied at a jump, throwing him and breaking his neck instantly.

His father had been an astute business man, but several unlucky transactions just before his demise had depleted his finances quite considerably. Mark Tarrington, the dowager informed her, had then taken over the reins at Winslade Hall, becoming notorious not only for his hell-raising and devil-may-care attitude, but also for his financial genius. He had, since taking over his inheritance, increased his wealth beyond any conceivable expectation, and was now, Alice

145

Milbrook informed her with narrowed eyes, one of the wealthiest men in the country.

Sarah could tell from the expression on the old woman's face that she expected some comment from her on this information regarding her nephew's sizable fortune, and she, feeling unable to comment further as soon as the conversation returned to the earl, had merely risen at this point, saying that Emma really should be in bed quite soon and thanking the dowager for an interesting afternoon. She then left, unaware of the old woman's keen gaze as she did so.

The large library held a great fascination for Sarah, and whenever she had idle hours she would wander in there and scan the rows and rows of leather-bound books for something to read, curling up with her legs under her in the windowseat for hours, alternately engrossed in the book in her lap or the view of startling beauty through the window. She was doing this on the day of his return, her head leaning against the window post, staring sighlessly into the distance, her thoughts once again troubled by the uncertainty of her future.

By the time she had registered the static in the atmosphere, he was standing quite close, hands thrust deep into his pockets, watching her. She jumped up at once, knocking the book from her lap and onto the floor, noticing irrelevantly as she did so that his clothes looked dusty from riding, and a fine, greyish powder covered his hair.

"You frightened me, my lord," she exclaimed, trying to cover her discomposure at his unexpected appearance.

"Still?" He said it with gentle mockery, and she could feel the spontaneous rush of color to her cheeks.

He bent and picked up the book from the floor, studying it. "Jane Austen again. I had no idea you read this romantic drivel also."

"I do not, usually," she said quickly, unable to keep the defensive note from her voice. "Besides, I understand the prince regent also seems to like romantic drivel."

He looked at her and smiled inquiringly, as though indicating he knew more of the prince regent's ways than she did, and dropped the book onto the seat she had just vacated.

"Am I forgiven yet?" His voice was soft, yet she dared not meet his eyes or reply, merely tracing the lettering of the book with an unsteady finger, and he murmured, "No? Well, no matter."

She searched desperately in her mind for some reason to excuse herself, finally using the one she inevitably did. "Emma—I have to go. It is nearly her bedtime."

"Not yet. I have to talk to you."

She tried to voice some further excuse, moving away as she did, but he caught her arm, pulling her around slowly to face him. "Are you not interested in the plans I have made for your future?"

She did stop then, the sapphire eyes staring at him with uncommon directness. "Have you found someone else to employ me?"

He laughed, releasing her arm. "No." He paused for a while and then said, watching her face closely, "I have a house in London. I only use it rarely, as I spend most of my time here now. However, I intend to move back to London quite soon, for a while at least. You will go also." It was a statement rather than a request, and she stared at him uncomprehending for a mo-

147

ment.

"I do not understand. What would I do? Do you mean as a housekeeper?"

"If you like." His voice was mildly taunting, and she could see a spark of humor darkening the gold of his eyes, and as a vague uneasiness stirred, she said coldly, "What does that mean?"

"It means that I am not sure Mrs. Brookes would be too pleased by the arrangement—she is the house-keeper there." He was keeping his tone mock solemn and his face impassive, and as she felt her anger stirring and her suspicions increasing, she said coolly, "I cannot see what possible use I could be there, then, and can only repeat my request for a reference before I leave here." She made as though to go, but he moved also, slowly backward, so that he stood between her and the door. She stopped abruptly, not wanting any physical contact with him. She forced her eyes up to meet his and noticed that all traces of mockery were gone now.

"You will have the house to yourself. I shall not stay there; I have other residences in London. You will be mistress of the household; the servants will answer to you and all the financial arrangements will be taken care of. You can buy whatever you want, change the furniture if you like or redecorate as you wish. It is up to you."

She stared at him, unable to keep the bitterness from her eyes or voice. "Just mistress of the house-hold?"

"No." His answer was brief, and his eyes held hers for a moment before she looked away, fury knotting her stomach.

"I am, of course, deeply sensible of the great honor

148

you do me, my lord but I am afraid I have to decline your kind offer." Her tone was sweetly sarcastic and he laughed saying, "I was not actually asking you to marry me, Sarah." He spoke lightly and yet his eyes were intent, watchful for any reaction.

But she simply returned, with honeyed disdain, "A fact of which I am sure we are both extremely grateful. No, I merely thought that a man of your arrogance would no doubt deem the honor the same." She moved forward again, making a detour to the door, but he moved also, blocking her way. "I think you misunderstand, Sarah." His tone was hardening. "I was not, in fact, giving you a choice in the matter. I have no intention of supplying you with a reference, and I am quite sure you realize that without one you will not work." He added with an ironic smile, "Even if you did manage to find someone willing to take the risk, I am quite sure that I could make them change their mind."

Sarah stared at him in horrified disbelief and then abhorrence as she realized what he was implying, her wrath white-hot. But she managed quitely, "I had no idea, my lord, you found it necessary to go to such devious lengths to acquire your mistresses. In any case I would have thought, from common gossip, that you had more than enough already."

He said nothing, merely watching her with a kind of patronizing humor, as though her virulence amused him.

She clenched her hands in an effort to calm the violent rage that was threatening her self-control and continued steadily, "Besides, I am quite sure you would not find me at all satisfactory in my duties . . . you see, I have no experience as a whore."

149

"If I wanted a whore I would go to Haymarket." The irritation was apparent, and she knew that his patience was at an end, yet could not prevent herself from adding impetuously, with feigned sweetness, "Surely not, my lord, I had heard there was somewhere much closer."

She met his eyes, the accusation bitter and uncontrollable, and he laughed, his hand moving slowly to his forehead in an almost embarrassed gesture, but he said with mock gravity, "No, it would have to be Haymarket . . . I gamble in town, nothing more." And then repeated, with almost coaxing softness, "Nothing more."

She was not appeased, merely tossing her head slightly as she turned away in disdainful disbelief, and she said in the same sweet tone, "Well, in that case I really think you should go there then, my lord. I am quite sure you would get much better value for your money."

She saw his eyes raise slowly heavenward in utter exasperation, but he said with soothing tolerance, "This is getting you nowhere, Sarah. This wrangling of whether or not you will become my mistress is nonsensical. If I remember correctly, you have already done so. The best thing you can do is to accept the inevitable gracefully, while you are still in a position to dictate terms."

"I would rather starve than go anywhere with you, my lord," she spat viciously.

"Perhaps, my dear, but I think your daughter will probably make you more prudent in the event."

She glared at him, biting her lip. She had, of course, forgotten about Emma. She was the burden that would determine both their futures. She looked at him with a mixture of hopeless pleading and venom and whispered quietly, "I hate you," her eyes bright with unshed tears.

He smiled sardonically at this impassioned declaration, knowing too well that the violent emotion he had managed to incite in her was the wrong one and not what he wanted at all, but he merely said remorselessly, "I shall give you a week or two to get used to the idea. And, in the circumstances, I think you could drop the formality now—my name is Mark." And without a backward glance he walked from the room.

Sarah sank back down into the windowseat, her head falling slowly into her hands. She sat numb, oblivious of the abrupt hefty crash resounding from the region of the study door, although the rest of the household were startled into apprehensive awareness of it, several pairs of eyes meeting in anxious question before lengthy and imaginative discussion commenced as to the cause of this latest tantrum.

Sarah rose slowly some time later, unsure how long she had been sitting thus, and made her way to her room.

Sarah was washing a playful and squealing Emma with much noise and splashing of water. She halted as Sarah entered, allowing the wet child to sink onto the floor amid a pile of towels, which she proceeded to roll in. "He is back, then." It was a statement, and Sarah simply nodded, sinking onto the edge of the bed.

Maggie said nothing, although Sarah knew the girl was anxious for some explanation as to the reason for her misery, and she murmured tonelessly, "He wants me to go to London with him as his mistress."

The other woman was silent, and Sarah looked up at her slowly. "You do not seem surprised."

151

Maggie smiled ruefully. "I am not. I am only surprised that it has taken this long." She sat down on the bed next to Sarah's trembling form and her arms went about her gently. "Don't worry. I shall come with you."

Sarah pushed her away angrily and stood up, rounding on her accusingly. "You are convinced I shall go, then."

"What choice have you?" Maggie's tone was soothing. "You stand no chance on your own with the child. You have been more than fortunate thus far. If it was not him it would be someone else; less wealthy, less attractive, certainly not as generous."

Sarah stared at her wide-eyed, her voice astonished as she said, "You sound as though you like him."

Maggie looked away, ill at ease. "Well, I do. He has been very kind to me. Sometimes he allows Stewart time off when I am free so we can be together." She halted, aware that mentioning her own happiness at such a time was not very diplomatic, and changed the subject hastily. "Look, Sarah, if you do not go, what *do* you intend? You will be alone, penniless, and will probably be hounded by various unsavory characters wanting to set you up in some poky establishment, turning you onto the street again when they tire of you."

"He intends just the same thing, Maggie. Does it make a difference that I shall be an expensive whore, then?"

Maggie looked at her with an odd expression and then said falteringly, "Stewart told me not to say anything, but . . ." She hesitated, "but . . . he thinks the earl is in love with you," she finished in a rush.

Sarah stared at her for a moment and then laughed

with shrill incredulity, almost hysteria, and said despairingly, "Forcing me to sleep with him hardly seems like affection to me. I am quite sure he does not even like me very much." She turned away and added on a defeated sigh, "He is certainly avenging himself well. . . ."

Maggie watched her, noting the wretchedness, and wondered how the girl could have been married to a lecherous whoremonger for over a year and still seem so naive. She said placatingly, "But it does not mean that he does not care. . . ." and added coaxingly, "He has been patient. . . ." But she could tell her words were not easing Sarah's grief in the slightest, and she hesitated and was silent.

Sarah studied her hands, twisting the ring slowly in rhythmic rotation, and said in a low tone, with almost a return to self-composure, "In any case, I doubt he is capable of any such emotion. As soon as my usefulness is finished, I will be dispensed with as the rest have been."

Maggie brightened perceptibly. "But I heard Lady Susan say once that his mistresses were all pensioned off extremely generously."

Sarah could not prevent a shaky, hysterical laugh at the girl's practical attitude. "Oh, Maggie." The exasperation was apparent, and Maggie laughed too, repeating, "I shall come with you."

Sarah shook her head. "No. Stewart would prefer you to stay here, wouldn't he?"

Maggie nodded slowly, saying, "Yes, I think so."

"Well, you must stay, then."

"No." Maggie's tone was adamant. "There is plenty of time. Besides, perhaps I am fooling myself as to his intentions, and I do not want him to think that he can take me for granted . . . just yet," she added with a wry smile.

Sarah smiled also, shaking her head at the other woman, and then, taking a towel each, they attempted to dry the still wriggling Emma.

Chapter Eleven

Now that spring had arrived, the weather was illogically displaying wintery tendencies. Late frost rimed the solid earth and intermittent snow flurries littered the atmosphere and shortened the days once more. The chilled-wine air was throat-achingly refreshing, and Sarah, riding slowly away from the stables, inhaled the razor cold with self-punishing thoroughness and then blew a large, steaming breath in front of her.

Sarah was riding alone today, because Joanna was packing for a trip to stay with a friend of her mother's for a couple of weeks. Sarah enjoyed her rides. They took her away from the house, where she was beginning to bow beneath the oppressive weight of her uncertain future. She rode slowly, unable to do anything else. Her ability was just about adequate to keep her seated at a steady pace, and luckily the docile grey mare she rode seemed unanxious to increase speed.

She had been riding for about fifteen minutes in a different direction from the one she and Joanna usually chose when the mare stopped suddenly, veering slightly to the right, and Sarah, clutching the reins overtightly in her fright, nearly made the nervous horse unseat her.

She scanned the wooded copse to her right where she thought she had seen a vague movement and spied a small boy of perhaps six, attempting to hide himself amongst the scrubby undergrowth.

"What are you doing there?" She spoke softly, not wanting to alarm him, and the boy, emboldened by the quiet friendliness in her voice, came out and stood staring at her.

He was so thin that he looked almost skeletal. His trousers were patched and repatched, tattered beyond belief, and his jacket looked almost threadbare. She noticed he was without shoes or socks, and she said, in stunned disbelief at the sight of him, "You must be frozen."

He did not answer, merely staring at her with wide-eyed alarm.

Sarah turned suddenly at a noise from behind, and a woman displaying the same ragged bearing and carrying a basket, pushed through a screen of bushes and into view.

She stopped at the sight of Sarah, her expression showing petrified fear. "He didn't mean no harm, my lady, really," she began. "He were just looking for a bit of wood for a fire." She beckoned frantically to the boy to join her and he did so, wiping the back of one filthy hand across his streaming nose.

"Wait. Don't go," Sarah called quickly as they showed signs of disappearing into the bushes. "Is that your son?"

The woman nodded, looking at Sarah warily, repeating, "He didn't mean no harm, honest."

Sarah smiled reassuringly at the woman, noting that, despite her bedraggled appearance, she was probably not a lot older than herself.

"He must be frozen. Has he no shoes?"

The other woman laughed bitterly. "It is not the cold, my lady, but his empty belly that worries him most."

"Where do you live?" She asked it quietly, but the woman started to back away, the fright apparent in her eyes again. "Do you live on Winslade land?" Sarah could not believe her eyes. She had been told by various people that all the tenants on the Winslade estates were well cared for, their cottages in good repair and their lives, by all accounts, pleasant. She felt an uneasiness stir in her at the sight of this all too obvious poverty, her own misery palling into insignificance in comparison.

The woman darted a furtive glance around her, as though expecting to see someone else, and looking back at Sarah, said, "Are you mistress at the big house?" She inclined her head toward Winslade Hall as she did so, and Sarah almost laughed with bitter irony that the woman had very nearly proved right in her guess.

She merely said, "No. I work there as governess, that is all." She noticed a slight flicker of relief cross the woman's face and said again, "Do you live near here?"

The woman nodded slowly. "In a cottage on the estate. We should not be here, really," she continued, looking at her rough hands as she spoke, "but we had to have some shelter; my young 'uns are sick and we had to stop somewhere."

She ended on an imploring note, and Sarah said, "Have you other children, then?"

The woman nodded vigorously. "My name is Sally Turner, and this is William. He is six, and then there's Jenny, she's four, and the baby, Adam. He's only six months and he's terrible sick."

Sarah saw the start of tears to the woman's eyes. Dismounting slowly, she went over to her, not knowing how to comfort her, and said, "Show me. Perhaps I can help."

The woman shook her head hopelessly. "My husband will kill me. He told us to keep out of sight. If we are seen we'll be moved on again. You won't tell, will you?" Her eyes were round with pleading, and Sarah shook her head, swallowing hard. "Show me where you live. I shall explain to your husband."

The woman said nothing, simply turned with the boy trotting at her heels, and made her way back into the copse.

The cottage came into view after a few minutes. It was not even that, thought Sarah, aghast. More like a ramshackle hut. The door was half off its hinges and the windows were partially covered with bits of filthy cloth.

As they approached Sarah heard strident coughing, and the woman paled, murmuring hoarsely, "That is the baby."

The door opened as she was speaking and a man appeared. He was dark-haired, swarthy, and heavily set, and as he turned toward them as they neared, Sarah noticed that one of his arms was a stump of no more than six inches.

The woman, seeing the direction of Sarah's gaze, said bitterly, "He lost that arm fighting the Frenchies." She laughed bitterly. "He served king and country, and when he returned he was no use to anyone."

The man's face had hardened visibly at her words, but she continued, "He can't work, and now we're on the run, moving from place to place like rats because he stole a chicken to feed us when we were starving. The farmer caught him, but he managed to get away. If they catch him he'll probably be deported." She laughed again hysterically. "What will I do then? I can't manage with three children and a man. What will I do without him?" She was close to tears again, and Sarah said quickly, "But this is ridiculous. Surely if you were starving, something could be done." Her voice trailed off as she saw the hopeless misery etched in lines of grief on the woman's face.

She turned to the man, but he merely returned her stare with distrustful resentment. "I work at Winslade Hall," she explained. "My name is Sarah Thornton." She stopped, the child's abrasive coughing breaking into her words. "Can I see the child?" He did not answer, simply opening the door wider on its broken hinge so that she could enter.

The cottage was filthy. There was a small fire burning, but the warmth it gave out was negligible. A pot of some indistinguishable-looking food stewed slowly, its smell turning Sarah's stomach. She noticed a small girl staring at her from beneath a mass of matted dark hair, her eyes wide with terror. She smiled at her in what she hoped was an encouraging fashion, but the child backed away, clutching at her mother's tattered skirts. Her feet were also bare and her clothes looked in a worse condition than those of her brother.

The barking cough erupted again, and Sarah turned to a small basket near the fire. She gazed down into the tiny, chalk-white face, and she noticed that the small nose and fever-bright eyes were encrusted

159

with some yellow matter, one eye practically closed with mucous. She felt unable to breathe suddenly as the small face swam beneath her vision, interchanging slowly with the face of her daughter. She watched horrified as the tiny body bounced frenziedly amid the ragged coverings with the violence of the racking cough. Turning abruptly, she said, "I shall bring you some food. I shall speak to the earl. I am sure he will have you housed somewhere else and have a doctor sent to the baby."

The man and woman stared at her as though she had taken leave of her senses, and then the man laughed with bitter humor. "I think if you want to help at all, you should say nothing. Give me a chance to move us out of here."

The woman shook her head slowly. "Jed, I can't go anywhere else." Her voice was hopeless with defeat, and Sarah merely said, with a ferocity that surprised even herself, "I shall bring you some food, at least, later," and mounting the grey mare, she turned its head back in the direction of Winslade Hall, the pathetic family watching her dull-eyed.

She changed quickly, steadying her nerves with difficulty as she dragged the brush through her hair. Her cheeks were pink from the ride and her breathless determination.

She had to speak to him about it. It was inhuman to allow any such suffering, and they were, after all, at present resident on his estate. The child's face, in all its horror, moved slowly before her sight, and she made quickly for the door before her resolve failed her.

She realized suddenly, with dawning self-hatred, that three years ago such a thing would not have moved her to such stricken horror. It was only the fact

160

The Publishers of Zebra Books Make This Special Offer to Zebra Romance Readers...

AFTER YOU HAVE READ THIS BOOK WE'D LIKE TO SEND YOU
4 MORE FOR *FREE*
AN $18.00 VALUE

NO OBLIGATION!

MORE PASSION AND ADVENTURE AWAIT... YOUR TRIP TO A BIG ADVENTUROUS WORLD BEGINS WHEN YOU ACCEPT YOUR FIRST 4 NOVELS ABSOLUTELY *FREE*
(AN $18.00 VALUE)

Accept your Free gift and start to experience more of the passion and adventure you like in a historical romance novel. Each Zebra novel is filled with proud men, spirited women and tempestuous love that you'll remember long after you turn the last page.

Zebra Historical Romances are the finest novels of their kind. They are written by authors who really know how to weave tales of romance and adventure in the historical settings you love. You'll feel like you've actually gone back in time with the thrilling stories that each Zebra novel offers.

GET YOUR FREE GIFT WITH THE START OF YOUR HOME SUBSCRIPTION

Our readers tell us that these books sell out very fast in book stores and often they miss the newest titles. So Zebra has made arrangements for you to receive the four newest novels published each month.

You'll be guaranteed that you'll never miss a title, and home delivery is so convenient. And to show you just how easy it is to get Zebra Historical Romances, we'll send you your first 4 books absolutely FREE! Our gift to you just for trying our home subscription service.

BIG SAVINGS AND FREE HOME DELIVERY

Each month, you'll receive the four newest titles as soon as they are published. You'll probably receive them even before the bookstores do. What's more, you may preview these exciting novels free for 10 days. If you like them as much as we think you will, just pay the low preferred subscriber's price of just $3.75 each. *You'll save $3.00 each month off the publisher's price.* AND, your savings are even greater because there are never any shipping, handling or other hidden charges—FREE Home Delivery. Of course you can return any shipment within 10 days for full credit, no questions asked. There is no minimum number of books you must buy.

that her own uncertain future made it possible for any such nightmare to become her own reality that made it of such immense importance to her.

She descended the stairs slowly, wondering if Mark would think to make any aid to the Turners' dependent on her acceptance of his offer. She doubted it, somehow. His conceit would not allow him to bargain with her, she thought acidly. Besides, he had no need to do so. He still held the outcome of her future well within his grasp.

She knocked at the door, realizing as she did so that it was the first time she had ever stood there and hoped he would be within.

She breathed deeply as she heard the command to enter.

He and Stewart Palmer were poring over an open ledger on the desk and it was Stewart who looked up first. His glance was keen, and she knew instinctively that he was aware of the new situation between herself and the earl.

He looked up frowning at Stewart's silence, the golden eyes darkening as he saw her. He straightened, and without needing to be told Stewart made for the door, smiling at Sarah easily as he left.

She could tell from the expression on his face that he thought she had come submissively to inform him she was prepared to do his bidding, and the knowledge that she was about to frustrate his expectations gave her a comforting sense of malicious satisfaction.

He indicated that she should sit down, and he sat also, his hand going to the small ornate dagger on the desk that he obviously used as a pocket knife and she stared mesmerized for a moment as his fingers ran smoothly along the gleaming length of it. His skin looked unnaturally dark against the whitish metal, and she glanced away quickly, not wanting to acknowledge what memories his slowly moving hand evoked.

He had not spoken and sat watching her closely until Sarah, sensing her resolve eroding already, said quickly, "I wanted to speak with you about some people I saw when I was out riding this morning." She saw the shuttered look appear on his face, the slightly mocking inquiry in his eyes that appeared when he thought she was concerning herself unduly with unacceptable matters.

She continued quickly before her determination failed completely. "They are starving and are living in some sort of derelict cottage that looks as though it is ready to fall down. One of the children is dying, I think." She could not keep the tremor from her voice as she said it. "He is only six months old, and I should think the other children will die also. They had no proper clothes and are so thin that they look like skeletons. The man cannot work; he was crippled in the war, and his wife . . ." Her voice trailed away at the memory of Sally Turner's prematurely aged and grief-lined face. "You must help them." She said it with quiet pleading, but there was no compassion in his face and he repeated with soft menace, "Must?"

"The children will die; they have no proper shelter or food. It is inhuman, monstrous that people should be allowed to live that way."

"The man is a thief, I believe. No doubt if he had served his own landlord fairly, he would still be resident there."

"But he only stole because they were starving." As she said it, the realization dawned that he already knew of their existence, and she said in a horrified whisper, "You already knew they were there and have

162

let them stay in that hovel."

He cut in sharply. "I will deal with the matter in my own way. It is none of your concern. They are fortunate that I have not thus far had them forcibly evicted." Seeing her stricken face, he continued soothingly, "You know nothing of these matters, Sarah. If I allow this family to stay, before I know it, every wandering vagrant for miles will be settling on Winslade land."

She stared at him, stunned, and then said with violent contempt, "You are despicable. The food that is thrown from your table after one meal could probably keep them fed for a week."

He had moved round the desk and now stood behind her chair, bending forward so their heads were close. "This admirable sympathy you seem to display in such abundance—I think it might benefit you more if you directed a little of it my way."

She started to rise, wanting to avoid his proximity, but his hands on her shoulders pushed her back down before he moved away slightly, and she said scornfully, "I had no intention of benefiting myself, my lord, something I am quite sure you would be incapable of comprehending."

She rose then as if to go, but he caught her face in his hand, turning it so she could not avoid his eyes. "Mark." He said it softly, but she remained silent, and he added with treacherous gentleness, "Do not be foolish enough to try to cross me in this, Sarah." He was watching her intently, the golden eyes narrowed, and she let her lids drop, shielding the fiery defiance from his astute gaze, and jerked her head angrily away from his touch.

"Have you nothing more to say to me, Sarah?"

"I am afraid not, my lord." She used his title with

163

insolent politeness, well aware of the annoyance it provoked.

"I shall be leaving for town at the end of the week." His implication was explicit, but she merely turned to him with affected innocence and said, "Then it can only remain for me to wish you a pleasant visit, my lord," and with that she closed the door, her small victory tasting sour in her mouth.

It was nine o'clcok. Sarah sat on the bed, clenching and unclenching her hands in an agony of indecision. She had been determined that she would go to the Turners with food that night, but her courage had slowly diminished. She was fearful of his revenge should he find out, and the knowledge of her cravenness filled her with disgust. Yet still she sat there. She had even gone to the lengths of having a cold evening meal in her room and had wrapped all the untouched food in a cloth ready to take to them.

She stood up abruptly, moving to the window and gazing out into the frost-bright sky. The moon was rising and the stars shone with the brilliance that heralded a freezing night. She turned back into the room, sighing hopelessly, and started to undress. The sheets felt silkily cold, and she snuggled quickly into the covers, not wanting to think of those with no proper shelter, let alone a soft bed to sleep on. She closed her eyes, trying to erase the disquieting vision of the small, thin faces that haunted her, and tried to sleep.

She was unaware how long she lay unmoving, but her quiet was broken suddenly by a hacking bark. She shot up in bed, reliving the nightmare she had witnessed that morning. It was probably one of the servants coughing, and yet the sound had eliminated her drowsiness completely and rekindled the horror she had felt. She hugged her knees up under her chin for a moment, trying to invoke some courage, and then got up and dressed quickly in the warmest clothes she possessed.

She looked down at Emma, noting the pink chubbiness of her face and the rounded plumpness of her arms, and turned abruptly away, moving to the door, picking up the bundle of food as she went.

She made her way silently toward the servants quarters, aware that there was a small side door leading toward the stable area that was left almost unfailingly with the key in the lock. She had often wondered why this was so, and it had finally dawned on her that some of the servants were obviously indulging in a little idle dalliance. She wondered now whether Matilda Davis was unaware of it or was too softhearted to bring an end to these romantic episodes by locking the door and removing the key.

She swung the door outward silently, and as she closed it soundlessly behind her she prayed fervently that tonight of all nights she would not be locked out by a vigilant Mrs. Davis. The icy air made her breath catch sharply in her throat. Not daring to wake anyone in the stables, she started to walk quickly, hoping desperately that she would remember the way. The night was bright and clear, with barely a cloud to mar the luminescence of the heavy full moon. The ground beneath her feet was frozen solid, and she stamped her feet into the unyielding hardness, trying to warm some life into her already numb legs.

The unfamiliar muted sounds of the night made her start incessantly, and her pace quickened almost to a run until the only sound available to her was the blood drumming rhythmically in her ears. Her eyes scanned

165

the inky shadows feverishly and she drew her cloak about her tightly as she moved further away from the warm security of the house and into the unknown night.

Mark Tarrington stared at the figures in front of him, wondering how many more times he would need to read the page before some of the information penetrated. His eyes moved to the empty glass and his hand reached automatically for the decanter, and then he hesitated, his fingers drumming irritated denial against the desk for a few moments. He was drinking too much and even beginning grudgingly to acknowledge the fact. His hand moved to the small tray, picking up a chicken drumstick, and he studied it for a moment wondering if he wanted it.

He looked up casually as Stewart Palmer entered and then looked back at the ledger for a moment before the other man's agitation registered and his eyes raised again.

Stewart blew into his numb hands, saying quickly, "I have just seen Philip Locke . . . the groom," he explained unnecessarily, and then, conscious that this information had suddenly afforded him his employer's undivided attention, he continued hastily, "You wanted to know if anyone left the house tonight."

The chicken drumstick remained in midair and Mark half-smiled, turning the meat slowly in careful examination as he asked, "Has she taken the grey mare?"

"No . . ." The reply was uneasy, Stewart too conscious of the other man's mood, and Mark Tarrington looked toward him sharply, repeating questioningly, "No? Which then?"

"None . . . she did not go to the stables. She is

walking.

Mark Tarrington turned toward the window and scanned the dark night, then back to Stewart, grating out, "Christ, it's freezing out there tonight." He threw the untasted meat back toward the tray, standing up as he did so, and Stewart said speedily, "There's something else . . . Locke thinks this might have been about half an hour ago, perhaps longer." He hesitated as his employer stopped abruptly by the door and half-turned toward him, asking with dangerous quiet, "What?"

Stewart laughed nervously, trying to ease the tension a little, and explained with forced lightness, "I think the poor lad got a little sidetracked; when last I saw him he was wearing one of the kitchen girls around his neck. . . ."

The bantering died as he saw Mark Tarrington smile unpleasantly and then make some foul observation regarding his groom's sexual habits. He flung the door open, and Stewart, wincing at the crudity of the language, followed his master uneasily in the direction of the stables.

The young man scrambled untidily from the hay as he heard his name and stood staring uncertainly at the two men, oblivious of the comic disarray of his remaining few clothes.

Mark Tarrington beckoned brusquely and he moved forward, still wary.

"You saw someone leave tonight?" The question was even and the youth relaxed a little.

"Yes, your lordship. A woman, some while ago now; walking that way." He pointed vaguely through the stable door.

Mark Tarrington nodded thoughtfully, adding almost reasonably, "I thought I made it clear I wanted

167

to know of this at once."

Philip Locke shuffled nervously, saying "I am sorry . . . I forgot, my lord." He glanced toward the hay in unconscious explanation, aware of the girl still huddled there.

Mark Tarrington turned slightly, as though dismissing the incident, and the young man's breath escaped audibly in a relieved sigh before the blow knocked him backward into the hay he had so recently vacated. His hand went almost absently to his bleeding mouth, the astonishment on his face more pronounced than the pain.

The girl behind him whimpered, trying to back further into the shadows, and Mark Tarrington yanked the boy up, shifting his weight slightly as though to hit him again. He heard the sharp intake of breath as Stewart realized his intention and he inhaled heavily, calming himself before pushing the boy back against the wall, biting out deceptively quietly, "When was it . . . exactly?"

Philip Locke opened his mouth several times as though to speak, but appeared unable to do so. Then he stammered quickly, "Not . . . not more than twenty minutes ago." He turned toward the girl, desperate for support, saying, "That's right, isn't it?"

The girl glowered at him as though accusing him of making known her presence, then nodded several times in agreement, saying nothing.

The earl's eyes slid to her and she pushed herself up in undignified haste, smiling at him falteringly and overeagerly, unsure whether to use feminine charm or humility to best advantage.

He jerked his head, saying curtly, "Get in the house," and she sidled past him carefully, as though uncertain whether he might strike her also, and then stumbled sobbing toward the servants' quarters.

Mark Tarrington stared after her for a few moments and then looked at the night sky. He hunched his shoulders slightly against the bitter cold, muttering in a voice as raw as the night, "She could be anywhere by now . . . if she loses her way she could wander all night." He swore again, kicking viciously at loose shingle underfoot before starting toward the house, snapping over his shoulder to the still stupefied groom, "Saddle the horses."

He turned the door handle slowly and it yielded immediately to the slight pressure. He smiled tightly, knowing there was no need to investigate further. He was well aware that the door was kept unfailingly locked when she was within.

He walked into the room, instinctively toward the bed, and looked down at the disarranged covers. He stared at it, sensing his jaw grit as too often suppressed memories surfaced, and he turned abruptly, moving back toward the door. He passed the crib, glancing down casually, and then back-stepped slightly, watching the child's face, pearlescent in the soft moonlight gaining access through the small window above the cot. The likeness was uncanny, and his hand moved toward a lightly clenched fist lying on the coverlet, one finger sliding into the curled palm. His thumb brushed the silken skin lightly and he felt the spontaneous grip, and then, as she relaxed again, he withdrew his hand carefully and continued to the door.

Sarah walked for what seemed like an age, her feet frozen to numb heaviness, but the certain knowledge that the Turners would probably be no less cold and

169

frightened than she herself kept her moving steadily forward. The cottage came into view at last, and she noticed a tiny glimmer of light showing from beneath one of the limp rags at the window.

They greeted her with unconcealed incredulous astonishment, and Sarah realized that they had certainly never expected her to keep her promise to come back that evening. She handed the package of food to Sally, who stared at it unmoving for a few moments before taking it quickly and turning away mumbling her incoherent gratitude.

Sarah went slowly toward the small basket and peered into the baby's face. He was not coughing now, but his breath rasped and rattled in his small throat, filling the room with its raucousness.

Sally had opened the parcel of food tentatively, and Sarah noticed young William and Jenny unmoving, staring at the food as though entranced. Their mother cut some of the bread and ham carefully and then gave them each some, but they still looked at it bewildered, as if they had forgotten what they should do with it, and Sarah could feel the prickling behind her eyes as she stared at the two pathetic faces, hating Mark Tarrington fervently and wondering despairingly which, if any, of these children would survive to enjoy the warmer weather.

She looked back to Sally Turner and said softly, "There is some milk for the baby." Sally merely nodded, keeping her tear-wet face averted from Sarah as she rummaged further into the parcel.

Sarah picked the cold, listless baby out of the basket and sat down in a corner, holding him close, trying to warm him with her own body heat, watching as Sally warmed the milk near the fire.

Jed Turner had been watching the proceedings with

170

a kind of stupefaction, but as Sarah turned to look at him now she saw his expression change slowly to one of hunted terror.

She turned hastily in the same direction and saw that Stewart Palmer stood in the half-open doorway. Sarah started to rise, sure he must have come to turn them out, and then sank back as she saw who stood immediately behind him, the cold she had felt before nothing to the drenching chill now saturating every part of her. She clutched the baby tightly to her and she heard the small whimper as the baby acknowledged this overzealous embrace. She sat rigid, aware of the blood echoing painfully in her ears again and the nauseous tightening of her stomach, and as she looked towards the Turners she saw that both Jed and Sally were staring in the same direction now, terror and panic showing in their overwide eyes.

Jed stood up suddenly and moved jerkily forward, placing himself between the two men and his family, but Stewart, seemingly oblivious of any aggressive mood in the man, simply walked past him. Sarah noticed he was carrying a bundle of wood. He bent, kindling the small fire to a brightness and placed more wood on the heartening glow. Sally watched him for a moment, and then her eyes, like those of her husband, returned as though magnetized to the arrogant dark figure standing silently in the doorway still.

Sarah was sure he had not seen her. He had given no indication of noticing her presence, and she shrank back into the shadowy corner, still rocking the baby to and fro with automatic skill. She noticed at that moment that another, older man had entered behind him. She had never seen him before, and he walked slowly into the dimness and toward her. He took the baby from her unresisting clasp, saying, "I am Dr.

171

Sheldon. Let me see the child."

He placed the baby back in the blanket and started to examine him slowly. Sarah looked feverishly back to where the earl stood, sure he must have noticed her now, but he gave no sign of having done so. He was watching Stewart as he dropped some bundles of blankets onto the floor.

Jed and Sally still stood in petrified silence, and Mark Tarrington turned toward the man slowly and their eyes held, clashing in silent combat for a few moments before Jed Turner looked away, his expression subdued and stark defeat showing in the drooping of his shoulders.

The earl spoke then and his voice was silken peril. "One chance only." The man nodded once, not meeting his eyes, and then said harshly, "Thank you, my lord."

He did not answer, but turned her way now, and as their eyes met across the flickering patches of light and dark she realized that he had been aware of her presence all the time.

His hand raised slightly and his fingers moved once, and she went forward instinctively at the command. She kept her eyes lowered, acutely conscious of the intensity of his scrutiny compelling her to meet his gaze. She fought his control desperately, but as she neared him she looked up involuntarily and noticed that behind the slightly smiling mask of cold fury there was another barely concealed emotion, which she could not at first identify. She walked past him and out of the door, feeling the freezing air stinging her face, and then sudden knowledge touched her with equal chill. It had been triumph. He had warned her not to challenge him on this, but she had defied him, and by doing so she had enabled him to force another certain confrontation.

She walked quickly away from the cottage, pulling her hooded cloak tight about her head and body, feeling the frost weight her feet heavily.

"Sarah." His voice was quiet and yet it carried easily on the silent, frosty air.

She hesitated, wanting to run and yet knowing the futility of such an act. He walked toward her, leading the black stallion he always rode, and as he neared her he mounted it slowly.

She turned away and started to walk again, but he cut across her path, saying, "What are you doing, walking back?" His tone was indolent mockery, as though they were merely exchanging insults in the drawing room of Winslade Hall.

She said nothing, trying to pass him, but he moved the horse slightly so that it blocked her way again.

She looked up at him then and said in a trembling voice, "I walked here; I think I can manage to return the same way." She attempted to push past him suddenly, as if making to run, but he stooped, lifting her easily in front of him. She struggled instinctively and then stopped, simply remaining rigid in his arms, unwilling to participate in any further undignified tussles with him.

He made no attempt to pull her back against him, merely saying derisively, "You shall fall off like that," and she averted her face disdainfully. She felt him shrug as though unconcerned, turning the stallion's head in the direction of Winslade Hall, and then he had kicked the horse, without warning, into action so abruptly that the startled animal leaped forward and the sudden motion threw her back against him heavily. She felt his arm tighten around her, but she remained passive and turned her face into the warmth

173

of his coat to protect it from the chafing cold.

The ride was no more than a few minutes. He dismounted, lifting her down, and she made to turn at once, but he swung her back roughly, saying menacingly "Wait there. I have not finished with you yet," and lead the horse away toward the stables, calling harshly for the groom.

She stood petrified for no more than a moment, and then without thought ran in through the thankfully unlocked door and up the stairs as fast as her frozen limbs would allow. She was gasping breathlessly by the time she reached her room, and, not daring to look behind, she slammed the door, groping frantically for the key. She felt the shape of it beneath her numb fingers and started to turn it. But suddenly he kicked the door open, with such force that she was knocked, staggering, back into the room, her hands going out for support.

She watched mesmerized as he walked slowly toward her, and she felt her own feet moving backward in time with his advance, her hands searching frantically behind her for direction. She felt the edge of the bed suddenly and changed direction hastily so that she was retreating toward the wall, feeling the cold harshness of it against her back and the palms of her hands. He was no more than a few paces away now, and she made to dart suddenly to one side, but his hands came up, one on either side of her head, blocking her escape.

A slight noise from the cot at her side made her start, and she looked down at Emma with almost hysterical relief. Keeping her face turned away, she whispered, "You have woken the baby." She stared hard at Emma, willing her to wake, scream, create as much noise as possible, but the child turned restlessly for a few moments and then seemed to resettle, one tiny thumb caught between her teeth.

He was also watching the child, cursing silently that he had forgotten she was in the room. "You had better come downstairs, then, if you want her to sleep."

His voice sounded thick, and she swallowed hard, saying desperately, "I will settle her first and come down in a few minutes."

His head fell forward slightly, and she knew he was laughing silently. Then he looked back at her and murmured with wry humor, "You really never give up, do you."

She knew then that any such plan along these lines was doomed, and she preceded him slowly to the door and down the stairs, wondering forlornly how the noise he had made had not roused the whole household. He opened the study door and she entered, not looking at him, standing just inside the door with the wall at her back.

He walked to the desk and poured a drink from the decanter and walked back toward her with it, holding it out. She shook her head, looking at it with suspicion, and he smiled, acknowledging her fear, and said, "Drink it." It was a command, not a request, and she took the glass, holding it untasted. He watched her for a moment and then, taking the glass back, placed it to her mouth, tipping some of the fiery liquid between her lips. She spluttered and choked, the back of one hand pressed to her mouth, and he said drily, "It is easier if you do it yourself. Finish it. You look frozen, and I do not want you fainting on me."

She sipped the amber liquid, feeling the warmth of it starting to spread slowly through her chilled limbs.

He caught hold of her arm, pulling her away from

the wall and into the room and stood facing her in silence.

She looked away from him, her teeth clenched to stop their chattering, and she heard him say mildly, "Well?" As he was speaking he removed the glass from her hand and placed it on a small table, and for some inexplicable reason she now felt an illogical reluctance to let it go.

She studied her hands, her shaking fingers twisting the gold band around fast on her finger. "I apologize for my disobedience in ignoring your express wishes." She looked up, defiance making her sapphire eyes spark jewel-bright in the pale oval of her face. "Will that do, my lord?" Her tone was filled with unsteady insolence, and he smiled and said quietly, "I think there was another matter also."

"I have nothing more to say about it," she murmured coldly, and tried to retreat. But the hand abruptly on her arm stopped her.

"How do you intend to support yourself and the child then? Roll in the gutter for a pittance with anyone who has the price?"

"Even that might be preferable," she stormed, knowing as she said it that it sounded ridiculously childish. She saw his hand raise and turned her head sharply, sure he was about to slap her, but he released her with a slight push, asking harshly, "What do you want, Sarah?"

"I have already told you."

"A reference to teach someone else's brats. Do you really intend that shall be the entirety of your future?"

"It is what I know. I do not know how to be a whore." Her voice broke, and she quickly turned away, not wanting him to see her distress.

He pulled her back to face him, saying soothingly,

"We have been through this already, I think. You will be my mistress. There is a difference."

She jerked her arm away from his touch contemptuously. "Really? You will pay for my keep as long as I sleep with you. A mistress sounds remarkably much the same as a whore to me." Her tone was bitter, and he smiled suddenly at this outburst, saying, "I am sure Mrs. Fitzherbert would be most gratified to hear that."

She glared scornfully at him. "That is different. Why, it is even rumored that Mrs. Fitzherbert and the prince regent are married."

"A secret marriage that is invalid and unrecognized is surely no marriage."

"Besides she added heatedly, "It is quite obvious that the prince regent is in love with her."

He was watching her face closely now, and he murmured, "Why, does that make a difference?"

She stared at him for a moment, unsure whether she was saddened or scornful of his cynicism, but merely managed quietly, "Of course."

"Shall I tell you that I love you, Sarah?" His voice sounded strange, and she looked up, meeting the golden eyes, and was unable to look away again. She felt as though the breath was slowly being knocked from her, and she was aware that one of his hands was raising slowly as though to caress her face, but the gold ring glinting on his finger broke her trance and she turned away abruptly.

"Of course not. Such an obvious lie would serve no purpose." She swallowed hard waiting for him to reply, but he was silent, and she continued caustically, "And how long do you think my usefulness would last, my lord, a month or two? Six months, perhaps? I am quite sure you would then be more than willing to let me roll in the gutter with whomever I chose."

He smiled sardonically. "Well, perhaps I might then give you the reference you so earnestly desire."

"Indeed? In which capacity, my lord, my role as governess or whore?" She spoke with affected sweetness, but there was a tremulous note to her voice, and she could feel the start of hot, uncontrollable tears to her eyes at the hopelessness of her situation.

His scrutiny was perceptive, and he replied, laughing with cruel mockery. "Whichever you proved to be most apt at, my dear."

The tenuous grip she still retained on her self-control finally snapped, and with a sob, one hand flew savagely up toward his face. He caught her wrist easily, pulling her slightly off balance, so that she fell against him. She twisted in his arms, attempting to bring the other hand up, but he knocked it away and caught both her wrists, holding them behind her back with one hand, forcing her close as he did so. His other hand splayed across the back of her head, twisting into the golden hair, holding her still, and she felt the violence of his mouth on hers, not knowing why it should suddenly release some of the throbbing tension within her. She could feel the treacherous heat she remembered too well starting to burn slowly, and she kicked out viciously, trying to tear her mouth away, aware that he had started to walk forward, his strength forcing her to walk backward with him. She did not realize why until the backs of her legs touched against the sofa and she felt herself sinking into it.

Her mouth was free now, but because it was impossible to get up and she turned her face into his shoulder.

"Let me go." Her tone was beseeching, but he did not move or reply, and she whispered again, "Let me go . . . if you let me go now . . . I will come with you. I have no choice. I realize that now." She halted, her voice too unsteady to be trusted further, acutely aware that he was still silent and had not moved.

She was not sure how long they remained thus, she with her forehead still resting lightly against him, and then he stood up abruptly and moved to the desk. Kicking the chair back from it slightly, he sat down, turning the chair sideways and bringing his booted feet up to rest on the extreme edge of the desk.

She saw his hand go to the small silver knife, turning it over and over, hilt to blade, his fingers measuring the length of it, his eyes fixed unwaveringly on the opposite wall, and she realized he had dismissed her already.

She got up slowly, feeling there was no further need for haste, and moved to the door, closing it softly as she left.

He heard the door click and a muscle jumped at the side of his mouth, his eyes closing momentarily before moving to the silver dagger. He brought it closer, turning it and studying it intently for a few moments, and then, with an almost imperceptible movement, he had hurled it savagely into the wood paneling opposite, where it came to rest with the hilt vibrating frenziedly.

Chapter Twelve

Sally Turner was walking slowly, a bundle of washing beneath her arm, and as Sarah called her name she turned, her face breaking into an immediate smile of greeting.

She quickened her pace toward where Sarah sat under a large oak with Emma on her lap.

"How is baby Adam, Sally?" Sarah's voice was concerned. She had not seen the Turners for three days now, and she had feared the worst regarding the baby's health.

Sally smiled slightly. "He is improving slowly, ma'am. The cough is a bit better now, and regular food helps, of course. As the weather is brightening now, I think he stands a chance."

"Where are you living now? Have you been moved from that hut?" Sarah was frowning as she spoke, but the other woman laughed, and Sarah noticed that her face did not now seem so heavily lined as when last she had seen her.

"We have been given another cottage." She pointed in a vague direction away to the north and added, "Jed is helping in the gardens. There is not a lot he can do, but it is work, and I," she moved the bundle in indication, "help in the laundry; when I get a chance, that is. It is a bit difficult with the children, but . . ." She trailed off, her eyes looking suspiciously bright, and said, wiping the back of her hand across her face, "I don't know how to thank you, ma'am." She snorted noisily, and Sarah smiled kindly at her, shaking her arm slightly.

"You do not have to say anything. All I did was bring a small amount of food." She halted, noticing the woman's questioning gaze.

"You spoke to the earl, didn't you?"

Sarah laughed shortly. "Yes but . . ." She hesitated, not wanting to discredit him as he had, despite indications to the contrary, helped them, after all.

Sally laughed suddenly, a rare display of humor. "You don't think he did it for us, do you?" She sounded almost incredulous. "He had already warned us to move on, not personally, of course, through the manager." She looked at Sarah shrewdly. "He did it for you, not for us."

Looking at Sarah's hand and then at Emma she said quietly, "Where is your husband?"

"I am a widow. My husband died a year or so ago."

Sally looked suitably solemn for a moment at this news and then said brightly, "Well, who needs a husband when you have got an earl." She winked slyly and then added, "I have to go, or I might be out of work before I even finish a week." She moved off, smiling and waving, and Sarah frowned, watching her disappear in the direction of the laundry.

Sarah, Emma, and Maggie moved to London at the end of that week. Mark Tarrington had left the morning after the incident at the Turners' cottage, and Sarah knew bitterly that he was confident enough of her submission to leave her alone at Winslade Hall for a few days. There was nowhere else for her to go, and they were both well aware of the fact. She had not seen him again, and he had merely left her a concise, formal note informing her that John, the driver, and one of the grooms would take her to the address in London at the weekend.

Joanna, now that her schooling was finished, had gone to stay with a friend of her mother's on the same day that her uncle had left. Lady Jean Winton had a daughter of about Joanna's age, and the girl had been filled with pleasure at the prospect of enlightening a less fortunate peer as to her exciting forthcoming plans. And Sarah was glad that Joanna was not there to see her go, not knowing how to explain the reason for her move or for her presence in her uncle's house in London.

The dowager, coming out to wave them off, had merely smiled at Sarah's strained face and said enigmatically, "I would not worry, my dear. It will not be for long." So that Sarah, thinking that the dowager probably knew her nephew better than she, realized that his constancy was undoubtedly going to wane even sooner than she had anticipated.

Mrs. Davis looked suitably bland, not asking questions of any sort, although Sarah was sure that she and probably the entirety of the household knew of this new arrangement she had with the earl.

Stewart and Maggie exchanged hard looks, and then Sarah saw Stewart turn swiftly around and mount his horse, riding off at a thundering pace. Sarah looked quickly at Maggie, but instead of tears, she saw the girl's mouth curve suddenly into a gratified smile.

The London house was close to St. James's Park and was as magnificent, in its own way, as Winslade

Hall. This did not surprise Sarah, for she knew Mark Tarrington well enough now to realize that he would not put his name to anything less.

Mrs. Brookes, the housekeeper, was a thin red-haired woman of perhaps thirty-five. She met them at the door with a show of studied politeness bordering on insolence. Sarah had used the same ploy many times herself and recognized it instantly. Most of the other servants displayed a similar attitude, and Sarah knew instinctively that they resented her presence there. Only Samuel, the butler, seemed to display a genuine show of welcome as they dismounted and he showed them into the wide, marble-pillared hall.

Sarah's room was on the first floor and there was a room for Maggie slightly down the corridor. Emma would now have to sleep in another room, of course, and she unpacked the child's clothing and gave the things silently to Maggie, who took them to Emma's room without a word.

Sarah's bedroom was decorated in pink and blue and was much more expensively furnished and decorated than her room at Winslade Hall, but she hated it instantly, not knowing whether it was because of the color-scheme or the unwanted thoughts it provoked. There was a communicating door and she turned the handle, swinging the door wide. She knew that it was his room, and she found herself wondering sourly whether he would ever bother using it, as he had already made it clear that his sleeping would be done elsewhere.

Lady Susan Morton arrived not long after they did. Sarah could not hide her amazement at seeing the woman. She had not seen or heard from her since she had left Winslade Hall just after Christmas.

Susan laughed at Sarah's confusion, saying, "I must have been blind not to have guessed his intention at Christmas. His eyes never left you. Speculation was rife at Christmas, apparently, when he opened this house and started hiring servants. Rumor had it that he was moving back here himself. You are quite an enigma, you know. Not many men in his position will hand over their main London residence for their mistress's use." She gazed at Sarah's astonished face and laughed. "It seems his mistress was the last to know of his intentions."

Sarah could feel her anger starting to stir at the realization that he had obviously intended to take her as his mistress long before she had been caught out in his room. Susan continued hastily, seeing Sarah's fuming countenance, "He asked me to welcome you to London, but I expect he will visit later." She hesitated, aware that this news did not seem to ease Sarah's fury in the least, and attempted to change the subject. "You will have to have some clothes, Sarah. Shall we go out tomorrow and visit some of the warehouses? You could probably have the things made up very quickly. Mentioning the earl's name helps, of course." She laughed and added, "I always do it when I need a new gown quickly—well, he pays for them—most of the time."

Sarah, wanting to refuse any new clothes that would be paid for by him, merely nodded and smiled brittly, knowing that now that she was in London she could not possibly manage on the few meager dresses she did possess. Besides, she thought viciously, why should she not spend his money. He would expect her to do so, after all.

As soon as the light started to fade she felt a knot starting to tighten in her stomach, and she put Emma to bed early, not knowing why she did not want the baby to see him. The hours ticked by slowly, until at eleven o'clock she undressed and went to bed, lying

184

awake for as long as possible, just in case he chose to arrive late.

He did not, and the next few days were the same. She heard nothing from him and wondered hopefully if perhaps he had changed his mind about the arrangement.

Her relief was short-lived, however, as she realized that if this were so, her future would be just as uncertain as it had been at Winslade Hall. She was still trapped, with no way to turn.

A week passed. She and Susan were sitting in the library with Emma and Maggie. Susan was enthusiastically discussing the clothes they had bought, and Sarah realized with wry humor that the older woman's eagerness for visiting the warehouses had not been so much for Sarah's benefit as for her own. She had quite blatantly picked out several new materials for gowns, charging them to the earl's account as though it was Sarah who would benefit. She had looked at Sarah inquiringly while doing so, as though asking her permission, and Sarah had merely shrugged, smiling, saying nothing.

The dress designs had left Sarah wide-eyed with amazement. She had always thought Susan's clothes rather daring in style, but what she saw displayed in the dressmaker's window and on some of the customers left her acutely embarrassed. Material so sheer that it was transparent, sometimes with little or nothing worn underneath as a shift. Necklines that were cut so low across the breasts that they barely covered the nipples. She had looked aghast as Susan held one of the designs up against her slim form and had stammered something about its not being decent, but Susan had laughed, proclaiming loudly, "Mark will love it, then," reducing Sarah to scarlet-faced embarrassment in the middle of the shop.

She had chosen quite a few new outfits, but not nearly as many as Susan would have liked. She cajoled her mercilessly to buy more, but Sarah felt she could not and selected the bare minimum of items she thought she would require, not wanting even those.

Susan turned to Sarah suddenly and said, "Have you seen Mark yet?"

"No." She said it swiftly, not wanting to acknowledge that the fact was beginning to disturb her. The servants were also, she noticed, beginning to look at her askance, as if they were not now sure what the arrangement between herself and the earl was.

"Lady Pauline Trent is holding a card evening. She is very keen to meet you, Sarah. She asked if we would go later."

Sarah looked at her uncertainly. "I don't know, Susan. Suppose he should come tonight?"

Susan laughed. "It is quite an early card session. I think it starts about seven o'clock. As long as you are back by retiring time," she raised a sly eyebrow at Sarah, "what is the difference? Besides, I do not even know where Mark is. No one has seen him for a few days. He asked me to welcome you to town the day you arrived, and I have not seen him since."

Sarah smiled and said acidly, "No doubt he is trying to placate some superfluous female before making my presence known." She spoke venomously, feeling a dull misery filling her at the thought.

"Well, shall we go? It might be quite eventful, I think," and Sarah saw a glimmer of interest light the older woman's eyes and knew she was thinking of some particular conquest.

"All right. Why not." Sarah shrugged, pushing her misery out of sight beneath the anger she felt at what she was sure was his reason for not visiting so far.

Lady Trent welcomed her enthusiastically, and Sarah wondered if she knew of her relationship with the earl. As she noticed the many pairs of eyes turning her way, sharply curious, she realized that not only did Lady Trent know, but so did everyone else present. She became conscious that most of the woman were studying her with summarizing intent, while a lot of the men were eyeing her with frankly appraising interest. Susan introduced her to some other people who had just entered, and she found herself smiling and greeting people, knowing as she did so that she would never remember all the names or the faces that went with them.

Aware that Susan was now deeply engrossed in conversation with a man who looked to be about five years her junior, and noting also that she was batting her eyelashes with alarming regularity and trilling coyly, Sarah moved away, feeling ill at ease. She heard a voice she thought she recognized call her name loudly and she hesitated.

"Why Mrs. Thornton, the governess. I hear you have improved your prospects quite considerably since last we met."

Sarah, turned, seeing Celia Maynard with two other girls of about her age, watching her intently. She managed to return her greeting adequately, trying to move away quickly, but Celia was not about to be put off.

"Where is the earl?" She looked about her exaggeratedly in mock search. "Surely he has not forsaken you already?" Sarah heard the girls giggling behind their hands and could feel the blood draining slowly from her face.

She was conscious suddenly of other faces turning her way and watching eagerly as her discomfort grew.

She looked around frantically for Susan, but she and the young man had moved away further, and Sarah, turning back to Celia, said quietly, "I have no idea. He does not keep me informed of his movements."

Celia laughed contentedly. "No. I did not think that he would," she returned, gratified. "Well, Mrs. Thornton, as you have come to this little gathering, you might as well spend some of the earl's money for him." She indicated a vacant chair near a table where a game was being prepared.

Sarah shook her head quickly. She had never mastered the art of any card games, and looking now at Celia's flushed face she realized that the girl had guessed this. Someone close by held a chair for her, and she turned to stammer some excuse and leave but Celia caught her arm, her nails sharply restricting. "Come, Mrs. Thornton, if you patronize these little entertainments, you must join in the fun." She sat down herself in the chair next to the one held out for Sarah, and Sarah, aware now that there was quite a small crowd gathering and relishing her humiliation, sat down also.

She looked around stunned as she saw not only the spiteful looks on some of the women's faces, but also quite a few men watching, their faces alight with barely concealed leering amusement. Someone was dealing the cards now, and she watched numbly as the menacing stack began to pile in front of her. All eyes were directed her way as she picked them up with clumsy fingers, and she gave one last despairing look over her shoulder, scanning the room for Susan, but she was lost to sight.

She stared at the colored shapes and faces, seeing them dance before her eyes, scrabbling hopelessly in her mind for some of the information the dowager had imparted at Christmas regarding card games. She was conscious of an expectant quiet, and looking up noticed that practically everyone around the table was staring her way. She realized with frozen shock that it was she and not the cards that would provide this particular evening's entertainment. Her hand started to raise slowly toward the cards, hovering, not knowing which to choose, and then she felt it moved slightly and saw the flash of gold against the tanned skin as he rearranged the cards in her hand.

She closed her eyes momentarily, leaning back in the chair, instinctively seeking his closeness as he selected a card and threw it forward. She could sense his weight leaning casually on the back of her chair, and she felt his fingers, moving away from the cards, caress softly reassuring across her neck before resting on the chair back. She was aware of a throbbing quiet permeating not only the area immediately around their table but the whole room, and looking up slowly, saw that all eyes were now not on her but on the figure standing immediately behind her.

She watched Celia's face register disbelief, and then she smiled at him with intense sweetness, moving her head forward slowly in greeting, as though nothing was amiss. Sarah watched the other faces as the malice was replaced by shamefaced shuffling and saw quite a few people moving away from the table, ill at ease. A few of the women present who had, minutes before, been regarding her with vicious amusement, were now trying to catch her eyes with honeyed smiles, but she ignored them all, her eyes on the cards in front of her again.

It dawned on her slowly that it was only his presence that made her acceptable, and by this open display of protection he was establishing not only his exclusive rights to her as far as the speculative men were concerned, but also securing her future acceptance by the hostesses present.

He played the hand through, and then, unaware of the outcome, she felt his head bend close and he said, "Come."

It was almost a command still, and she felt like laughing hysterically as he moved the chair back and she stood up. She felt his hand firm on her arm as he lead her back to where Susan was still standing deep in flirtation with the young man. He said something to his sister in passing, steering Sarah toward the door. He stopped by Lady Trent, who looked crestfallen to see him departing so soon after his arrival, but he said something soothing and Sarah saw the woman smile, and then they were outside in the chill evening air.

She saw him make some signal and a carriage drew up next to them. She thought of Susan and said, "How will Susan get home?" but he said harshly, "Susan can look after herself," and then the carriage door was shut and they were moving forward.

She sat in the corner furthest away from him, her head turned away in contemplation of the diamond-bright sky. She could feel his eyes watching her restlessly and she turned relentlessly and said, "How did you know where we were?"

"Maggie told me you had gone out with Susan. It did not take a lot of working out; she is very friendly with Pauline Trent." She was aware of the harsh note still in his voice and queried innocently, "Am I not allowed out without your permission, my lord?"

He stared hard at her for a few moments and said quietly, "Susan's reputation leaves a lot to be desired. You will not go out alone with her in the evenings."

She turned to him with a bittersweet laugh and murmured, "I believe mine does also . . . besides, was I supposed to sit in alone, my lord, until you found time to visit?"

She saw the smile starting to curve his mouth at this retort and studied her hands, spinning the ring on her finger.

"Never say you have missed me, Sarah." His tone was softly mocking and she felt her anger at herself for what had sounded like petulance.

"Not at all, my lord. I am well aware that you have other affairs to see to." Her meaning was clear, and seeing his smile deepen she added fumingly, "I really would prefer it if you attended to them all the time."

He changed the subject abruptly, saying, "Why do you wear that still?"

She noticed he was watching the gold band turning beneath her fingers and she snapped, "I am a widow with a child. Why should I not?"

He leaned forward suddenly, and taking her hand started to draw the ring off. Realizing his intention, she curled her finger hastily, but he was too quick and she saw him drop it into his pocket. She made to start forward, demanding angrily, "Give it to me, it is mine," and then checked herself, sinking back into the seat, realizing the proximity she had nearly forced.

She looked out into the starry night again, furiously aware that he was greatly amused by her heated display.

The drive was short. They entered the house, facing Samuel bland-faced as he opened the door.

Sarah preceded him, through the door he held open for her, into the library, where he moved to the blazing fire, standing with his back to it, studying her.

She sat in one of the chairs and picked up a book from a nearby table, turning the pages idly.

He moved to the table, passing her chair, and picked up a crystal decanter. As he returned to the fire she felt one hand trail across her shoulder, and he

191

said, "This is nice. I received the bill this morning—how much of it was on your account?" He spoke drily, and she realized he knew Susan even better than she would have imagined.

She looked away from the book, saying with icy contentment, "Not a lot, my lord."

"Why, do you not like new clothes?"

She looked back at the book, flicking the pages over casually. "Of course."

"You do not like my buying them for you, though." It was a statement, and she merely said without looking up, "No, since you ask."

A sudden stirring idea was beginning to surface and she asked innocently, "Am I to have an allowance of my own, my lord?" She could not meet his eyes as she spoke and concentrated on the fluttering pages.

He was silent for a while and then said briefly, "No."

She looked up, meeting his shrewd observation, and he said, "You can charge anything you want to me. Why do you want money, Sarah? To enable you to disappear to some remote spot?" He smiled tauntingly at the guilty flush that had started to stain her face, and she looked back at the book, reading it with increased diligence.

The silence between them stretched. She sat in apparent conscientious study for a while, and then he said, "I saw Alfred Cunningham today."

She looked up at him at this unexpected piece of interesting news, saying, "How is Anna; and the children, are they enjoying it in Italy?"

He smiled at her enthusiasm, saying, "Anna is, I believe, traveling to Italy quite soon to stay with her sister and the children."

Sarah's expression was incredulous. "But she told me that she hated the idea of sea travel. Are you sure?"

He said laughingly, "I think it might have something to do with the fact that Alfred has been noising abroad his desire for a son and heir before he gets any older."

Sarah could not help smiling herself at the thought of Anna's journeying grey-faced all those miles merely to avoid poor Alfred's unwanted attentions.

The strained atmosphere seemed to have eased slightly, and Sarah, wanting to retain this new and bland harmony for as long as possible, said quickly, "Anna told me that you served with Wellington last year." She saw him look up frowning and added hastily before he changed the subject, unable to keep the note of eager inquiry from her voice, "Were you really a British spy? Was it successful?"

He watched her face, free from wary distrust for a change, and his expression softened. "Yes, but I can assure you that had I known Anna Cunningham was privy to my activities, I would not even have attempted the mission."

She laughed aloud, unable to suppress her humor at the notion of Anna's being entrusted with secrets of any kind, and he watched her animated face, smiling slightly.

Sarah would never have thought it possible that they might be able to talk or laugh together with relaxed ease, and the knowledge that they could made her withdraw suddenly, her hands turning the pages of the book once more.

Aware of her abrupt detachment, he sat also, and she realized after a few silent moments that he was waiting for her to make the first move toward the bedroom.

She sank back in the chair, watching the flames of the fire flicker and dance and then burn, as the long

193

minutes passed, to a dully glowing mass.

She could feel the atmosphere pulse once more, and as she heard the decanter knock against the glass again, she looked up startled, and he said softly, "It's all right, I don't intend getting drunk."

She was silent for a moment, and then said with forced brightness, "What a shame, I was really quite hoping that you would." She looked away, seeing the slow smile starting to curve his mouth, and back to the dying embers of the fire, and he murmured, "You will find that I am not quite so easily deterred, Sarah. Besides," and the wry humor was apparent in his voice now, "I think you will find there is no key in the lock. Not very gentlemanly, but. . . ."

She cut in quickly with dulcet sarcasm. "Oh, do not worry, my lord, I had never confused you with any such. That is something even your vast wealth could never buy for you."

She could no longer meet the darkening anger that shone clear in his eyes, and she heard him say quietly, yet with undisguised threat, "At times, Sarah, you try my patience too far."

But she was unable, despite the failing recklessness, to refrain from adding sweetly, "Well, that is encouraging news at least, my lord." She rose as she was speaking, unwilling to dwell on what form his revenge for these latest insults was likely to take, and made her way quickly to her room.

She undressed hurriedly, not knowing whether it was worth putting on her nightgown, remembering the tattered remnants of the last one she had worn. She dismissed the thought abruptly and let the shift fall over her head and climbed into bed, pulling the cold sheets tightly around her. She lay still, trying to control the tremulous shivering that she knew was not wholly due to the cold. She had already decided that

194

she would remain submissive. It was useless to fight, and besides she had forfeited all right to do so when acquiescing to this arrangement. But she was determined to remain passive; he would not shame her further by making her a participant as she knew she had been once before, and her hands clenched with the force of her purpose.

She heard the door open and close softly and shut her eyes tightly. She could hear him moving quietly about the room and then felt the bed ease as he lay down. Her fists tightened, her nails scoring deeply into her palms, and despite her resolution that she would not, she felt her skin flinch from his touch.

He drew her slowly toward him, and their eyes held momentarily before she let hers close and felt his mouth on hers. His kiss was tender, reassuringly gentle, and this unexpected ploy threatened her mood slightly, but she lay unresisting and unresponsive as he caressed her, willing herself to resigned rigidity. As though guessing her intention, his kiss became deeper, more exacting, and she could feel an answering flicker of warmth starting to kindle, but she crushed it mercilessly, her mind concentrating on her belief that yesterday he had been doing exactly the same thing with someone else. She ignored the coaxing persuasion of his slowly moving touch, until eventually he rolled onto his back and got up abruptly, swearing softly. He walked to the window, staring out and she could see the broadness of his shoulders and the play of muscle along his arms, outlined against the shadowy darkness.

She pulled the sheets up to her chin, hugging her victory about her like another cover. Becoming aware that he was moving back slowly toward the bed, she closed her eyes tight again, unable to keep a slightly triumphant curve from her mouth. His hand flashed out suddenly and she felt the covering sheet ripped from her grasp. She sat up at once, attempting to retrieve it, laughing slightly with what she hoped passed for composure, saying, "Really, my lord, I am cold."

"It had not gone unnoticed, my dear. We shall have to attempt to warm you somewhat." His voice and eyes were flinty irony, and she could feel her brief elation evaporating rapidly. He sat down on the edge of the bed near her, and she suddenly swung her legs over the side, all thoughts of surrender vanished now. Pushing at him, she said breathlessly, "My lord, I have to check, Emma is. . . ."

He held her easily still, his hand going to her face, and turning her to look at him, said harshly, "Mark. My name is Mark. Say it." His grip tightened on her face, and she could see the dangerous flare in his eyes. She opened her mouth to utter the name, but it seemed to choke in her throat and she looked away, remaining silent.

He released her face with a savage flick of the hand and pushed her back abruptly onto the bed. And then she felt his mouth on hers again, all traces of tenderness gone now.

She lay looking up at the moving shadows on the ceiling, her eyes feeling hot and wide with suppressed tears. She had not been able to remain unyielding this time any more than she had the last, and she felt the pain of humiliation more keenly, knowing that her carefully laid plans had been thwarted too soon. She listened for his breathing, wondering if he was asleep, not knowing when he would leave, whether he would go soon or want her again. She shut her eyes wishing she could sleep, feeling the threatening tightness in her throat and the dull ache of misery settling in her stomach.

His arm went around her suddenly, pulling her close, and the unexpected contact made her start violently. He held her, stilling the trembling slightly, and turned her to lie in the curve of his arm so her face was resting against him. She was aware of the thumb of one hand moving in an idle caress across her cheek, and after a while, despite herself, she felt her body starting to relax and her lids falling frequently in drowsiness, and then she slept.

Her consciousness roused slowly and she wondered vaguely what had broken her sleep. Her eyes were too heavy still to open and she lay quiet, aware of his arm still holding her and the sensation of his skin beneath her cheek rising and falling slowly with the evenness of his sleep. The realization surfaced that she could move away now, but she lay unmoving, the warmth and comfort too tempted to be relinquished, and she felt herself drowse again lingeringly into slumber.

She woke suddenly, her eyes opening quickly, as her inner time-clock perceived the lateness of the hour. She turned her head without thought, but he was gone, the pillow still indented where he had lain. She looked toward the window, and noticing the brightness of the day behind the heavy curtains, knew she had overslept.

She got up, washing and dressing quickly, and made her way to Maggie's room. She opened the door without care, and as she stepped inside she saw Maggie's finger go to her mouth in explicit warning. She pointed to the crib and shrugged, smiling, as

197

though indicating she was unaware why the child was asleep, but was grateful for it, nevertheless. Sarah smiled and retreated slowly, shutting the door quietly. She made her way downstairs, not knowing why, as she did not feel hungry at all.

Mrs. Brookes had been amazed at her reluctance to eat in bed in the morning. Apparently it was something expected of her, but Sarah was used to rising and working early, and it was not a habit she wanted to break.

She opened the dining room door, without caution, and then froze. She had expected him to be long gone, and the sight of him sitting casually in the corner, one booted foot resting on the other knee, with an open newspaper resting across him, stopped her dead. He looked up as she entered, watching her, and, not wanting to retreat before him, she shut the door and went to the sideboard where various covered dishes were laid out. She poured a cup of coffee and took it to the table, sitting with her chair turned slightly, so she faced away from him.

"Are you not eating anything?"

She shook her head. "I am not hungry." It was the truth, after all, she thought acidly.

"You should eat something. You are too thin."

She did not turn toward him, but merely said, her tone icy, "Well, in that case, my lord, I wonder that you bother coming here at all."

She could sense his amusement at this remark, and after a while he said, changing the subject, "Do you like the house?"

She was silent for a moment, not wanting to express her dislike of it for some reason. "It is very . . . grand."

She hesitated, unable to think of any other comment to make about it, and after a while he said, with

198

mock seriousness, "What do you not like about it? All of it, or just upstairs?"

She said nothing, and he continued evenly, "You can have it redecorated if you want; buy furniture if you like."

She turned then and said with a strained attempt at dulcet nonchalance, "Do you think that my length of stay here will merit such expense? You must have the most oft refurnished and redecorated house in London. I am sure the local tradesmen must rely greatly on your inconstancy." She turned away again, unable to control the feigned indifference further, her eyes riveted on her coffee as she watched the dark liquid rock back and forth in the cup.

"No one else has stayed here." His voice was quietly impassive.

She continued in the same honeyed tones, still watching the frenzied coffee. "Oh, of course, I was forgetting about your other London residences."

"Or there." He said it now with undisguised exasperation, as though the fact that he was explaining irritated him.

"You do not have to account to me for your activities, my lord."

"I am well aware of the fact, but as you seem anxious to know, mistresses usually have their own residences; it suffices that I should merely pay for their upkeep."

"How extremely inconsiderate of me, then, to be a pauper. It must inconvenience you dreadfully." She spoke with caustic sarcasm.

He stood up suddenly, throwing the paper into the chair, saying in a soft sigh, "Would you like to go somewhere this evening?"

She was silent for a moment, knowing too well that she would, but she merely replied with what she knew was childish petulance, "I thought it was my place to entertain you, my lord; you need not feel obliged to do the same for me."

She heard him mutter something beneath his breath, and then he said harshly, "I shall call for you at eight o'clock. Be ready." And the door slammed after his departing figure.

Chapter Thirteen

It was May 5th and Sarah's twenty-first birthday.

She watched her grubby-faced daughter, smiling as the child attempted to push yet another lump of sticky cake into her mouth. Maggie's eyes met hers over the top of the golden curls and they both laughed.

Sarah said, "I think you are wasting your time wiping her with that cloth before she has finished. It was very kind of you to make this cake, Maggie. How did you know? I had almost forgotten myself."

The girl smiled. "I remembered your telling me the date last month."

Sarah raised her eyebrows in mock surprise. "I am quite amazed you were allowed into the kitchens to do so. What did Mrs. Brookes have to say?"

Maggie scowled her opinion of the housekeeper and said, "That woman! Why do you not dismiss her? You could if you wanted to. You know he would say nothing."

Sarah shrugged, turning away. She had no intention of making even the slightest alteration to his household, unwilling to display any indication that she thought her stay might be a lengthy one.

She knew Mrs. Brookes was still resentful of her

presence and knew also that this was aggravated by the privileges she afforded Maggie. When they had arrived in London, Sarah had elevated Maggie to the position of companion, much to the other young woman's consternation. But Sarah was adamant, and Maggie now ate with her in the dining room rather than with the other servants, and did nothing all day apart from looking after Emma and herself. Sarah was eternally grateful for Maggie's company, not knowing how she would have coped had she been brought to London alone, and it was the only way she knew of repaying her a little for her unselfishness.

Watching Maggie's futile attempts to clean some of the cream from Emma's evasive cheeks, Sarah said, "Have you heard from Stewart lately?"

Maggie looked her way, smiling. "He must write every other day, I think. It is a good job I managed to learn to read a little. There are some words, though . . ." She looked at Sarah, frowning. "Perhaps if I show you later?"

Sarah smiled. "Of course. I will read them to you if you like. If you are sure that there is nothing . . . ?" She hesitated and they both smiled.

Maggie looked at Sarah, sighing wistfully. "I miss Winslade Hall, do you?"

Sarah nodded, not meeting Maggie's eyes. It was something she would never have imagined she could truthfully admit to, but she yearned now for the peace and tranquility, the fresh greenness and the unhurried life she had known there. But mostly she missed the unaffected friendliness of the people there and the knowledge that she probably would never see the house or the staff again moved her to hot-eyed misery.

She had been in London for just six weeks. He had stayed with her almost every night so far, leaving the house sometimes quite late the next morning. On the few occasions that he had not visited she had said nothing, never asking him about his absences, and he never explained, but her unspoken query charged the space between them with her suspicion.

On the evenings that they did not go out, she was surprised anew at the ease with which they were able to converse once he had managed to thaw some of her frozen detachment. He told her of his business dealings and explained about his various commercial interests. She knew that her ability to grasp the technicalities confused him slightly, and she gained satisfied delight from asking him some pertinent financial question, watching his bewilderment with gratified contentment. She had soon become aware from the way he spoke that he was a staunch Tory, and Sarah, never having held any strong political affiliation in her life, soon discovered a passionate sympathy for all Whig policies. He was well aware of her contrary attitude and usually assumed an air of amused superiority to her goading political retorts, answering her monosyllabically and with mock solemnity, studiously avoiding being drawn into any blatant confrontation.

She was well aware that women were not expected or encouraged to make any political contribution. She could remember well enough her father's condescendingly patronizing manner whenever her mother had attempted to speak to him on any such issues, although he had illogically encouraged Sarah to learn about and query all aspects of current affairs. She had realized at quite a tender age that her father was, in fact, giving her the education and encouragement he would have given a son, which he had ardently desired, but never had.

Occasionally she was able, by some skillfully subtle manipulation, to draw Mark into a lengthy and

furious debate about some current politically conten-
tious topic, and, once she had succeeded in provoking
him into treating her as a serious opponent, she
withdrew from the discussion at the crucial stage,
smiling sweetly and with undisguised triumph, forcing him to acknowledge her equality. He would then
smile also, knowing well enough that her victory
would be short-lived, and as the hour grew late and
the silences between them longer, she would rise
abruptly and go to her room, unable to bear the
straining expectancy any further.

The silent battle of wills behind the closed bedroom
door far exceeded any of the bitter verbal warring they
had participated in at Winslade Hall. She was seldom
victorious. It was rare that her self-imposed frigidity
could outlast his skill or patience, and on the few
occasions that she had managed a bitter triumph, she
could feel the force of his frustrated anger lashing her
as they lay silently in the dark room.

Although she knew nothing of men other than what
she had learned from him, she was instinctively sure
that he was a considerate and attentive lover. She
knew that his painstaking attempts to arouse her far
exceeded what was necessary merely to insure his own
gratification. Long after her assumed indifference to
his attentions had been broken and she lay compliant,
he caressed her still, with unhurried devotion, waiting
until she reached for him of her own volition, her arms
encircling his neck and pulling him close, before he
moved to join her.

The first night he had stayed with her, the sensation
of his skin sliding against hers had made her tense
instinctively, her nails cutting into his neck as the
movement evoked the memory of the pain as well as
the pleasure she had experienced. Her eyes had
opened, seeking his in silent entreaty, and he had bent

his head to hers again, murmuring into her mouth, "Relax. I won't hurt you," before she felt the stress melt beneath the insistent pressure of his mouth on hers. And in the event, she realized that he had, after all, spoken no less than the truth.

But the warm languor of satisfaction could never quite obliterate the core of emptiness deep within her that yearned for something more to fill its void. Sometimes, while still drugged with lazy contentment, she wanted to speak to him, to murmur some endearment or affectionate words, but she always swallowed them unuttered as her self-possession returned, and with it her pride. And she reminded herself, with stinging self-ridicule, that he had never given any indication that she meant more to him than any of the numerous others who had preceded her, or those who would undoubtedly follow. She retreated into the coldness inside, nurturing it lovingly, hardening herself desperately against him, feverishly determined that she would not feel any emotion other than relief when it was her time to be cast aside. She explained away his tenderness cynically, sure it was something he afforded to all and no more than a means by which he could secure another clingingly adoring female to feed his vanity. The need for her total response was not, she was certain, for her benefit at all, but merely to brutally emphasize his utter dominance of her and the humiliation she felt when forced to acknowledge the fact.

And yet, sometimes, when their eyes met at rare moments, she was sure she could see, behind the tight control, some spark of the sadness she felt so keenly mirrored in his own eyes. On one such occasion she had attempted to defeat him and the treachery of her own body by feigning arousal before she felt any, wanting to thwart him by withdrawing frigidly at the height of his passion. But in her eagerness not to be foiled herself she had moved too soon, pulling him close almost before he had kissed her once, and she had felt him tense suspiciously, muttering, "Sarah" with a mixture of mockery, threat, and despair. He had kissed her then with a sensuous savagery that left her drugged, the deceitful embrace turning involuntarily to one of need. Her hands were in his hair almost before she had sensed them moving, but he had jerked his mouth away, asking harshly against her cheek, "Do you want me to leave?"

She had lain panting softly against his face, her hands attempting to pull him back, but he had resisted her, demanding, "Tell me," his tone abrasive still and yet with a strange, pleading edge that had puzzled her.

But she was unable either to deny or agree and had merely moved her face until her parted mouth rested lightly against the side of his own once more, and he had turned back to her with a groaning, almost inaudible profanity.

She had seen many places during the time she had been resident in London. Vauxhall Gardens had enthralled her with its brightly lit splendor, and the same was true of Convent Garden and Drury Lane, but the opulence had palled slightly after a while with the knowledge that beneath the glittering facade presented by the majority of the haute monde lay spiteful insincerity and malicious contest.

The entertainment provided by these places, she knew, was second to that provided by the participants. People went not only to see but be seen, to scrutinize what others were doing, saying, and wearing, and she was unable to reason why the fact that he had shunned the superficial attraction of life in London in favor of life on his estate should make her feel strangely contented.

When they went to one of these social gatherings, she was always acutely aware of how highly coveted was her position of mistress to the earl of Winslade. Even while she was with him, he was a prime target for the many bright-eyed, hopeful debutantes and their fawning and equally aspiring mamas, who, although well aware of her presence, obviously deemed her as no serious threat. They, after all, were interested in higher stakes than supporting her as his mistress.

She was also conscious of the others, not suitably qualified to be considered in the marriage mart, but nevertheless just as eager to move into his bed should the opportunity arise, and it was these, with their hard-eyed smiles or openly hostile stares that depressed Sarah most. She often looked around at the multitude of glossily bright females and wondered which of those present had already filled the office she now held. They flirted quite openly with him, even when she stood quite close, and although he rarely left her side and seemed overtly unimpressed by this ardent female attention, Sarah would nevertheless turn away from him with studied indifference and move to some eager-eyed admirer of her own. She knew that she had gathered quite a small band of gallants herself, and although she also realized that they were apt to be rather scarce in his presence, she was usually able to tempt one of them to indulge in a little innocent flirtation. Joseph Ashton, she knew, was always willing to oblige her, a gleam of amusement in his eyes as he looked from her to the earl. She knew it enraged him from the flint-eyed impassive stare he directed her way, but she would ignore him completely and display an even greater coquettish interest in the man at her side.

This interlude was usually brought to an eventual close with his steely grip on her arm steering her toward the door or the carriage, and they then returned to the house in hostile silence, she acutely aware of his murderous gaze for the duration of the journey.

She sometimes wondered if he was perhaps jealous, but dismissed this vanity instantly, sure that it was no more than extreme possessiveness for his new toy. She knew that at times she quite deliberately tempted his patience beyond bearing and was just as sure, with a kind of exhilarated terror, that there would be a time when she would taunt him too far and the confrontation between them then would terminate their relationship irrevocably.

His revenge following these flirtatious bouts had so far been limited to the lingering torment of her betrayal in the bedroom. He could manipulate her quite ruthlessly to almost pleading ecstasy, reasserting his dominance of her totally and with strangely passionless resolution, and his mastery of her at these times swamped her with self-loathing. She lay afterwards, cold and mortified, staring up at the ceiling with brimming eyes, despising herself as bitterly as she hated him and she attempted to push away the arm that moved to hold her close while she slept. But he was unrelenting in that, too, merely restraining her rejecting hands until she calmed and lay quiet against him.

She knew that she was slowly becoming obsessed, and unhealthily so, with knowing which other women she shared or had shared him with, and she had soon discovered the identity of at least one.

Sarah was standing slightly apart from him that evening at Vauxhall Gardens, chatting idly to Pauline

Trent, with whom she had become quite friendly, when that woman spying her errant husband disappearing into one of the dark walkways with an unknown brunette, had set off hurriedly in hot pursuit. Sarah turned back toward the earl, who had been standing some way behind with Joseph Ashton and various other acquaintances. There was no sign of Joseph or any of the other men, but the earl was standing there still, and Sarah was halted in midstep at the sight of a darkly attractive woman of perhaps twenty-five clutching at one of his arms possessively and smiling up at him with frankly suggestive brilliance. She was quite startlingly beautiful, her black hair glinting with glossy blue highlights as she moved her head toward him enticingly. She was leaning provocatively close, her gown so low-cut that her almost bare breasts were pressed hard against his arm.

Sarah was stunned, as much by the blatant display of sexuality as by the look of avid hunger in the woman's eyes as she gazed up into the disinterested face close to hers. The desperation presented such a contrast to the sophisticated poise of her appearance that Sarah could not miss her misery. She felt overwhelmed by compassion suddenly, and was unable to look or move away. As she watched them unwaveringly, she saw him disentangle himself from the grasping hands with callous indifference and say something to the woman, his manner one of vague irritation. As though sensing Sarah's presence, he looked up sharply and their eyes held for a moment. The tedium on his face was quickly replaced by some unreadable emotion and she saw his lips move slightly and knew he was swearing to himself.

Sarah turned hastily, scanning the shadowy night for some familiar face, and seeing none started to walk blindly toward the walkway she had seen Pauline

Trent disappear into. She walked quickly, uncaring where, not wanting to acknowledge that at some time she would no doubt evoke just such contemptuous boredom. She knew instinctively that the woman was one of his mistresses. There had been too much intimacy in her attitude for it to be otherwise.

She was so absorbed by the pathetic scene she had just witnessed that she did not notice the three shadowy figures detach suddenly from the gloom and start to walk noiselessly behind her, fanning into an arc at her back. She was vaguely conscious of several people on the same path, but barely noticed them, aware only of the movement of air as they passed. But a spiteful-sounding tittering made her look up suddenly, mildly curious as to the cause of such malice. She saw a man and woman walking toward her arm-in-arm, and as they drew closer she noticed the woman's eyes fixed intently on her face. Then she looked past Sarah at some obviously amusing spectacle behind her and then at Sarah's face again, the disgust plain in her attitude as she turned to her companion with a whispered aside and swished her skirts away disdainfully as they passed.

Sarah suddenly felt the hair at her nape prickle pitilessly and turned quickly, her heart starting to thump slowly and heavily as she saw the three men standing silently blocking her retreat. She looked feverishly after the man and woman, but they were disappearing into the darkness. The men were walking steadily closer, and she could see the leering smirks as they acknowledged her obvious fright. She noticed with abstract terror that they all were young, probably younger than herself, and from their dress and swaggeringly arrogant bearing, were obviously of the peerage. Sarah looked around frantically, scouring the shadowy half-light for some sign of escape, but there was none—only hedging and shrubbery as far as she could see, and she knew despairingly that she would never be able to outrun them. Her senses strained for some sound indicating that there might be someone close by, but it was silent apart from the blood pulsing dully in her ears, and she realized that she had walked much farther than she had ever intended. She backed away, feeling twigs from the hedge tearing into her bare arm as she pressed herself against it, noticing the grins widening as her fear became more pronounced. She stifled a choking sob with the back of one hand just as the man nearest her lunged forward, dragging her close with brutish fingers. She brought her free hand up spontaneously, pushing it hard into his face, freeing herself as he yelped in surprise and pain and then cursed foully. She backed away again, stumbling, watching the lazy amusement in their faces harden to vindictive intent.

She was brought up sharply by the sensation of a hand on her shoulder pulling her back hard against a male form, and she turned, sobbing with panic, her hands coming up defensively, and then sensed his presence even before she could see him clearly. Her arms moved about his neck and she held on to him desperately. She felt one arm move around her, turning her sideways so that he was unobstructedly facing the three men still, and through the hammering in her ears she heard a voice mutter his name with wrathful disbelief tempered with unease, and then say with forced joviality, "Well, Lord Tarrington. Sorry, old man, had not realized you had prior claim to this one." She heard one of the others mutter something that sounded suspiciously argumentative, as though he was not about to be put off by one man when there were three of them, but the first man was laughing almost apologetically now, his tone sly and yet with an

211

undercurrent of thwarted fury as he added, "Just having a bit of a laugh . . . a bit of fun. . . ." His voice faded as he became uncomfortably conscious of the other man's continued silence.

The earl smiled suddenly with chilling brilliance and said quietly, "Well, I like a laugh as much as anyone. We could joke about it further tomorrow if you like, say five o'clock. I shall leave any other arrangements up to you. Or, you could apologize."

There was tense silence for a few moments, and Sarah, desperate just to be rid of the men as quickly as possible, started to murmur pleadingly to him, but the arm holding her gave a slight, silencing shake and then the aggressive voice cut in with scornful disbelief. "You must be mad. Why bother for a . . ." He was halted at that point by a swift dig in the ribs from a companion's elbow, and Sarah heard sibilant whispering as the belligerent youth was advised by some obviously more quick-witted colleague as to her identity.

The silence stretched interminably and Sarah was on the point of begging him to let the matter drop when someone uttered in a tightly controlled undertone, "I apologize on behalf of myself and my companions, Mrs. Thornton. We had mistaken you for . . . for someone else."

The men moved off then, one of them still making threatening noises, but the other two had pulled him away with brash attempts at good-humored nonchalance.

Sarah looked at him warily, and he said, his voice so controlled it was toneless, his eyes still intent on the disappearing youths, "Did they hurt you?"

She shook her head quickly, becoming conscious that her hands were still fastened tight to his neck. Feeling foolish, she started to draw them away as unobtrusively as possible, attempting to step back as she did so. But his arm tightened and he brought the other one around her also, moving her close again murmuring with more than a hint of wry amusement in his voice, "Be still. I promise I will not take it as a sign of capitulation."

She sensed his mouth closing with hers, and as the reason for her flight resurfaced and she saw again the anguished eyes of the dark-haired woman, she turned her head hastily at the last minute, feeling his mouth brush against her cheek. He remained unmoving for a moment, and she froze, wondering if he would force her face around. But his head moved back. She could sense his annoyance, but he merely said, with tight humor, "Is that all the thanks I get for rescuing you from a fate worse than death?"

Sarah laughed acridly, saying with impetuous bitterness, "I think it is rather late for that."

She felt him tense and knew at once the implied accusation had struck home. But he said softly, "It would have been much different this time."

She attempted to pull free, saying with thoughtless stupidity, "I really do not see how," but he held her still and said with steely inquiry, "Well, would you like a demonstration?"

She remained rigidly before him, her head bowed slightly as she examined the diamond pin in his cravat with unwarranted fascination, and he rasped suddenly, "What made you foolish enough to come wandering out here on your own—only soliciting whores walk these pathways unescorted."

Sarah looked up then with a taut smile and a ready, slick rejoinder, but noting the warning in his eyes as he read her thoughts, she glanced away again and merely said coolly, "I was looking for Susan or Joseph."

"What was wrong with looking for me? I was standing just behind you."

Sarah curled her hands, replying with as much indifference as she could muster, "You appeared to be otherwise occupied. I did not like to interrupt." She knew furiously that she had not, after all, been able to exclude the note of accusation from her voice.

He said, with soft emphasis, "She means nothing to me."

Sarah laughed with increased bitterness and returned harshly, "Oh, don't worry, you made that perfectly plain."

"Would you prefer it if she did, then?" His tone was hardening.

Sarah pulled herself free, saying distantly, "I am sure it does not matter to me either way," and then spoiled it completely by blurting suddenly, "Is she your mistress?"

He smiled wryly, saying with quiet irony, "I had thought *you* held the obviously dubious honor."

She swung back to him, saying with the affected sweetness that had become second nature, "And I had not believed you to be so niggardly with your favors, my lord."

He was watching her through narrowed eyes, and she heard him say tonelessly, "She was my mistress . . . some while ago now."

Sarah stared at him, not knowing why hearing him admit what she had already guessed should wound her so, and she dismissed it with flippant spite and said, "Of course, it is not so much a question of those who are or have been, but the few you might have been careless enough to have overlooked."

She moved then as though to go, but he caught hold of her arm, asking with controlled exasperation, "Am I to be constantly apologizing for my past for the rest of my days, Sarah?"

She hesitated slightly, not knowing what to make of this enigmatic query, but merely replied with a forced smile, "I have not the slightest notion, my lord. Should you marry, perhaps your wife might require some explanation for your past excesses, but you will be relieved of any such necessity for the next month or so, at least. As I have already said, it interests me not at all."

She watched his eyes narrow again, strangely and abruptly aware of the dusk and silence enveloping them as he questioned softly, "Month or so?"

Sarah shivered, feeling the chill in the night air suddenly, but managed with deliberate and exaggerated query, "Week or so?"

Their eyes held interminably, and then he said evenly, "Why do you persist with this childish defiance? It affords you nothing." His hand moved to her face, tormentingly slowly, his thumb brushing her mouth lightly as he added, without any hint of threat, "I could break you so easily, Sarah. You do realize that, don't you?" and continued gently, almost appealingly, "Don't make me do it."

Sarah was silent for a moment, knowing well enough the truth of his words. She had known it from the first insult delivered at the Cunninghams' what seemed now like an age ago. She regarded him steadily and challenged softly, "Why do you not, then? I am quite sure you would gain the greatest satisfaction from doing so."

He smiled slowly, his eyes intent on the fingers still caressing at her face. "I know other, more enjoyable ways of gaining satisfaction from you, Sarah." The softly worded reply was explicit, and she felt the blood starting to burn her face mercilessly. Turning quickly, she made to walk away. His hand moved out, jerking her back against him again, and she twisted in his grip, bringing her hand up savagely to slap at his face. He evaded the blow easily, and restraining her hands said, half-laughing, "You are going the wrong way. I have no intention of playing knight errant for the rest of the evening."

"No, I can appreciate how difficult it must be for you trying to act so far out of character." It was out before her thoughts were rational, and as she saw his eyes harden and a muscle tighten near his mouth, she knew she was treading dangerously close to disaster.

For no apparent reason, she could suddenly hear Anna Cunningham's words before she had left for Winslade Hall, regarding her required future behavior. The absurdity of her continued disregard of Anna's advice made her give a spontaneous choke of hysterical laughter.

He studied her silently for a few moments and then asked drily, "Dare I ask what amuses you now?"

And for some inexplicable reason she told him. "I was thinking of Anna Cunningham's kindly advice on my expected future attitude while residing in your household. I think it had something to do with curbing my reckless impulses," and she laughed again, the despair honing the hysteria.

She thought for a moment he was about to say something, but he reached for her slowly, his head moving lingeringly closer, and she knew he was taunting her with the opportunity to turn away once more, but she remained unresisting as he kissed her with wooing sweetness.

His head raised and he said, some of the laughter back in his tone, "Well, that is an improvement, at least," and then asked quietly, his eyes intent, "Shall we go home now?"

She hesitated, trying to judge whether he wanted to

leave or not, her uncontrollable perversity making her want to choose the opposite. She saw the sudden wry twist to his mouth as he acknowledged the reason for her hesitancy, and she asked with blunt sweetness, "What would you prefer, my lord?" unable to prevent the betraying smile from curving her mouth.

He smiled also, looking over her head, and said solemnly, "Oh, I think I would much prefer to stay here."

She laughed, moving unconsciously closer in an unguarded, shared moment of humor and affection, murmuring almost coyly, "Well, we appear to be in agreement for a change then, my lord."

He took her hand, holding it for a few moments before drawing it through his arm, and they started to walk back the way they had come. He muttered, smiling still, "I thought we might."

Sarah, reliving the incident a few days later, could not prevent a vague, wishful sigh. Sometimes . . . she reflected wistfully . . . but her reverie was curtailed sharply by the arrival of a breathlessly excited Susan.

Maggie, standing up at that moment, lead a chocolate-faced Emma from the room, holding her mucky hand gingerly, smiling welcome at Susan as she went.

"You will never guess what Sarah," Susan murmured.

Sarah looked at the dark woman with suitably arrested attention.

"Joseph Ashton has intimated that he will take me under his protection." She was nearly inarticulate with agitation, and Sarah frowned, saying, "Does that please you, then?"

Susan laughed gaily. "Of course. He is very rich and generous. I have been angling for his attention for ages. You would think as we lived so close for so long

217

that we might have . . . well, never mind. I have seen the most marvelously expensive emerald necklace; it is quite beautiful. I must have it." She sank down into a chair, her bottom lip caught between her teeth as she mused covetously, unaware that Sarah was regarding her with stunned horror.

"What do you mean, Susan? Are you going to ask him to buy it?"

"Well, not right away. There has to be a little subtlety about it. A few hints here and there in a few weeks' time." She looked at Sarah's shocked face and said soothingly, "Jewelery is a good investment. Money is spent too easily. Expensive baubles are always convertible to cash when your looks have gone and you need capital. Has Mark bought you any trinkets yet?"

Sarah shook her head hastily. "No, and if he did I would return them. I want nothing from him."

Susan sighed. "You do not warm toward him at all, do you Sarah?" She looked reflective then, and added with wry humor, "Which is just as well, of course. . . . I would hate to see you hurt, and you would be if you allowed yourself to become fond of Mark. He is totally unfeeling—a complete bastard, actually." She giggled at Sarah's expression, continuing with a dismissive gesture, "Oh, it is all right. As his sister, I am privileged, and can admit aloud to what others merely think. Oh, he is generous, it is true, but only with his money. Well, he has enough of it, after all. That is why you should not feel badly about being mercenary. He expects it . . . prefers it. . . ." She hesitated, becoming aware of Sarah's silence and averted face, and said coaxingly, "Look, if he will not let you have an allowance of your own, you should . . . encourage him to buy you things of value. You can always sell them if you need to." She smiled then, with a broad wink, and said, with a return to frivolity, "Of course, you might find that your expected gratitude will render you sleepless for a couple of nights, but what are a few dark circles? Surely it is worth it for a few thousand pounds' worth of jewelry?"

Sarah stood up, moving to the door, unable to keep the look of disgust from her face.

"Oh, Sarah. Do not be such a prude." Susan spoke with amused tolerance. "You are in a worse position than I am. Be sensible. Of course, you will probably be provided for by Mark for a while after his protection has finished, but you must have some finances of your own." She was trying to be helpful and tactful, but realized ruefully that she was making a worse mess of the situation, and she fell silent.

But Sarah turned back, smiling overbrightly at the woman, and said, "I am sorry, Susan. I forget sometimes what my position here really is, I think." And she returned to the chair she had just vacated and sat down.

Sarah tensed as the sobbing came again. She wondered with mounting melancholy whether he was deaf to or just uncaring of the child's distress. The noise ceased as abruptly as it had started, and she relaxed a little, lightly sighing unconscious relief into the slow, clinging mouth covering hers. Her hands started to raise, away from the sheets, sliding skimmingly along the hard smoothness of his back to his shoulders, and then, as a fresh bout of wailing erupted, they tightened and removed spontaneously.

His mouth relinquished hers with leisured reluctance and his head moved back, their eyes meeting in rare contact. He looked at her frank, appealing gaze and anxious face and then rolled onto his back, saying with an exasperated sigh, "Go on, then."

She got up at once, moving quickly and silently to the door.

Maggie was rocking a screaming Emma to and fro in her arms, and she looked up astonished as Sarah entered. She held her arms out for the child, and Maggie surrendered her gladly.

"I think it is her teeth. The side of her face is bright red and burning hot."

Sarah nodded, stroking the flushed face and whispering soothingly as she paced slowly back and forth in the room.

Maggie looked at her and said laughingly, "How did you get away? Is he asleep?"

Sarah shook her head smiling ruefully. "Perhaps he will be when I get back though?" She could not keep the note of expectation from her voice and realized suddenly, as did Maggie, that she was provided with quite a reasonable excuse not to return at all.

Maggie looked at her shrewdly. "Well, what are you going to do?" She nodded at Emma. "Wake her again?"

Sarah looked at the child, sleeping now quite peacefully. She replaced her in the cot and stood looking at her for a while. "She might wake in a few minutes. I ought to stay for a while." Maggie said nothing, but Sarah knew she was watching her intently as she sat in a chair near the bed.

Maggie sat also, and Sarah said suddenly, "Turn up the lamp and I shall read your letters for you." Maggie jumped up at the suggestion and pulled two envelopes from a small drawer.

Sarah read the letters through slowly, twice each, smiling at Maggie's red-faced confusion at the closing endearments.

"He wants to marry you, then." Maggie said nothing, merely nodding, and Sarah said wistfully, "You shall be going back to live on the Winslade Estates. You shall like that."

Maggie smiled, unable to look at the other woman and with a sigh Sarah got up and moved back to the cot, peering in at the now content child.

Maggie, she knew, was probably tired and waiting to sleep, and after standing undecided for a few moments, she said, "Goodnight, Maggie," and closed the door softly as she left.

He was lying on his back still, with one hand thrown across his forehead. Sarah hesitated, and then when he did not move she walked noiselessly around the bed and stood close, gazing down at him. He was asleep, the dark lashes curving against his cheeks. He looked younger while asleep, not so much older than herself, and it dawned on her suddenly that she did not even know how old he was. She studied him for a few minutes with a rapt attention she did not understand. She never looked at him for long during the day; avoiding his eyes was a habit she found hard to break. Now she stood unmoving, one hand starting to move involuntarily, slowly toward him, and then abruptly she withdrew it and returned to her side of the room.

She had not expected him to be asleep, despite saying so to Maggie, and the knowledge that his desire had been so fickle illogically nettled her, until she realized that he had not expected her to return, either. She lay down without any perceptible movement of the bed and stared up at the dancing shadows, her mind alert, and all notions of sleep gone for a while.

"Is she settled now?" His voice pierced her meandering reverie abruptly, and she stammered, "Yes . . . yes, it is her teeth troubling her, but . . ." She halted,

221

sure he was not in the least interested in any of her daughter's ailments and wondering how long he had lain beside her awake.

"What were you thinking of that makes you sigh so often? Not me, that is for sure." His tone was soft, self-mocking, and she returned irritably, "No, my lord, I was thinking of my late husband."

He was silent for so long that Sarah was sure he would not bother making any reply, and then he murmured, with steely calm, "What of him?"

She hesitated for a moment and then said quickly, "I was thinking that if I had treated him more . . . more fairly, perhaps things might have been different between us."

He pulled her close so sharply that her hand went up in reaction as though to slap defensively at him. He caught her wrist in a painful grip and bit out menacingly, "Do not ever say that again."

She stared at him in startled incomprehension for a moment and then said sourly, "Does it irk you my lord, that perhaps my husband might have cared for me?"

He moved his head slowly forward so that his mouth was only inches from hers and murmured softly, "Do I not care for you, then, Sarah?"

Their eyes locked for a moment before she allowed hers to slide away, saying with toneless deliberation, "Very well, my lord. I want for nothing."

He was silent again, merely lowering his mouth to hers completely and taking the imprisoned hand up around his neck, holding it there until her straining dwindled and her fingers twined into his hair.

Chapter Fourteen

Mark Tarrington walked briskly, whistling softly, his hands thrust deeply into his pockets. He frowned, wondering vaguely why he was in such good humor when he had just lost five thousand pounds on a business deal, something that would normally have rendered him vengefully furious, not only with himself but with the unfortunate winner in the transaction.

Perhaps he should let her take over the running of his business affairs. He smiled. It was not even as though she would be incapable of it, he thought wryly. His thoughts turned to her father, Sir Paul Brent. She had certainly not gained her financial acumen from him. He remembered him vaguely; a likable enough rogue with a hopeless commercial head and a penchant for large redheads, if his memory served. Their paths had crossed once or twice, even to the extent that the man had once asked him to visit. He cursed fate now that he had never taken him up on the offer. Had he seen her three or four years ago, when she was still under her father's protection . . . he cut his musings short abruptly. There was no sense in it. He had not, and she had married someone

223

else. His hands curled into fists in his pockets, unable to reason why even the thought of Charles Thornton could reduce him to such intense rage; he had never even touched her, after all.

He entered the house quietly, wondering what she would think at seeing him so early in the day. He never visited before dinner in the evening, and he smiled ruefully, wondering if she would remove stony-faced to the bedroom at the sight of him. His need for her now far exceeded mere physical desire, and he knew with a wry self-honesty that it had always been so.

He opened the library door, knowing that she used that room most, swinging it wide, but the room was empty, and he walked softly to the small salon.

Maggie and the child were sitting at a table. As he entered Maggie looked up startled. "Your lordship. I was not expecting to see you so early. I am afraid that Sarah is out with Lady Susan. They have been quite a while, though—shopping I think—they will probably return soon."

He frowned in mild exasperation, not knowing why it should vex him so that he could not see her; it was the middle of the afternoon, after all.

He smiled slightly at Maggie's worried countenance and moved to the table watching the child, her face mucky with cake.

"What is this?" He indicated the chocolate mess she was attempting to cram into her mouth, and Maggie laughed, saying, "That is the remainder of the birthday cake. She will not be satisfied until she has eaten it all."

Mark Tarrington looked at the child thoughtfully and asked, "How old is she now—two?"

Maggie was silent for a moment as she realized what he thought, and she stammered slightly. "She had her second birthday last month. Sarah was twenty-one two days ago."

He did not look away from the child's face but merely took a piece of the cake from the plate and tasted it. Moving away, he sat down in the wing chair in the corner of the room.

Mistresses were usually notorious for bringing to light every conceivable anniversary possible, even to the extent of inventing a few; it was typical of Sarah, he thought with amused sadness, that she would not even mention to him her coming of age. He sat tapping his feet impatiently, one hand flicking a day-old newspaper over idly, and he wondered acidly how in six weeks she had managed to make him feel alien in his own house.

He was aware of the child moving closer. She stopped in front of him, studying him with frank curiosity. He looked up at the small face, one corner of his mouth lifting slightly at her candid scrutiny, and as he took in the golden hair and delicate features he found himself pondering how he would deal with the throng of ardent admirers in fifteen years' time. The notion and all that it implied did not surprise him; he acknowledged it with calm detachment, wondering now how he had ever imagined that it could be any other way. He had known that he loved her for longer than he cared to remember, and with some sign that she had softened slightly toward him he would have told her so. Besides which, she had the remarkable power of provoking him to almost uncontrollable fury sometimes, parrying any tentative affectionate overtures with some withering sarcasm. He knew that his pride would not allow him to speak of marriage before he was sure she would not scorn him.

The knowledge that he had handled the situation badly grated remorselessly on him, the more so now he knew her well enough to realize that she would be quite capable of sacrificing them both in some fit of vindictive pique. He knew with equal certainty that if he proposed and she spurned him, the arrogance he found so hard to control would not allow him to ask her again, nor would he let her go. His mouth twisted slightly in sardonic humour as he wondered how, after years of skirting carefully around mentioning anything that could be mistaken for some sort of commitment, he now found himself desperately trying to think of words that might possibly be acceptable to this angelic-faced shrew.

It puzzled him why she would not relent a little. He knew she felt something for him; she was too innocent to respond to him the way she did and allow it to mean nothing. Besides which, there were times when he looked up unexpectedly and caught her studying him without any trace of fear or hatred in her eyes, but with such intensity that for a few moments she would not even realize that he was watching her. As her awareness returned, he would note the guarded wariness shutter her face before she turned away, as though she was desperate not to betray too much of the inner self she protected from him so fiercely.

He thought about the first night he had made love to her here, wondering if even now she would call it that. He should have spoken to her then of his feelings. The longer he left it, the more effective she was becoming at goading him to a retaliatory mood. He had nearly told her, so engulfed with love and tenderness had he felt, but even as he had hesitated, trying to gauge her reaction to any such declaration, he had sensed her freezing beneath him again. Her arms and legs had fallen away from him with swift neatness, as though she believed he might object to any further, unnecessary, contact. He had looked at her, but this time she had not turned away, merely stared past him vacant-eyed at something he knew only she could see, and as he had watched her he had noticed the beginnings of a frown, as though she were desperately trying to focus some inner thoughts.

He had felt the frustrated disappointment overwhelm him as he moved away, the exasperation making him want to get up and slam out, leaving her to languish alone in the virginal innocence she was so reluctant to give up. He knew her pleasure had been no less than his own, indeed, he had taken great care to make it so, and yet she had lain beside him so silent and still that he could have been alone, only the damned misery throbbing between them, suffocating him slowly, forcing him into constant awareness of her presence. He had realized suddenly that she expected him to go now, that she was waiting with noiseless patience for him to leave so that she could cry, and the wounding poignancy had stifled his anger and the gnawing ache that made him want to reach for her again, out of his own need rather than for her comfort.

He could not remember making a conscious decision to stay. He never usually remained longer than the bare minimum of time required for some show of gallantry. Sex was one thing. Trying to sleep with someone clinging to you was something else. But once he had felt her relax and her hand had moved across him in the unconsciously reciprocating gesture of sleep he knew he would not leave. There was nothing cloying about her, and morning had found him still holding on to her with far greater tenacity than she was to him, and he could remember well enough wondering ruefully who, after all, had needed comforting most. He had moved away carefully and got up, knowing that if he stayed longer she would

227

misconstrue his motives and probably be proven right in doing so. He was not sure, either, why he had waited two hours for her to wake so he could speak to her before he left. He had soon enough wished he had not bothered.

He reflected on the sarcasm that morning, and his mouth curved slightly as he tried to reason how she could be so childishly vulnerable and emotionally immature and yet possess such a sharply adult wit that he winced now at the memory of it. It was no doubt Paul Brent's fault for providing her with such an expensive and successful education. He wished at times, with totally ludicrous illogicality, that both her father and Charles Thornton were still alive so he could have the immense satisfaction of killing them both. More so Paul Brent, for ever having left her alone and susceptible that she had been forced to marry Charles Thornton, or to fall into the clutches of someone such as himself, for that matter. He knew well enough that if it had not been he it would have been someone else, and his knuckles whitened and his jaw clenched as he dwelt on the likely treatment she could have expected as payment for the spirited willfulness she could not control. There were times, he knew, when he was certain she would push him too far. . . . He sighed, flicking the paper over again, trying to make some sense of why, when she was giving him such a hard time, he should feel so fiercely protective toward her that he could even despise himself for his own need and for making her yield to it.

He was suddenly aware of a small hand resting tentatively on his knee, breaking his reflective mood, and he looked back at the small face staring solemnly at him. Emma, now that she had managed to regain his undivided attention, withdrew the hand at once and hid it quickly behind her back, and as he noted the gesture he realized drily that the girl was starting to resemble her mother in more than looks alone. He held his hands out slightly, and after hesitating for a moment the child went to him and he lifted her onto his lap, leaning back in the chair with her. As he touched the golden hair he promised himself wryly that her education would be limited to sewing or piano playing or whatever it was young ladies were supposed to excel at. Two intelligent females in the house could be crippling. . . .

Emma sat still for a while and then struggled down and ran to the corner where her toys were stacked. Picking up various items, she started to bring them back to his chair, climbing onto his lap again between journeys, both of them unaware of Maggie's contented smile as she watched the scene.

Sarah entered slowly and suddenly noticed Susan's eyebrows rise with humorous disbelief in her direction and the woman nodded forward as though indicating something amusing.

Sarah turned and stood motionless at the sight of her daughter sitting on Mark's lap, the dark head bent close to the fair curls as he attempted to replace the limbs of Emma's wooden doll. As she watched for a moment, transfixed, she saw her daughter lean forward slightly and kiss his cheek. It was something she was wont to do when in good humor, and she saw him raise the fingers of one dark hand and caress her face casually, without looking away from the broken toy.

Sarah turned away abruptly, reflecting bitterly that he had managed the conquest of yet one more adoring female, and she retorted sharply, "You are wasting your time, she pulls them out again straight away."

He looked up at her, his eyes narrowing slightly as

he sensed her annoyance, and then he lifted Emma down and stood up, walking toward her.

They stared at each other for a few moments, unaware of Susan and Maggie exchanging gratified glances, and then Susan moved forward and looked up at him coyly, saying, "We have been shopping again, Mark; I hope you are not going to scold when you receive this bill." She fluttered her lashes at him, smiling sweetly.

He said drily, "You are wasting your time, Susan, I am your brother, remember?"

She pouted at him and turned to Sarah, saying, "I can see you will have to ask Mark for my tolerance in future," but he cut in harshly, "She cannot, I'm afraid. She finds the name sticks in her throat."

Sarah, feeling the atmosphere starting to charge and slightly ashamed of her uncharitable outburst earlier, said quickly, "I am sorry I was out. I was not expecting you so soon. Have you been waiting long?"

"No. I was merely passing." He stood looking at her, wanting to reach for her, but he simply moved to the door, saying, "I shall be back later. Tell Mrs. Brookes I shall eat here tonight." And then he was gone, the door closing quietly after him.

He watched her over the rim of his wineglass as she churned the food in front of her to a pink, frothy mess, and he asked with exaggerated interest, "Are you going to eat that now?"

She pushed the dish away from her slightly, saying, "I am not hungry."

"Do I have the ability to remove your appetite completely, or is it that you never eat more than a few mouthfuls?"

She looked up meeting his eyes, uncomfortably

aware of his perception, and she said quickly, changing the subject, "Susan wanted me to speak to you about some furniture she bought today." She hesitated, aware that his eyes had hardened slightly and he was looking down at his fingers, toying with the stem of his glass. "It is rather expensive, I am afraid, but she says she is in desperate need of another table. . . ." Her words faded, and as the ensuing silence lengthened she cursed Susan inwardly for involving her in this humiliating toadying.

He looked up, meeting her watchful eyes, and said quietly, "If you want it so. You know I can deny you nothing."

She looked away flustered by his words and the intentness of his gaze, unmarried by mockery for a change, and returned lightly, "Indeed, my lord? I seem to remember something."

"Ah yes, the reference. Do you still want it, Sarah?" His tone was softly inquiring, but she replied with subdued sourness, "I don't think even a glowing recommendation from the earl of Winslade could secure me a position as governess now."

He was silent for a moment, and then he said in a tight voice, "Is it so hard to soften toward me a little, Sarah?"

She was silent also, knowing bitterly how easy it could be, but she merely picked up the spoon again, watching steadily as she mixed the syllabub slowly and said with weary sarcasm, "I am sorry, my lord. I had not realized it was a necessary part of my duties to do so."

He changed the subject abruptly, his tone harsh. "Well, I hear that Joseph Ashton is likely to be taking the brunt of Susan's ever increasing expenditure upon himself soon, poor fool."

Sarah did not look up then and said with mild

surprise, "Do you not mind? She is your sister after all."

"What is to mind? Susan's reputation was shot to pieces before Alex Morton was cold in his grave." His tone was sneeringly cynical, and Sarah studied the stirring spoon, thinking of the emerald necklace, wondering if Susan would be victorious in a few weeks' time.

As though his musings were treading the same path, he said, "I have something for you." His hand went to his pocket, and she saw him draw out a black box. Leaning across the table, he placed it in front of her.

She stared stupidly at it for a few moments, feeling the ice starting to spread slowly, and he said softly, "Are you not going to open it?"

Her fingers went automatically to the lid and she raised it with slow reluctance.

It was a diamond and sapphire bracelet, so magnificent that she knew she could not even begin to realize what it had cost.

One finger went out and touched one of the blue stones. It felt cold, and she withdrew it instantly and heard him say evenly, "Do you not like it?"

"It is very beautiful." She stared at the glowing jewels, mesmerized for a moment by the colored lights sparking from the diamonds, and as she sat entranced she could hear Susan's words regarding her expected gratitude for such gifts. She looked away from it sharply, smiling with brittle sweetness, and said, "What I meant to say, my lord, was that it looks very expensive. I do hope that you find I provide good value for your money." And then she added, with what she knew was self-destructive rashness, "Besides, I am sure if you find me wanting, you could probably return it tomorrow for something less valu-

232

able." She snapped the box shut abruptly with a contemptuous flick of the fingers, aware that he appeared to be studying his glass with fanatical intent. And then he looked up, meeting her eyes steadily, and she saw the satanic rage there, all the more terrifying because he was controlling it so well.

"You should know me well enough by now, Sarah, to know that I can always get the best of any deal." He was holding her gaze easily, and she felt the icy fingers expand, saturating her with a paralyzing chill as the glow in his eyes intensified. "You are looking tired, my dear. You should retire now, I think."

She stared at him numbly for a moment, not wanting to understand, and then she rose and started to move toward the door. As she passed where he sat his hand snaked out gripping her wrist, his fingers biting deep into her flesh.

"You have forgotten tonight's payment. Get it."

She tried to pull away, but his fingers tightened and she gasped with the pain and then turned, picking up the box from the table. She moved trancelike to the door and shut it quietly, and as she heard the glass shatter within, she knew that her hour of reckoning had finally come.

She undressed quickly, slipping the nightgown on with trembling fingers, and the slight sound behind her made her swing around instantly.

He was watching her from the doorway, and she wondered uneasily how long he had been there, but merely said, with viciously assumed coyness, "Such impatience, my lord. I had barely time to undress."

He kicked the door shut and started toward her slowly. Unable to look at him, she turned back to the dressing table. Opening the box, she took out the bracelet and fastened it about her wrist, acutely aware of the unaccustomed weight on her arm. She swung back toward him, noticing that he was now no more than a few paces away, and she lifted her arm, allowing the soft light in the room to fire the stones, and said overbrightly, "I think I should wear it, don't you?"

"Why not." His voice was cool, but meeting his eyes briefly she could see the hellish light glinting furiously, and he continued with treacherous calm, "As you are so determined to be a whore, my dear, I really think you ought to learn a few more tricks."

His hand reached for her and she tried to back away but the dressing table immediately behind blocked any escape. She felt his fingers caress her throat lightly and then hook casually into the top of her shift, and he drew her slowly toward him, saying evenly, "First, whores are not usually so consistently meticulous about covering what they are selling."

She closed her eyes, guessing his intention, wanting to retreat from this nightmare before it stifled her completely, and she stammered, "My lord, I am sorry for my . . ." But the words would not come, and as she attempted desperately to express her remorse, she heard him say with deceptive mildness, "Mark." And then his fingers twisted and she felt the material rend, and he started to tear it slowly, the noise harsh in the silent room.

She managed again in a trembling rush, "I apologize for my ingratitude," but he merely murmured, "Mark," as his fingers ripped lower, and then he was pushing the nightgown from her shoulders and she stood naked before him.

She was acutely conscious of his deliberately lingering appraisal, and she let her head fall further forward, the heavy curtain of hair partially screening her nudity. She felt him moving it away again, and, unable to endure the humiliation further, her hands

234

went up in spontaneous aggression. But the defiance was failing fast, and as she faltered she saw the compassionless cruelty she had glimpsed so often but never before been subjected to darken his eyes humorlessly as he acknowledged her ultimate defeat. His hands moved to her raised wrists with insolent leisure, and he moved them outward and back down to her sides as he said with poisonous mockery, "No. You really must not do that. Well . . . not unless you are asked to; then you could charge more."

She felt his hands slide back to her shoulders and he started to push her slowly down until she was kneeling in front of him, one hand resting on her head and holding her still. He stared down at the bowed, bright head and the shaking form for a few moments, feeling the hair silken beneath his fingers, and then, swearing savagely, pulled her up again and threw her backwards onto the bed in one fluid movement, with such force that she had to grasp swiftly at the covers to prevent herself from bouncing off again.

She lay gasping, trying to breathe, and watched hypnotized as he removed his jacket casually and flung it onto a chair, and then he had turned toward her and was walking toward the bed, and she realized with detached horror that he was not even going to bother undressing.

She looked at him, the pleading vivid in her eyes, but he merely jerked her brutally toward him, holding her hands at her sides. She could feel his clothes grazing her skin as he leaned over her, and then his mouth crushed hers with such barbarity that she tasted the metallic salt of blood and knew her lip had split. His kiss was a calculated insult, and she was aware of his hands loosening his own clothing and positioning her crudely, and she squirmed beneath him and attempted to twist her head away from the pain, but she merely increased it with her efforts, so she lay tense and still, the degradation more wounding than any physical injury.

She could sense the hurting misery building slowly, thickening her throat, and then as she realized that this was to be her final memory of their time together, she tried to swallow, to remove the choking grief before it betrayed her, but her throat had closed and the sob tore from her painfully, making her convulse against him.

His head lifted slightly, and as it did so her arms went up instantly around his neck and she clutched at him hysterically, her head moving in frenzied negation. She could feel him straining against her and she tightened her grip, clinging to him frantically, as though by holding him close she could prevent him shaming her further, and she turned her face into his neck, her tears soaking his hair as the uncontrollable weeping threw her against him in racking spasms.

He relaxed against her slowly and then his hands went up, attempting to disengage himself from the feverish clasp, but she whimpered, pulling him closer, her head starting to shake again, and he let his hands fall away.

She was unaware how long they lay so, but as her sobbing quietened and her arms slackened slightly she felt him duck suddenly so that he was free of her, and, dreading his purpose, she curled her fingers, her nails tearing into his shoulders as she felt her hold loosening.

He caught her flailing hands in his, and, taking them up by her hair, he bent close, stilling her head with both their hands, and whispered, "Hush, it is all right. Be still."

Her own anguish made her oblivious of the hoarseness of his voice and the strange brightness glazing his eyes. He murmured to her and she felt his mouth caress her face ceaselessly as he attempted to soothe her fear.

Her trembling lessened slowly, and one of his hands moved casually to her shoulder, sliding unhurriedly the length of her arm to the bracelet, and she felt his fingers move beneath it, twisting, until she sensed it snap, and then he had flung it backwards without looking at it, and she heard it smash into the mirror. Then his weight lifted, and the door rocked on its hinges as he left.

She got up slowly and walked unsteadily to the dressing table, her arms going about her in a protectively warming caress. She looked down at the shimmering bracelet, then picked it up and studied it impartially, realizing it was probably worth even more than she had at first thought. She opened the box and dropped it in, about to shut it again when she noticed the small card half-hidden in the lid.

She removed it with shaking fingers and read the few words, feeling the desolate tears start to her eyes again. "Belated Birthday Wishes."

There were no names, just the greeting, and she crumpled it in her hand and let it drop to the floor before returning to the bed.

Chapter Fifteen

Sarah sat by the window in the small salon, looking out over the front of the house, watching carriages and strollers pass by in unending procession.

She realized that she felt quite hungry. Turning back into the room, she looked toward Maggie. The young woman's hand was moving slowly, her tongue caught between her teeth, as she diligently copied out the letter to Stewart that Sarah had drafted for her earlier that day.

Sarah started to rise, intending to go to the kitchens herself, and then sank back into the chair slowly as the nausea rose into her throat once again. She closed her eyes, holding her breath until the sensation subsided slightly, and she heard Maggie say quietly, "Are you all right?"

Sarah nodded. "It is just a chill; it leaves me giddy."

Maggie was silent for a moment, and then she said in the same even tone, "When are you going to tell him?"

Sarah's eyes opened and she saw Maggie regarding her steadily. Looking at her hands, she said quietly, "I am not."

Maggie snorted her disgust "Why not? He has a right to know, and you have a right to some support; it is his child too, after all." She regarded Sarah's strained, averted face and the uncharacteristic fullness of her figure and continued calmly, "Besides, he will know next time he lies with you."

"Well, he will never know then, will he?" Sarah stormed, her voice breaking on a sob.

She turned away from Maggie's worried face and back to the window, gazing out sightlessly at the moving scene.

She had not seen or heard from him for nearly three weeks now. And instead of the estrangement's being what she thought she had so desperately desired, it filled her with an aching misery. She had wanted to explain it away as being solely caused by the uncertainty of her future once again, knowing well enough that she would soon be homeless, but she was too wise to the loneliness of separation; she felt as though part of her was lost, and the nights she had come to await with a kind of anticipated dread were now filled with cold seclusion.

She turned in the night, in the chill expanse of the bed, to where he had once lain, moving toward the warmth and comfort he had always provided, and her lack would leave her staring sleeplessly at the ceiling wishing for him to be there as desperately as once she had wished for him to be gone. The knowledge that she loved him was no consolation at all: it merely made the pain more acute with her awareness that had she not been so stubborn she could have kept him with her longer.

She realized now, with bitter self-wisdom, that her virulent displays of dislike and frequent attempts to goad him mercilessly had not been caused so much by her hatred as by her need. She had been desperate for some word that she was more than just another idle pleasure, but he had never spoken. There were never even any meaningless endearments murmured at night in passion, and she was unsure whether to be grateful or sad that he had never flattered her slightly with lies for his own sake.

From the first time she had seen him staring at her at the Cunninghams', Sarah had known with terrified certainty that he, of all men, had the ability to threaten not only her person but also, the warm cocoon of innocence that she had wound about herself so protectively, and she acknowledged now that the intense aggression she had felt toward him had been born not only of her fear of him but also of her fear of herself. She had resented him for forcing her to step from girl to woman so abruptly, certain that it was not what she had wanted. But she realized now that by behaving as a spoiled child she had destroyed by her willfulness what she desired most.

Although she still received various invitations in her own right to social gatherings, she went nowhere. Not that she was depriving herself, by any means; she had never managed to feel at ease in the gay social whirl of London's polite society, even when he was by her side, and now that she was alone she spent almost the entirety of her day indoors, the only break in the monotony being the daily trip to the park with Emma and Maggie.

Susan, she knew, was well aware of the rift between her brother and herself, and Sarah had once or twice nearly found enough courage to ask the older woman if she knew if there was someone else now, but her pride always made her swallow the query unuttered. Susan never volunteered any information about her brother's prolonged absence, tending almost to avoid his mention whenever possible. A few times the older

240

woman had tried to draw Sarah out to some entertainment in the evening, but Sarah had refused all such attempts, knowing well enough that if she relented and went and then met him there with someone else, she would fall to pieces. And now that Susan's expenditures were being met by Joseph Ashton, she did not try to persuade Sarah to accompany her on constant spending sprees as she had once done, and Sarah spent nothing at all now on herself.

She waited daily for Mrs. Brookes or one of the other servants to come and tell her that the household bills were unpaid or that tradesmen would no longer deliver. She wondered uneasily if he would expect her merely to leave without needing to be told, and the knowledge that she had nowhere else to go made the bile rise into her throat again. She thought of Emma and the child she was now carrying, trying to imagine how she would ever cope. She realized dully that the pregnancy must be her fault. Something she had done, or rather omitted to do, that was necessary to prevent such undesirable occurrences. She should have asked Susan to explain; she must have known, after all, as she had had many lovers and yet only the two children of her marriage. She could remember well enough Caroline Brown's telling her, with peeved vexation, that she was usually much more careful about insuring against such unwanted complications, and she had also told her, with calm objectivity, of the pains she had been to when she realized she was pregnant to attempt to rid herself of the baby in the early stages, before Charles Thornton had made it clear he was prepared to make any such endeavors unnecessary. A bottle of gin and a hot bath. Sarah remembered the tale well—drinking gin in a steaming hot bath. She had been sickened by the notion at the time—disgusted—much to Caroline's obvious amusement. But she understood now; it was not so much a matter of callousness as survival.

She had, two nights ago, asked Mrs. Brookes to prepare her water for a hot bath. The undisguised contempt on the housekeeper's face as she uttered, not even bothering to hide the insolence for a change, "Very hot, madam?" had left Sarah in no doubt that the woman had not been fooled for a moment. Sarah had not known whether there was any gin in the house and had not dared ask, so she had taken the half-full decanter of brandy from the library, wondering forlornly if it would work in the same way. She had undressed, but a tentative touch of the burning water had made her rebelt her robe about her and sit for a while, knowing she would be unable to bear the scalding heat. She had stared unflinchingly at the amber-filled glass and watched as the misty steam rose slowly from the murderous water and condensed onto the cold windows in rivulets. But the slowly falling droplets had looked too much like tears, and as her vision blurred her resolution cooled, and with it the water, and she had thrown the soap into the bath despairingly, watching as the water started to milk. Then she had called to the girls to take the bath away, that she had finished.

She now found herself studying Emma with unusual intentness, imprinting the small features on her mind for no good reason. But at night she was not haunted by restless dreams of blue-eyed fair children, but by small boys with bronze-dark hair and eyes the color of the brandy she could not drink. She knew she would never tell him. She could not bear to see the derision in his face at what he would probably think was some deliberate and desperate attempt to keep him with her.

Maggie's voice cut softly into her musings, saying,

"Shall I get you something? A drink, perhaps?"

Sarah shook her head. "No. I think I might lie down for a while." She hesitated for a few moments, not knowing whether any movement might increase the nausea she felt, and as she sat undecided the door opened and Joseph Ashton and Susan entered.

Susan sank breathlessly into the chair next to Sarah and Sarah smiled a welcome, although her spirits had sunk at the sight of them. The last thing she felt like at that precise moment was entertaining.

"Have you time for some tea? I shall ring for some."

"No, thank you, Sarah. We were just passing. We have been shopping." She stared intently at Sarah, a sly smile touching her lips, and one hand went indicatively up to touch her throat.

An emerald necklace sparkled vividly against the lemon muslin of her gown, and Sarah saw one of Susan's lids drop slowly in an almost imperceptible wink.

Sarah stared at the green stones, entranced for a moment by the memories it stirred, and then she said, with forced gaiety and suitably surprised admiration, "What a beautiful necklace, Susan. Is it new?"

Susan turned toward Joseph Ashton, and smiling sweetly, said, "Joseph bought it for me. I really think it is a bit ostentatious for day wear, but I so wanted to show it to you." She broke off suddenly, noting the young woman's strained, pale countenance, and peering at her intently, said, "Are you well, Sarah? You look . . ."

Sarah stammered quickly into her words, not wanting the older woman's observation to become too perceptive. "Yes. I am fine. Just a slight headache, that is all."

Maggie snorted loudly and rose suddenly, saying,

"I shall see if Emma is awake yet," and banged the door shut as she left.

Susan looked toward Sarah, her dark brows raising. "What is the matter with Maggie? She looked positively fuming."

Sarah smiled nervously. "She misses Stewart, I think. That is all." Susan, studying her face keenly now, said quietly, "Have you seen Mark yet?"

Sarah knew that Joseph was also well aware of the rift between her and Mark by the unusual and marked omission of his friend's name whenever he visited, and she shook her head briefly, attempting to turn the conversation to some safer topic. But Susan cut in encouragingly, "Don't worry, Sarah, I am sure he will come soon," and then added, laughing slyly, "After all, Mark is not renowned for his powers of abstinence . . ." before she halted, flushing hotly, aware that she had again spoken without thought.

Sarah laughed with uncommon shrillness and simply said, "I am sure," and added quickly and brightly, "Is Joanna in London yet?"

"No. She will be arriving soon with Lady Winton. I just cannot believe that I am to have a twenty-two-year-old as a son-in-law soon. It makes me feel so old." She looked toward Joseph Ashton coyly, waiting for him to make some flattering refutation of this remark, and he obligingly murmured something soothing, his eyes fixed on Sarah's ashen face.

He was not sure what had caused this estrangement between his friend and the young woman, but whatever it was he knew Mark Tarrington was suffering equally painful withdrawal symptoms. He had been three days in a drunken stupor at his club, not even bothering to return to his residence at night, and all Joseph's tentative endeavors to extract some explanation for this inebriated excess had merely resulted in his nearly being knocked senseless for his pains. Mark now spent the best part of his time journeying between London and Surrey, for no more apparent reason than to waste as much time as possible.

Joseph watched Sarah's face, noticing the pallor and the forced smile. She obviously thought that there was someone else now. He wondered whether he should speak, tell her that to his certain knowledge there had been no other woman in the earl's life for months past. His memory dwelt on their trips to town in Surrey, remembering Mark Tarrington sitting moodily at the card table all night, ignoring the more interesting aspects of diversion to be had at the establishment. The scowling intensity with which he had refused to be drawn away from the gambling hall had mystified Joseph at the time, even to the extent that he had once, while disappearing up the stairs with a buxom blonde, shouted tauntingly to his friend, "What is the matter with you, anyway? Are you in love?" and watched amazed as he had stormed out before it was even ten-thirty.

He smiled to himself. He had been nearer the truth than he could ever have imagined, and it looked as though Sarah's emotions were of like intensity. He knew he should tell her, lighten the misery slightly, but some uncharacteristic vindictiveness stopped him. Not that he relished Sarah's unhappiness. It was his too handsome and too wealthy friend who needed to sweat a little. It would certainly be a novel experience for him, anyway, he thought drily. Besides, he had not forgiven him yet for not being more open with him about his intentions towards Sarah. He was still quite interested in her himself, and he ridiculed himself for not having spoken to her sooner of his own ardent feelings. Things might have been different . . .

He looked toward Susan and sighed. She was

245

beautiful, it was true, but unfortunately he knew he could never be sure just how many ways she was dividing her charms. Her trilling voice cut into his musings at that point and he rose, smiling, noticing that she was indicating that they were leaving.

"Sarah has a terrible headache, Joseph. She is going to lie down. Come. I really think there is time for a little more shopping before we return home for the evening." She smiled suggestively at him, ignoring the horrified look that had accompanied her mention of a further spending spree, and pulled him playfully toward the door.

Sarah leaned back in the chair, savoring the silence for a moment, and then stood up slowly, determined to rest in her room.

As she neared the door Samuel entered, saying, his face enigmatic, "There is a gentleman to see you, madam."

Sarah's spirits soared for a moment, before she realized that it was unlikely Mark would be announced in his own home. "Who is it, Samuel?"

"He would not say, madam, but he says it is extremely important." Samuel's face registered slightly supercilious indifference, and Sarah wondered whether he believed she had another lover in his master's prolonged absence.

"I have shown him into the drawing room, madam."

"Thank you, Samuel. I shall be there directly."

Samuel moved silently away, the door closing noiselessly, and Sarah hesitated for a moment, trying to scour her mind for some clue as to who it could be. Then, shrugging to herself, she moved forward again.

The man was tall and fair, and as he turned toward her she held her breath; he had an almost girlish beauty about his smooth face. His eyes were a wide greyish-blue, and his whitish hair was thick and straight. He looked just slightly older than she herself, and he smiled at the sight of her, and yet there was a chilling hardness about his features that contrasted so sharply with the fairness that it made Sarah freeze suddenly.

She thought she recognized him slightly and searched in her mind for some clue as to the identity that lay just beyond the boundaries of her memory, and as she stared at him the realization broke in on her suddenly that he resembled herself.

The dawning horror of what the notion indicated made her retreat slightly, and she knew by the unpleasant smile that he had guessed her thoughts.

He extended his hand, saying, "Mrs. Thorton. I am Peter Drew."

She stared at him stupidly for a moment, and then mumbled a formal greeting, waiting for him to speak again.

As though sensing her impatience, he was contrarily silent for a while, and then he continued quietly. "You do not know me, of course, but I believe we have a common relative." He smiled then, saying, "My choice of words leaves much to be desired perhaps. A child of about two?"

His voice was insinuatingly soft, and Sarah uttered through frozen lips, "Where is Caroline?"

He laughed coarsely. "How should I know?" Last time I saw her, she was raising her skirts around Whitechapel for anyone with the price of a gin."

He laughed at her shocked incredulity at these words, and then said with venomous quiet, "You, however, have done remarkably much better for yourself."

"Are you . . . are you the child's father?"

His smile deepened with genuine amusement. "Not

247

I. My brother James had the pleasure. . . ." He laughed then again at his unintentional witticism, and Sarah cut in quickly.

"Where is he?"

"Dead these past two years. Stupid bastard was killed in a duel over the slut." His mouth curled with the strength of his cynical despising and he continued again with mild amusement. "No. I am young . . . ?" He hesitated questioningly, and Sarah returned numbly, "Emma."

"I am young Emma's uncle. I thought it was about time I put in an appearance to see my kith and kin."

"What do you want?" Sarah's voice was an icy whisper.

"What else should I want but money?" His face was ugly now, twisted savagely with the strength of his purpose. "I am in dire trouble. I have to get away quickly or I shall be killed for my debts, and I do not see why I should not turn my rather interesting information to some benefit. I am quite sure that the Earl of Winslade would not like it noised abroad that his lady love is in fact mother to some whore's bastard and rearing it as her own." He smiled maliciously at Sarah's shock and added, "I shall not be too greedy. Just enough to get me clear of England and set up abroad somewhere."

"I have no money."

He looked at her threateningly, his eyes slitted, and she whispered again, "It is true—I have no money of my own. He owns the house and everything in it. I have nothing of my own."

"You are lying. All mistresses have an allowance. You must have something. Some jewelry I could sell." His eyes raked Sarah's figure for anything of worth, and he noticed incredulously that she wore no jewelry at all.

Sarah hesitated, remembering the bracelet in her room and the gold necklet she always wore beneath her bodice, but she said quickly, "I have nothing. If I had money of my own do you think I would be here?"

He laughed again then, as though she had uttered something uncommonly funny, and then said spitefully, "Well, I advise you to get some. Two thousand pounds by tonight, or I shall make sure that before I go under the whole of London knows the truth about the earl's lightskirt and her brat." He stared at her for a few moments, as though wondering if she were really without any funds of her own, and then added viciously, "It is all over town the earl is besotted with you—ask him for money."

Sarah laughed then with bitter humor. "Well, I am surprised, as you seem to know so much of the earl, that you do not also know that he has not been here for nearly three weeks. His protection is finished now, and no doubt I soon shall be in the same sorry financial state as yourself."

She could see some of the smug self-assurance wiping slowly from his face at her words, and he looked uneasy for a few moments, as though uncertain whether to believe this new information or not. Then he said vehemently, "It makes no difference. The earl's reputation—such as it is—" he sneered, "could still be dragged through the kind of muck that will stick forever."

He stared at her spitefully for a few moments and then said, "Jamaica Wharf tonight, at ten o'clock. It is your last chance—and mine," he added almost ruefully, and then he strode to the door, saying over his shoulder, "I shall let myself out."

Sarah stood petrified for a few minutes after he left, unaware that the door had reopened and Samuel was watching her.

Sarah turned to go, starting as she noticed him behind her, and he said quietly, "Is everything all right, madam?"

She nodded slowly, not knowing what else to do, and then, becoming aware of the sympathetic query in the man's face and voice, asked haltingly "Do . . . do you know where the earl is residing at present, Samuel?"

The elderly man shuffled uneasily for a few moments. He was not sure what the problem was between his master and the young woman, and he did not want to incur his legendary wrath by giving out his current address to perhaps a newly discarded mistress.

Sarah, seeing the man's obvious embarrassment and guessing it was probably caused by the fact that Samuel was well aware that Mark was staying with a new mistress now, started toward the door, not wanting her distress to be apparent to any of the servants.

Samuel, moved by the girl's dignified wretchedness, said hastily, "I could probably get a message to him, if you like."

Sarah hesitated for a moment and then sat down at the desk. She wrote a brief note, simply asking him to visit. She did not put his name to it and merely signed it Sarah. She looked at it for a moment and then added Thornton, with an acid smile, just in case it confused him.

Sarah sat alternately flicking the pages of the journal idly and watching the clock as the hands traveled slowly around the smooth ivory face.

It was nearly nine o'clock.

She fluttered the pages of the journal in her lap, swallowing her fears. She knew Samuel had taken the note. She had seen him return to the house hours earlier, at five o'clock.

She rose quickly and went to the bell pull, and he entered almost immediately.

"Samuel, did you manage to deliver the note I gave you to the earl?"

"Not personally madam. I left it at the residence he is using at present. Simmons, the butler, said they were expecting him back quite soon."

Sarah merely smiled and nodded at the man's uneasy countenance, indicating that that was all.

She sank back into the chair. So. He was not intending to come. The knowledge made her heart thud dully in her throat for a moment, and then she felt the humiliation of rejection being replaced by consoling spite. If Peter Drew had been serious in his threats to discredit him because of his association with Emma and herself, he could not blame her for not attempting to warn him of it.

She flicked the pages of the journal feverishly in her agitation and then threw it despairingly onto the floor. She let her head fall back against the cushioned chair back. She felt so tired. It was early still, and yet she had begun to feel weary most days long before it was time to retire.

She closed her eyes, not knowing whether it was worth waiting any longer; she might just as well go to her room and rest. She knew he would not come now. She could feel the fatigue weighting her lids, and she let the drowsiness possess her for a few moments before turning her head toward the clock once again. Nine-fifteen. It would soon be too late, anyway. She studied the gold hands, watching the numerals blur slowly into oblivion as her lids dropped once more.

Her senses strained and she moved her head restlessly, trying to regain the comfort of sleep, but it was tormentingly elusive and she opened her eyes slowly, staring at him with the unwavering frankness of new awakening. Control returned, and she pushed herself hastily upright in the chair, her eyes still locked with his.

He was sitting opposite, leaning back in the chair, his elbows resting lightly on the arms, watching her.

She was not prepared for the sheer weight of relief or depth of emotion at seeing him again that made her want to rise instinctively and rush to him, seeking the security he had always provided and she had readily abused. But she sat unmoving, staring openly, almost avariciously at him, until a gratified, acknowledging curve to his mouth made her look away hurriedly. Her still drowsy state hooded her caution further, and she stammered, unable to hide the reproach, "I did not think you would come . . . have I interrupted something . . . ?" Aware that it sounded prying, her fingers went to twist the absent ring before she continued more slowly, "I would not have asked you to come but . . ."

He cut into her muddled explanation, saying soothingly, "I have only just received your message. I have been in Surrey for a few days."

Sarah looked up, surprised. "At Winslade Hall?"

He nodded slowly, his eyes never leaving her face, and she was conscious of his scrutiny moving slowly across her features and the length of her form with such intensity that she thought he must have forgotten what she looked like.

She met his eyes briefly, searching for some spark of desire in the lingering appraisal, but there was nothing; he was keeping his expression and eyes shuttered.

She looked away, swallowing the disappointment that threatened her regained composure, and could not refrain from asking wistfully, "How is everyone? Your aunt and Mrs. Davis and Joanna—is she home yet?"

"No. She will be coming to London next week with Lady Winton to start preparations with her mother for her come out." She heard the derisive note in his voice as he mentioned the event, and it dawned on her slowly that she would probably never see the girl again, and she stared sightlessly at him for a moment as her mind dwelt on the security of Joanna's future life, before looking away, too conscious of his perceptiveness.

He was watching her closely, and he said evenly, "Do you not resent Joanna's having everything in life that she desires at sixteen, when you had nothing at eighteen?"

She frowned, vague surprise showing on her face as she attempted to comprehend his attitude, and she remarked guilelessly, "Why should my misery make me begrudge Joanna her happiness?" She colored slightly, wishing she had chosen her words more carefully.

"What would make you happy, Sarah?" His tone was mild, but she knew he expected a reply, so she merely shrugged dismissively, laughing uneasily, aware that she had rendered herself too vulnerable, and said shortly, "I am not sure that I know anymore." She started to change the subject hastily, but he was unyielding, asking again, "What did you want when you were sixteen, then?"

She studied her hands, and then a slight, secretive smile started to curve her mouth as her mind turned inwards, stripping away the seemingly endless, desolate years that separated her from her carefree youth. She thought of the Marston Academy for Young Ladies where she had been a pupil and of the girls she had known there. She remembered Betty Gillespie, her closest friend, and the way they spent idle hours discussing the handsome and eligible men they were sure they would one day marry, who were destined to fill their futures with security and joy, and as she wondered now if Betty had ever realized her ambitions, she murmured in a softly dreaming tone, her eyes glazing, "The same as most young girls, I suppose . . . a handsome prince on a white horse."

He was silent for a moment, watching the childlike innocence she usually protected so fervently from him, pure on her face as she drew the enchantment out to its limit.

"Why will you not settle for a handsome earl?" His tones was light, almost bantering, and as the words penetrated her distant senses, she looked up quickly, sure he was ridiculing her reverie. But the casualness was belied by the expression in his eyes, and as she stared at him uncertaintly he added with a smile and coaxing persuasion, "I could manage the white horse."

She looked away then quickly, confused as to what to read into the words, and then her eyes focused on the clock and it evoked a more recent memory, and she jumped up exclaiming, "It is a quarter to ten." She had completely forgotten the reason for his visit, and she turned to him, saying feverishly, "I almost forgot. It will be too late soon."

He stood also, frowning at her obvious distress, and she started to explain raggedly. "A man was here today. His name is Peter Drew and he is Emma's uncle. His brother was her father."

She hesitated, noticing the ruthless narrowing of his eyes at her words, and then continued in a whisper, "He wants two thousand pounds or he said he will let the truth about her parentage be known and he will discredit you because of your association with us."

She watched his face with wary intent, expecting to

see some sign of fury, but the gold of his eyes darkened slightly, and then she saw the hard, satisfied twist to his mouth as he gazed at something past her, and she said in a horrified murmur, "Do you not care?"

He looked back at her steadily, his eyes holding hers for a moment, and she could see the heat starting to burn as he said slowly, "Very much so." And then he turned away, continuing, "I had not expected after all my fruitless efforts to find them that they would be obliging enough to come to me . . . well, not quite so soon at least." There was definite contentment in the words, and Sarah stared at him bemused for a moment and then asked, frowning, "What do you mean? Have you been looking for them, then?"

"Of course . . . well, not personally. I have been trying to find Caroline Brown since you first told me of the matter. It seems she has disappeared into London's underworld somewhere." He turned back to her then, and noting the bewilderment in her face said softly, "You did not really believe that they would simply remain silent about this tale once your association with me became common knowledge, did you? It always had to be worth money to them. I had hoped to find them before they realized the fact."

Sarah saw his eyes narrow again and his mouth curl slightly as he added thoughtfully, "Not that I was expecting an uncle . . . it makes me wonder just how many of them there could be. . . ."

He looked at her anxious face and his expression softened into a reassuring smile. "It is all right. I don't mind. This matter had to be dealt with at some time. It is better now. . . ."

Sarah looked up then, asking in a hopeless tone, "But why did you bring me here if you knew it would provoke them to blackmail you?"

His eyes met hers and she noticed that they looked uncommonly dark, and as she stared at him she realized irrelevantly that his tan had faded slightly.

"Why indeed?" His words were so soft that she had to strain to catch them, and then he was moving slowly toward her as he added, his tone harshening, "No doubt something to do with my arrogance and your acid tongue."

She did not realize she had retreated from him until her hand went behind her to steady herself as she knocked into the chair. He stopped at once and she saw his mouth distort before he turned sideways and said tautly, "Where were you to take the money?"

"He said Jamaica Wharf at ten o'clock tonight."

He nodded briefly and started toward the door, and Sarah, still dazed by her stupidity, said, "What will you do?"

"I will deal with it. Do not worry further about it. Go to bed now."

"But . . ." She realized suddenly that he was leaving already and said rashly, "Will you come back later?"

He halted, his hand on the doorknob, and said without turning, "Do you want me to?"

But she was silent for too long, and as the door closed she whispered, "Yes."

Peter Drew stood half-hidden in the gloomy patchwork of shadow.

He stamped his feet briskly, trying to warm them; it was late May and yet the night felt damp and chill. Then he froze, abruptly aware of the noise he was creating.

He knew it was late and wondered uneasily whether she would come; not that he was expecting her to arrive personally. She would probably send some friend or servant.

His hand went to the smoothness of cold steel in his pocket and he stroked the razor sharpness with soothing devotion for a few minutes. He merged further into the shadows as he heard a noise, knowing too well that his pale hair made him an obvious target.

Two drunken revelers passed unsteadily, and he wrinkled his nose in disgust as the permeating stench of the area and the oily water splashing softly below pervaded his nostrils. His thoughts returned to Sarah, and his mouth curled as he wondered if she would try to cross him in this. If the slut thought he was bluffing . . . he hesitated, swallowing hard at the thought of the moneylenders who were out for his skin, and he cursed his rank stupidity at the sudden perception that he could probably have sold this information to them. They would certainly not have balked at the use of extortion.

He did not want to think of Mark Tarrington, either. The reputation preceded the man, and he shuffled restlessly, cursing bitterly that the bitch had not become involved with some equally wealthy peer with a less successsful dueling record. If she told the earl what the money was for he could be in bad trouble still, not that the two thousand pounds would worry the earl, but the principle that he was being fleeced was sure to. He dismissed the thought, however. It was unlikely that he would know anything about this sordid little tale; it was not the sort of thing an aspiring mistress would be likely to bring to light when acquiring such an influential protector. Nevertheless, he cursed his own idiocy again that he had not tried to bargain this information for at least more time to pay.

"Drew."

He swung around skittishly at the sound of his

name, scanning the inky darkness with slitted eyes. And then he saw him.

He stepped out leisurely from the night and into a shaft of pale moonlight so that he was visible, and Peter Drew laughed with nervous harshness.

"Well, well. My lord earl. I am flattered you should have come in person."

His brash words could not hide the slight tremor in his voice, and as he saw the flash of whiteness in the dark face, he knew that Mark Tarrington was acknowledging his weakness.

He walked toward him slowly until he was but a few paces away, and as the earl's sword arm raised slowly, he noticed the dull glint of steel and uttered in a whining tone, "My lord, I am unarmed."

He saw the smile deepen as the other man said softly, his voice rueful mockery, "Is that my fault?"

He allowed the point of the rapier to rest lightly against the fair man's throat and said with silky menace, "You should have come directly to me with this matter."

Peter Drew laughed uneasily, the sound abrasive in the still air. "Why? What is the brat to you?" He halted abruptly, feeling the blade nick, and then continued, a slightly confident edge honing his voice. "So. And she thinks you care nothing for her. The notorious earl of Winslade tamed by an innocent blond."

Mark Tarrington moved the blade slowly higher until it rested almost imperceptibly against the side of the other man's eye, and the laughter ceased at once. The earl queried softly, "Who else knows of this?"

"No one, except for Caroline Brown."

"Where is she now?"

"I already told your . . ." He yelped in pain as the blade cut slowly into his flesh, and he started again.

"She is a penny whore down in Whitechapel. She is riddled with pox and does not even know who she is let alone a child she has not spoken of for nearly two years."

Mark Tarrington nodded slowly and then said, "Your brother?"

"Dead in a duel," and added sneeringly, "He loved her true, more fool him."

Mark Tarrington's smile flashed white again, and he said smoothly, "So, that leaves just you."

The implication was crystal, and Peter Drew flustered desperately, "You do not think I would be fool enough to come here without telling anyone, do you?" But his tone was strident with fear, and he continued almost despairingly, "Besides, what is two thousand pounds to you? You could spare it without noticing its loss."

The rapier moved slowly again so that the cut intensified and Peter Drew stood rigid with shock and pain, not daring to move lest the blade take out his eye.

His hand went to his pocket and he felt the heaviness, not knowing whether he dared use it.

He lunged suddenly sideways so he was free of the taunting agony for a second, his hand coming up savagely in a vicious swipe, but the earl had moved backwards instinctively at the fair man's first tentative movement and the knife merely grazed his shoulder before the rapier, flashing violently sideways, had knocked the knife from Peter Drew's hand, sending it spinning high into the air.

Peter Drew heard the splash as it hit the water, and he started to back hastily away, but the rapier was under his chin again and he stopped abruptly, the sweat soaking his fair hair to lank strands.

"You cannot kill me. What would she say when she

found out; I am little Emma's uncle, after all." His voice was shrill with fear, and Mark Tarrington smiled easily, saying nothing for a moment.

"Where were you intending running to? Europe?"

"No. Anywhere. I do not care, as long as it is out of England for a while." His voice was filled with unconcealed pleading now, and the earl said almost pleasantly, "No. Not for a while. You go for good."

Peter Drew nodded vigorously, acutely conscious that the blade was once again resting lightly below his eye.

"I have a merchant ship leaving for the West Indies on the morning tide. You can have passage on that." And then Mark added, with mock concern, "Is that all right?"

Peter Drew, now that his fear of imminent death had passed, smiled sardonically, saying, "How very convenient. A passenger on one of your own ships. Am I to have any money?"

The earl's head moved slowly in negation, and Peter Drew's lip curled suddenly. "I could have spread this muck in any case, but I did not. You owe me something." His teeth bared viciously into a snarl.

Mark Tarrington said evenly, "You are right, of course," and he started to draw the rapier leisurely downward, leaving a bloody streak in its wake.

Peter Drew's hand flashed up disbelievingly to the wound. He pulled his hand away and stared mesmerized at the sticky, dark stain and screamed, "My face."

Mark Tarrington murmured, "Yes, too pretty by far. It matches your character more equally now, I think. Besides, should you decide to return in a year or so, it will make my task of recognizing you that much simpler."

He smiled with malicious satisfaction and then

said, "Come. I will show you where the ship is docked."

They walked in silence for about ten minutes, Mark Tarrington slightly behind the fair man, and on nearing a massive trader being prepared actively for impending departure he shouted up suddenly, "Get Abe Masters. Tell him it is Winslade."

A voice above bellowed something indistinct, and within a few minutes a large, pale oval frayed with unshaven blackness appeared and a grinning voice called down disbelievingly, "Mark? What are you doing here? Not reduced to pleasure-seeking along the waterfront, surely?"

The earl laughed, saying, "I have a passenger for you this trip." He indicated the man at his side contemptuously, and the big man shrugged easily, shouting, "All right. If you want. Tell him to come aboard."

Peter Drew started to moved slowly forward, and then he swung around and raged like a child in a tantrum, "I will not forget this, Tarrington," and his hand went instinctively to the ragged mark on his face.

Mark Tarrington merely grinned whitely, murmuring, "No. I did not expect you would." He watched as the fair head disappeared from sight, and then, staring hard at the looming hulk of the man above, said with slow deliberation, "I should imagine this trip could be rough. In fact, I am quite sure it will be. That last cargo, Abe, if it should be damaged in transit, it would not bother me overmuch."

They stared at each other in silence for a few moments through the shadowy gloom, and then Abe Masters laughed boomingly and said, "You're right, of course—cursèd weather," and he waved frantically for a moment before Mark Tarrington turned and disap-

261

peared into the night.

He entered the house silently, not knowing why he had come back. She would be asleep now. He stood unmoving for a moment, throwing his head back slightly, concentrating on something else, and then he walked to the library door.

Sarah jumped up as he opened the door, and they stared at each other for a moment before he walked into the room, saying, "You should be in bed." He halted and made a small gesture, almost to himself, as though indicating he had said the wrong thing, but she moved toward him slowly, her eyes fixed on the rent in his coat. Noticing the dark stain as she moved closer, she made a soft exclamation and rushed to him, saying, "You are hurt."

Her hands went to the wound tentatively, and she asked hastily, "What happened?"

"Nothing. It is only a scratch." He looked down at the golden head close to his face, feeling the warmth of her through his chilled clothes, and his hands clenched momentarily before he moved her firmly aside, saying, "Go to bed now, Sarah," and then, without looking at her, said again, "Go to bed. I shall be leaving soon."

Sarah swallowed hard. He was rejecting her and she could feel the hurt rising in her throat. "I am not tired now. I do not want to sleep. Have you killed him?" Her question was barely a whisper, and he sank into the chair by the fire where he had sat earlier that evening and said, "Why? Would it matter if I had?"

She bit her lip, frowning slightly. "No. I do not think so," and then added quickly, "but he is Emma's uncle."

He laughed shortly and she looked at him, saying uncertaintly, "What is funny?"

"Nothing. Just something Drew said."

Neither of them spoke for a few moments, and, frightened that he might in fact leave without further conversation, she broke into the quiet abruptly. "Where is Peter Drew?"

"He is leaving on the morning tide for the West Indies."

"Will he come back again?"

"No."

"But if he did in a year or so?" Her voice was raw. She was frightened. Nervous of what could happen to herself and Emma if he returned in a few years' time when she was alone and vulnerable. She would have no one to protect her from his malice then. The notion that he might be able to take Emma from her, perhaps legally, made her blood freeze suddenly, and she whispered again, "But if he came back in a year or so, when I am alone?"

She saw his eyes darken and knew he understood the implication, and he said, his voice harsh, "He will not come back, and if by some miracle he did, I would deal with the matter again."

She was silent, wondering what to deduce from this statement, and, unable to bear the uncertainty of their relationship further, asking haltingly, "Am I . . . shall I be leaving here soon?"

She had moved closer as she was speaking, watching her fingers intertwining in her agitation, and as she drew level with his chair his hand came out slowly and he caught one of her wrists lightly, his thumb moving lingeringly across her pulse, and he said softly, "What makes you think so?"

His touch burned relentlessly, and she stopped her pacing immediately, standing ummoving by his chair.

He started to draw her slowly backwards so that she was slightly in front of him again, and then turned her, twisting her slightly off balance, so that she fell into his lap.

Her hands went automatically against his shoulders and she felt him wince as she touched the wound. Her hands dropped away at once, and she whispered, "I'm sorry. Did I hurt you?"

He stared at her, noting the overt concern in her face, and then he laughed sardonically for a few moments and seemed about to speak, but he merely murmured, "No matter," and pulled her back against him, his arm tightening around her, holding her close. She was aware of his hand winding into her hair, moving caressingly, and she felt herself relax, her eyes closing as she luxuriated in his nearness. She wanted to turn toward him, to have him kiss her, but she remained still, scared that if she moved he might try to put her away from him again. And with this unwanted thought came also the one that she was still no nearer to knowing what her future was to be. She wanted to ignore the uncertainty, to merely savor the joy of the moment, but she heard herself say again, hesitantly, "Am I to leave here soon?"

He was silent for a long moment, and then he repeated softly, "What makes you think so?"

She sat up slightly, too conscious for his touch, and said slowly, frowning with the intensity of searching for the right words, "It seems my . . . it seems there is no further need for me to stay. You have not visited for so long that I thought perhaps you would expect me to leave."

"I thought that was what you wanted, Sarah . . . to be free of me. Was it not?"

His tone was goading, and she nearly screamed that it was the last thing she wanted, but instead she said, controlling her voice with difficulty, "I have nowhere to go."

She could feel the traitorous heat behind her eyes, and she let her head fall further forward so that her hair shielded her misery from him, and she heard him say quietly, "The house is yours now. I have had the deeds made over into your name. You have no need to leave."

She did not move for a moment, unable to believe what she had heard, and then she turned toward him and said stupidly, "How would I afford to run a house like this?"

"I will maintain it still."

She searched his face, unable to understand how the desire, brilliant at the back of his eyes, could contrast so sharply with what she had just heard.

She stood up abruptly, backing away from him as his meaning pierced her dulled senses, and she laughed bitterly and said with a return to sarcasm, "Your generosity is certainly boundless, my lord. I had not expected any such magnanimous payoff. You really should have let me have the reference I asked for; it would have proved so much more economical."

She turned swiftly, aware that he had risen as though to stop her, but she ran, slamming the door behind her, and sped to her room. She leaned against the door, her hand going automatically to the key, and then she laughed with despairing self-ridicule. There was no key, and certainly no need to use one, he had made that quite clear. She breathed deeply for a few moments, steadying her ragged nerves, and the back of her hand wiped shakily across her wet face. Then she walked calmly to the wardrobe and pulled out her old trunk, and after looking at it for a few minutes she lifted the lid and started to pack her things.

Mark Tarrington sank back into the chair, his head falling forward into his hands. He studied his nails, examining them intently, and wondered whether, if he went to her now, the sight of him in the bedroom would send her into some hysterical fit. He dwelt on the feel of her in his arms and knew that he had been right in his guess. His thoughts turned once more to the incident upstairs when he had thrown her violently onto the bed, and his mouth hardened and he turned his head away slightly in self-concept. She obviously had no intention of telling him, and he had been fool enough to think she had broken first and sent for him to do so; that it might make her meet him halfway. He would have come tomorrow, anyway; he knew that with unwavering certainty. Now that he had seen her again, he was not sure how he had managed to stay away for so long. He smiled bitterly; she was still winning every round easily.

His shoulder was throbbing dully, and he flexed his arm gingerly, standing up. He hesitated at the door, uncertain whether to risk going to her, and as he did so he acknowledged with rueful self-mockery that not only was she ruining his self-confidence, but that after years of talking his way into the affections of countless remembered females, now, when it mattered most, he could not quite seem to get the words right. He sighed; time enough in the morning to sort this mess out once and for all, and he let himself quietly out onto the damp night.

Chapter Sixteen

Maggie sat staring at the empty cup sightlessly, and as it focused she moved one finger to rub absently at a dark stain on the rim before her head fell forward into her hands and she felt the tears stinging her eyes again.

Her hands moved agitatedly in her hair as she wondered what on earth had gone wrong. It was obvious that Mark Tarrington was in love with Sarah and that she was also in love with him, despite any protestations to the contrary. Maggie tried to imagine Sarah coping alone with two young children, and her head dropped further forward.

Sarah had left with Emma that morning before five o'clock, her face ashen but set with unshakable determination, and no pleas or tears from Maggie to reconsider or at least let her accompany them had made any difference. Sarah had been terrifyingly calm. She had simply wished Maggie well in her married life, promised to write when she could, and then waved as the carriage moved out of sight, as though they were embarking on some pleasant outing.

Maggie thought of Sarah and she began to shake her head. Sarah had no idea. She still had the unspoiled innocence of a girl just out of the school-room, despite what she had been through. Maggie was certain that she really believed she could rake together some sort of life for herself and the children out of the debris of her past. Sarah had made her promise not to tell the earl where she was bound first, and the sapphire eyes had glazed suddenly and she had murmured, "There will be no need, of course. I doubt he will bother coming here again." But she had made Maggie give her word nevertheless, much to Maggie's tortured dismay.

She looked at the empty cup, brushing the back of her hand across her eyes, and as she did so she heard the voices in the hall and heard him say something to Samuel. She rubbed frantically at her red eyes, her stomach writhing painfully. She heard him enter and greet her, and she mumbled something incoherent in reply.

"Where is Sarah? Not in bed still surely?" His voice was mild, and when Maggie did not answer he said conversationally, "Is she shopping with Susan?"

Maggie shook her head, but she did not look up, and he gazed at the bowed head and then scanned the room quickly, saying, his voice grating slightly now, "Where is the child? Where is Emma?"

Maggie was silent, merely shaking her head slowly, and he stared at the dark curls for a few minutes in rigid disbelief. Then he turned, and she heard him take the stairs two at a time and the bedroom door slam back against the wall as he knocked it open.

He walked slowly into the room. It was immaculate, as though she had tidied it carefully to look as it had when she had first arrived. He moved to the wardrobe, opening one door almost casually. All her new clothes were there. He closed it with one finger, walking toward the dressing table, and stared down at the neat array of bottles and brushes. The black jewelry box was set out in the middle. He lifted the lid and gazed at the bracelet for a few moments before his attention was drawn to the small gold circlet he had never before known her to remove lying, perfectly formed, to one side. He picked it up, his thumb brushing the glossy length of it, and then he dropped it into his pocket as his other arm came out savagely, smashing everything else to the floor. He turned and went back downstairs almost leisurely and into the small salon where Maggie still sat in numb misery.

He pulled the chair opposite away from the table and sat down and said quietly, "Where is she?"

The note of mild inquiry in his voice emboldened Maggie to look up and meet his eyes, but the blaze behind the gold made her turn away hastily, and she stammered, "I don't know." She knew the lie was unconvincing, and he said almost pleasantly, "Maggie?" but she merely shook her head slowly.

He was silent for a moment, and then said with quiet friendliness, "Stewart tells me you two want to be married quite soon."

Maggie looked up then and whispered, "Yes," and sat, not meeting his eyes, her bottom lip caught between her teeth.

"Where were you and Stewart intending to live?" His voice was casual, as though he was quite genuinely interested, and as she met his eyes and noticed the expression there she mouthed, "You would

269

not . . ."

He said nothing, merely raising his eyebrows slightly, his eyes holding hers steadily, and she murmured brokenly, "You bast . . ." She halted sharply as it dawned on her whom she was in fact speaking to, and her face drained of color, but he simply sat watching her, his mouth curving slightly in a humorless smile.

She let her head sink forward slowly, whispering defeatedly, "She has gone to the dowager first for some money so she can get away." She looked up then at him, her eyes and voice flaring. "She has gone to try to borrow money from your aunt so that she can try and make a life for herself and the . . ." She halted, chewing her lip again, and then added despairingly, "Afterward I think she was probably going to throw herself on her stepfather's mercy." Her lips curled at the obvious absurdity of the suggestion. But he had risen, and she could see he was smiling now, satisfied, some of the panic gone from his eyes, and he murmured, almost to himself, "Has she indeed," and then he turned back sharply, saying, "When did she leave?"

"Five o'clock." His hand went automatically to his watch and he studied it intently for a few moments, and Maggie knew he was trying to estimate how far she would have traveled.

He started to the door and Maggie called out to him wretchedly, "You would not really have thrown Stewart and me out, would you?" Her voice quavered on a shrill, disbelieving note, and as he turned her way and smiled, she realized the truth.

Maggie stared hard at the closed door for a few minutes before she lifted the cup in front of her and

270

hurled it viciously after him, screaming, "Bastard!"

Sarah sat twisting her hands nervously in her lap, wondering how on earth she would go about asking for money she knew she had no way of ever being able to repay, and wondering also what sort of welcome she would receive in Manchester. She was well aware that her stepfather would not let her in the house once her condition became apparent, and her only reason for bothering to go there at all was to beg her mother to take Emma under her care. The notion of giving up Emma, probably for good, made the tears sting hotly to her eyes, but she brushed them away impatiently; she could not afford any emotional self-indulgence. She realized that it would be an impossible task finding any sort of work to support herself and the baby she was carrying, and it would be mere selfish folly to make Emma suffer the certain deprivation also if she could manage to secure some sort of reasonable future for her.

Sarah had arrived at Winslade Hall barely an hour previously, much to the astonishment and subsequent delight of Mr. and Mrs. Davis. Matilda Davis had then monopolized the gleeful but exhausted Emma and bustled away to the kitchens with her, old Mary in tow, fussing and clucking in broad Irish.

The dowager was just rising for the day, and Sarah waited now in her sitting room, painfully ill at ease as she wondered whether she should be honest and admit she was unlikely ever to be able to repay the money or to say she would send some when she could. She frowned with concentration, attempting to make her exhausted brain assess the minimum she would need, and her troubled calculation was interrupted

271

abruptly as the door opened and the old lady entered, leaning heavily on an ebony stick. She greeted Sarah enthusiastically in her abrasive voice, without any apparent sign of surprise at the young woman's unexpected arrival.

"Are you hungry? I shall send for some tea. I have not had breakfast yet. Never eat breakfast much before midafternoon."

"No. No, thank you. I shall not be stopping long. I have only come to . . . to ask you a favor, actually." Sarah noticed the shrewd look in the black eyes as the old woman moved closer and sank into a nearby sofa. Sarah sat again also.

She looked away from the piercing gaze and back at her hands and started quickly. "I was wondering if you would be kind enough to let me have some money. I have to journey to Manchester, and I have not even the fare." She twisted her fingers again, not looking up, adding quickly, "I am afraid I probably would not ever be able to repay you but . . ."

The old woman cut in sharply. "Where is my nephew?"

Sarah met the black eyes squarely then, saying calmly, "I have no idea. Still in London, as far as I know. Our . . . relationship is finished now, and I shall be journeying to stay with my mother." She could not prevent a flash of doubtful anxiety crossing her face at the thought of the reception she was likely to receive, and she heard the dowager say drily, "I had believed my nephew to be slightly more generous to his discarded mistresses?"

Sarah replied, attempting to keep her tone even, "Oh, he was. He gave me a residence of my own in London. I have no desire for London or the house."

272

"You could always sell the house," the dowager cut in astutely.

"I do not want his house or his money. But if you could let me have perhaps twenty pounds, I am sure he would pay you back." Sarah looked up pleadingly, meeting the narrowed eyes, and the old woman uttered matter-of-factly, "You are in love with him, then."

Sarah swallowed hard, about to make some vehement denial, and then merely nodded, repeating quickly, "I am sure he would repay you."

The old woman laughed. "You do not mind accepting his money then, in a roundabout way, of course," and then she continued quickly, seeing Sarah coloring miserably, "Does he know where you are?"

Sarah shook her head and smiled shakily. "In any case, I am sure he would not be in the least interested."

The dowager rose suddenly, saying, "I am quite famished. I must have some tea and toast. Will you join me, my dear?"

Sarah started to protest, reiterating her need to depart quickly, but the old woman waved her hand dismissively, saying, "There is plenty of time; it is early still."

She moved slowly to the door and opened it, calling loudly and saying something to a servant outside.

She moved back into the room slowly and sank back into the chair, her eyes traveling the length of Sarah's slim figure, and she said quietly, "You look exhausted."

"The journey was very tiring," Sarah replied hastily, sitting forward quickly, "and Emma was at mischief for the duration."

The old woman nodded, seemingly satisfied, and

273

they chatted amiably for a few minutes until the tea arrived. The dowager sat eating toast as though she was indeed starving and sipping her tea noisily, merely making general remarks every so often about the weather and questioning Sarah about what she had seen and done during her stay in London.

Sarah answered her politely but briefly, wondering with nauseating panic if the old lady was in fact going to refuse her request as she had said no more about the money. As she agonized whether to venture mentioning it once more she saw the dowager sit forward, startled, her face a study of incredulity as she looked at something behind Sarah, and then she choked, with a mouthful of toast, "Good God, Tarrington. That was quick. Did you fly here? I only sent Peters with the message, why, barely half an hour ago."

Sarah froze for a moment, sure she must have misheard, and then she turned slowly, her cup falling to the carpet from her nerveless fingers.

He was standing by the door, hands in pockets; his clothes smothered in dust and grime, and his eyes fixed steadily on her whitening face.

Sarah rose swiftly, and as the meaning of the dowager's recent words penetrated her dazed shock she looked toward her, bitter reproach in her eyes, but she merely said, not looking at either of them, "I am sorry, I should not have come."

She started to move toward the door nearest her that lead back into the hallway, and she heard the dowager snort, "Do not look at me with that sorry expression, my girl. Never known two people so stubborn. Not that it is all your doing, of course." She turned to her nephew standing there silently and said, "It is your fault, you know. Taking her to London as your mis-

274

tress instead of . . ."

"Shut up." His voice was like flint, and the dowager halted immediately, laughing almost contentedly, saying, "Yes. Perhaps I should. I think it is your turn now."

Sarah started quickly for the door again, and she heard him say quietly, "Please, Sarah."

She hesitated, something in his tone making her stomach churn, but she quickened her pace, her hand reaching for the doorknob, and he said, his voice a raw request, "Don't make me crawl, Sarah."

She heard the dowager snort loudly again and retort, "Why not? That should be a sight well worth the seeing." Sarah could feel hysterical laughter bubbling beneath the anguish at her words, and then the old lady mumbled placatingly, "Oh, all right, all right, I'm going," and she heard the door opposite close quietly.

She was conscious of his footsteps moving closer, and he halted just behind her, not touching her, and she heard him murmur, "Sarah?"

She knew he expected her to turn back to him, but she remained unmoving, merely saying, with a calm she was unaware she possessed, "Yes, my lord?"

"My lord . . . my lord," he mimicked softly. "Am I to remain nameless for the rest of my life, Sarah?"

She could feel the dragging misery choking her slowly, and, unable to bear the sensation longer, her hand tightened on the doorknob, about to open it, but his arm came across her shoulder, leaning heavily against the door, and as her head bowed with the weight of her despair, she heard him say, his voice hoarse with emotion, "I am sorry. Forgive me."

His hand moved away from the door and to her face

275

in the first tentative touch she had ever known, and then he spun her round and pulled her so close that she felt the breath leaving her body.

His face buried in the soft thickness of her hair, and he said in a muffled tone, "I love you, Sarah. Don't leave me."

As his words were slowly absorbed by her senses, she felt her tension relaxing into a rich, enfolding joy, and she attempted to free one of her hands to hold him close. But she felt his clasp tighten, as though he thought she was going to struggle free, so she slid her arms around his waist, her head falling forward onto his shoulder, and as she clung to him she realized almost disbelievingly that he was shaking nearly as much as she was herself. She had never known him to be anything less than totally self-assured, and her arms tightened and her hands moved slowly across his back in an instinctively comforting embrace.

He raised his head slowly after a while and his hands went to her face, pushing the hair gently away so he could see her eyes, and he said with tender mockery, "You could have told me. I have nearly killed two horses getting here so quickly."

She laughed then, with sheer, golden relief, and her arms went around his neck and she turned her face into his clothes again and whispered, "I love you."

She felt his arms tighten, lifting her off the ground so that her face was level with his, and he kissed her with fierce tenderness before he said, "Where is Emma? You are not going to rush off to put her to bed in a few minutes, are you?"

Sarah shook her head, smiling at the love in his eyes and wondering now why she had never recognized it as such before. "No. She is with Mrs. Davis and

Mary, eating her way through the kitchens."

His eyes caressed her face for a few moments, and then he said slowly, "I shall have to return to London, but I shall be back in a day or so."

She stared at him uncomprehending for a moment, and then laughingly said, "Well, am I not coming with you?"

"Why? I thought you would rather stay here?"

She looked at him, her eyebrows raised slightly, and said with mild censure, "I do not think even the earl of Winslade could get away with flaunting his mistress at his country residence."

"Are you not going to marry me then, Sarah?" His voice was gentle, and she stared hard at him for a moment, searching for some sign of mockery, unable to believe what she had heard, and then, looking away, said simply, "But I cannot."

His hand went to her face, turning it back sharply, and she saw his eyes narrow suspiciously. "Why not?"

She let her lids drop and said quietly, "It is not suitable. You will be expected to make a good match. I am a widow with a child. There will be gossip; people will think you have only married me because of . . ." She hesitated, her heart thudding and her happiness evaporating slowly as she remembered that he knew nothing of the child she was carrying, and she continued woodenly, "I have no dowry."

He laughed then, and she could see the undisguised relief in his face. He said quietly, "Is that all? Do you really think I am about to start worrying what others think now? When it matters not at all? Besides, if you want a dowry that much I shall give you one." He smiled, adding ruefully, "After all, I shall, no doubt, be providing Joanna with hers."

His hand went to her troubled face and he traced her mouth lightly with one finger, saying softly, "And I am pleased about the baby."

She was too shaken to react at all for a moment, and then, as the fingers near her mouth slid to cup her face gently, lovingly emphasizing his joy, she turned her face slightly into his touch and asked, her breath catching on a relieved sob, "Who told you? Maggie?"

"No." His tone was fondly amused, and she looked doubtful, flushing slightly at the expression in his eyes as he said softly, "It was not that difficult to work out. I had been in your bed every night for more than five weeks. If you ever had a valid excuse to refuse me, I am sure you would have used it."

She turned away sharply, and to hide her confusion said tartly, "Not every night."

"Ah, yes. Did you miss me, Sarah, the nights I did not visit?"

The laughter was still in his voice, and she retorted swiftly, "No," and then, defeatedly, "Yes."

"Good. Then it was worth the sacrifice." His eyes and hands slid the length of her slowly, and he said, the humor still in his voice, "Besides, you have nowhere to hide the extra weight."

She laughed then, her hand coming up to slap playfully at his face, and he let her hit him, saying with mock threat, "I shall allow you just that one."

Sarah looked up at him, a slight, taunting smile curving her mouth as she said, "I really think you only want to marry me to regain your house."

He smiled also, looking over her head, and murmured in a vaguely apologetic tone, "Oh yes, the house. I have a confession to make . . . I lied. It is not yours." His eyes met hers and he said, amused, "Well, you can have it if you want . . . why would I give you a house you hate?"

She stared at him, totally confused, and then uttered, "But why . . . ?"

"I thought if you believed I was prepared to allow you the house unconditionally, you might be prompted to tell me that you did not want your freedom after all." He paused, then said in a half-smile, "Just another of my noble gestures you managed to thwart."

She shook her head slowly at him, trying to keep her face straight as she murmured with mock sincerity, "Did I miss some?"

He pulled her close, his head moving to rest lightly on top of hers as he said softly, "My intentions always were strictly honorable . . . it's just . . . you never seemed to allow me the right moment to tell you about it."

He moved back slightly, his eyes searching her face slowly as he said quietly, "Will you marry me, Sarah?"

She was silent for a long moment, and then said with forced brightness, "You do not have to. It is enough that you care."

"It is not enough for me." His voice was tight now, and as she looked at him she noticed the panic flickering behind the gold of his eyes, and she smiled hesitantly.

His expression softened and he repeated, "Will you marry me, Sarah?"

She nodded then and simply said, "Yes."

He looked at her for a moment, sheer contentment curving his mouth, and then he murmured, "Yes what?"

She could feel the mischief rising, and she looked thoughtful for a moment and then said with a show of inspiration, "Yes, please?"

His mouth twisted slightly and his smile deepened, and he shook his head slowly.

She said laughingly, "Yes sir?"

His hand went to the scruff of her neck and he pulled her close, muttering threateningly, "Sarah," and she buried her face in his neck and said softly, "Yes, Mark."

He moved the hair back from her neck and kissed her, saying thickly, "I was beginning to think you had some terrible affliction that prevented your twisting your tongue around my name. Say it again."

And she obligingly did so.

Sarah stood unmoving, gazing out over the lake, its surface fired with the last rays of the setting sun, conscious of his hand at the back of her neck covering the gold necklace in a possessive caress. His free hand went to his pocket, and she saw him draw out her gold ring. He studied it for a few minutes and then, bringing both arms about her, he slid it onto his little finger, measuring its size. Then his arm drew back and she saw the sun catch it once briefly before it disappeared without a trace.

She stood silent for a moment and then said, thoughtfully, "If that lake ever dries up people might think that there was some terrible tragedy when they find a gold ring and a woman's petticoats." She was frowning solemnly, and he continued in the same tone, "There nearly was."

She nodded slowly, murmuring, "Poor Emma."

"I was not thinking of her." She could feel him laughing now as he added, "I nearly throttled you on the spot."

She started to turn toward him, but he held her still and his tone was different. "You scared me half to death sliding about like that."

She leaned back against him, luxuriating in his touch, and she heard him say thickly, "I should have left today; I could have been back within a day or so."

She twisted in his arms, and looking up at him suggestively, said softly, "You surely did not really want to go tonight?"

His eyes roved over her features slowly, lingering on her mouth, and he said with a hoarse laugh, "Oh, you will be quite safe. I would not be at all surprised to find my ever vigilant aunt sleeping across your door all night." He looked away from her abruptly, saying, his voice raw, "In any case we will be married soon . . . a few more days will not make much difference. It has only been three weeks."

She saw his mouth tauten and said softly, "Two weeks and six days."

He laughed, not looking at her. "Well, it seems like three weeks to me."

He was silent for a few moments and then said matter-of-factly, "I will bring a special license back with me. We can be married in the chapel here when I return. Perhaps Joseph will come back with me and act as best man. I shall have to warn him not to mention it to Susan, though, or before I know it she and Joanna will be ranting about double weddings. God, what a circus that would be."

He was almost talking to himself, and Sarah queried laughingly, "Shall I have any say in this, my lord?"

He looked at her then and smiled, saying, "This is one thing I will not indulge you in, Sarah," and then added conflictingly and coaxingly, "You could have a reception another time, if you want. If I had not been in such a tearing hurry to get here, I would have brought a license with me."

Sarah smiled and said with teasing mockery, "Such confidence . . . I might have refused you, after all."

He looked steadily at her, some of the arrogance visible again, and said softly, "It would have made no difference."

She stared at him, uncomprehending, and said laughingly, "How so?"

"I managed to coerce you into becoming my mistress. I am sure I could have done the same to make you my wife."

She noticed the curl to his mouth and the self-disgust darkening his eyes, and she said hesitantly, "You would not," and then added disbelievingly, "Would you?"

"Yes." He turned toward her and she could see the arrogance still as he said quietly, "It is hard to break the habits of a lifetime. I have always managed to get whatever I desire desperately enough."

She stared at him, stunned, and then looked away quickly and said, unable to keep the hurt from her voice, "How many others . . ."

But he cut sharply into her words, saying, "None. You surely do not think I would have bothered to go to all this trouble for anyone else, do you?" His tone was pure scorn, as though the very idea was ludicrous, and then, seeing the distress in her face he added gently, "There has never been anyone who I was ever

282

more than just fond of." He looked thoughtful suddenly, and said slowly, "There was a horse once that Joseph and I both wanted. A chestnut stallion."

She realized he was trying to make light of the situation, but she could not prevent herself from turning away, saying bitterly, "Well I feel very flattered that I at least rate as highly as a prized animal."

He caught her arm, pulling her close and holding her still, and said softly, "If it had been that way, I would have married you on your terms just to keep you with me. I cannot help needing you so much, Sarah. A year ago I would have laughed at anyone who said I would ever feel like this. I would have laid money against ever being this dependent; now I would give you anything you asked for to prevent your leaving." He paused, sighing unconsciously and deeply before adding, "Sometimes I think I love you too much; I have only to look at you to regret ten years of my life." He was silent for a moment, and then he shrugged and laughed, slightly ill at ease, as though he was vaguely ashamed of what he had just admitted. She stared at him for a few minutes and then said with a slight, shaky smile, "You . . ." but she left the name unuttered and her arms went up around his neck, holding him reassuringly close.

She felt him cling tightly, acknowledging her ultimate forgiveness with grateful avidity before he relaxed a little and said with assumed injury, "I am not sure why, but it seems everyone wants to challenge my birthright today. My mother must be spinning in her grave."

Sarah laughed, saying lightly, "Oh, I shouldn't worry too much . . . she must be well used to vertigo by now."

He caught her face in his hands and said slowly, "I often wonder, Sarah, if you will survive to celebrate your twenty-second birthday."

She was silent for a moment, thinking of the birthday gift he had given her, and she knew by the slight tightening of his hands that he also was thinking of the incident. She said quietly, "Will you have my bracelet mended for me?"

"No." His voice was harsh, and he cut into her words almost before she had finished speaking, looking at something over her head.

"I really do like it," she started persuasively, but he merely said, not looking at her still, "I shall get you something else." And then he smiled suddenly and added, "In any case, it is probably beyond repair now; it landed on the floor again when I found you had left."

He bent closer, his mouth caressing her face slowly as he murmured on a regretful sigh, "I really should have left tonight . . . I could have been back so much the sooner. There are several matters I shall have to attend to urgently, but . . ." He seemed preoccupied suddenly, gazing over her head thoughtfully, and added distantly, "But I shall be back as soon as I am able."

"Yes, of course." Her tone was frigid, and she withdrew from him, turning as though to start back to the house, but his hand came out, catching her wrist, and he drew her back and said quietly, "There is no one else."

"It does not matter." She tried to slip her wrist from his hold, but he retained his grip, repeating softly, "There is no one."

She remained silently before him, her head turned

284

away in apparent fascinated study of the lake, and he added, laughing slightly, "There has been no one else for so long that at one time I was contemplating taking a vow of silence also." His tone was coaxing, but she merely retorted acidly, "Yes, it is quite amazing how the weeks drag sometimes." She let her head fall forward, ashamed of her sarcasm, and said simply, "I'm sorry," and tried to disengage herself, feeling the tears start to her eyes.

"The last time was . . ." She cut in quickly. "I do not want to know."

But he repeated slowly, "The last time was . . ." He stopped, savoring the moment, and her hands went up to cover her ears, but seeing the abrupt wetness on her lashes he added gently, "The last time was just before you told me I was fortunate my wealth made me attractive. I think you shattered by self-assurance that day."

She remained rigid for a moment and then looked up, her expression astonished disbelief. "But that was . . . that was the first time I saw you. It was more than ten months ago."

He smiled sardonically, saying with unintentional harshness, "I know well enough how long it has been, Sarah."

She stared at him for a few moments, and then, as realization dawned on her she accused, "You intended I should become your mistress right away."

His mouth lifted slightly in wry humor and he murmured, "Well, there was that, of course." But he could see behind the mild reproach in her eyes the doubtful distrust, and as she looked away from him again he released her abruptly and moved towards the lake's edge. He picked up a few pebbles and tossed them in his hand for a few moments before he started to skim them viciously across the smooth surface, and then he said with savage self-mockery, without turning toward her, "There is no need to look quite so astonished, Sarah. I can assure you that I am no less amazed."

She watched him for a few minutes, noticing the bitterness in his profile, and she was suddenly aware of supreme self-confidence and she knew that she trusted him implicitly. She moved toward him slowly, her hands sliding leisurely up around his neck, and she kissed his cheek, her mouth parted and tantalizingly close to his as she murmured with soft suggestiveness, "You should have said. Had I known I might have been kinder sooner." She pressed herself closer, sensing the taut hardness of his body along the entire length of hers, and, letting her lids fall slightly, asked softly, "Did you love me even then?"

He was silent for a while and then said, "It would seem so." His voice sounded odd, and she was acutely aware that his arms were still at his sides. This was not the reaction she had expected to her first attempt at flirting with him, and she started to withdraw a little. Her hands began to drop away uncertainly, and her eyes opened quickly. But as she looked up at him, she saw he was laughing.

She made to pull back at once, infuriated, but he moved swiftly, catching her hard against him once more, his mouth seeking hers urgently, and then he had swung her up in his arms and started back toward the house.

A COMPROMISING SITUATION

Sarah opened the door to Mark Tarrington's bed-chamber, holding her breath lest the valet still be there. She walked in, closing the door quickly behind her. Avoiding looking at the massive bed which dominated the room, her eyes scanned the most likely places. She headed for the pile of books lying on a desk in the corner.

She was unaware the door had opened until a slight flickering of one of the lamps made her look up. Tarrington, a decanter and glass in one hand and his coat in the other, was entering the bedchamber, the valet following.

The valet paused, his face a study of incredulous astonishment, quickly masked by a look of bland indifference.

Noting the change in the man's attitude, Tarrington turned into the room. For a few moments he and Sarah stared at each other in pulsating silence. Then with a few words to the valet, he kicked the door shut after the man's hurriedly departing figure.

He walked slowly toward her.

"I can explain . . ." she said quickly, then halted, unable to think of anything else to say. She moved away from the bed, making a detour of the furniture towards the door.

"There is no need," he said, smiling enigmatically in the shadows.

He placed the decanter and glass on a table and threw his jacket towards a chair and as he did so she made a sudden, furious dash for the door.

He caught her easily, dragging her close and said with frightening quiet: "It has taken you long enough to get here—I think you should stay awhile."

THE BEST OF REGENCY ROMANCES

AN IMPROPER COMPANION   (2691, $3.95)
by Karla Hocker
At the closing of Miss Venable's Seminary for Young
Ladies school, mistress Kate Elliott welcomed the invitation to be Liza Ashcroft's chaperone for the Season at
Bath. Little did she know that Miss Ashcroft's father, the
handsome widower Damien Ashcroft would also enter her
life. And not as a passive bystander or dutiful dad.

WAGER ON LOVE   (2693, $2.95)
by Prudence Martin
Only a rogue like Nicholas Ruxart would choose a bride on
the basis of a careless wager. And only a rakehell like Nicholas would then fall in love with his betrothed's grey-eyed
sister! The cynical viscount had always thought one blush-
ing miss would suit as well as another, but the unattainable
Jane Sommers soon proved him wrong.

LOVE AND FOLLY   (2715, $3.95)
by Sheila Simonson
To the dismay of her more sensible twin Margaret, Lady
Jean proceeded to fall hopelessly in love with the silver-
tongued, seditious poet, Owen Davies—and catapult her
entire family into social ruin . . . Margaret was used to
gentlemen falling in love with vivacious Jean rather than
with her—even the handsome Johnny Dyott whom she se-
cretly adored. And when Jean's foolishness led her into the
arms of the notorious Owen Davies, Margaret knew she
could count on Dyott to avert scandal. What she didn't
know, however was that her sweet sensibility was exerting a
charm all its own.